GOOD INTENTIONS

Jane Adams

A SIGNET BOOK

NEW AMERICAN LIBRARY

Publisher's Note

This novel is a work of fiction. Names, characters, places, and incidents either are the product of the author's imagination or are used fictiously, and any resemblance to actual persons, living or dead, events, or locales is entirely coincidental.

NAL BOOKS ARE AVAILABLE AT QUANTITY DISCOUNTS WHEN USED TO PROMOTE PRODUCTS OR SERVICES. FOR INFORMATION PLEASE WRITE TO PREMIUM MARKETING DIVISION, NEW AMERICAN LIBRARY, 1633 BROADWAY, NEW YORK, NEW YORK 10019.

Good Intentions was previously published in a hardcover edition by New American Library and simultaneously in Canada by The New American Library of Canada Limited.

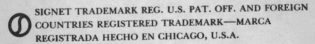

SIGNET TRADEMARK REG. U.S. PAT. OFF. AND FOREIGN COUNTRIES REGISTERED TRADEMARK—MARCA REGISTRADA HECHO EN CHICAGO, U.S.A.

SIGNET, SIGNET CLASSIC, MENTOR, PLUME, MERIDIAN AND NAL BOOKS are published by New American Library, 1633 Broadway, New York, New York 10019

First Signet Printing, June, 1986

1 2 3 4 5 6 7 8 9

PRINTED IN THE UNITED STATES OF AMERICA

TO J.S.A. AND C.S.A.——THIS IS FOR YOU.

1 A front had moved in from the Pacific that morning, bringing with it an autumn rainstorm that passed over the city at noon and then moved on as quickly as it had come. The squall left the sky clear, blue, and cloudlessly innocent, and the air, this close to the waterfront, was tangy with brine. A century before, loggers hauled fir, cedar, spruce, and hemlock trees from the slopes of the Cascades to the top of the steepest hill above Elliott Bay and skidded them down to be towed to the sawmills that dotted the islands of Puget Sound. Now Skid Road was slicked and polished for the tourists, but some reminders of its past hung stubbornly on, like the shabby, toothless old Indian sleeping in a doorway across the alley from the Public Defender Building. Anne watched from the window of her office as he woke, tasted the salt breeze with his tongue, picked up a shapeless bundle, and moved out of her line of vision. She wondered where he would go when the fern parlors and boutiques of nearby Pioneer Square finally pushed him out.

She had been waiting for a verdict for less than an hour when her telephone rang. Before she answered it, she shrugged into her raincoat and picked up her briefcase. If she won her case, she thought, she might just take the rest of the afternoon off, stop at the gym for a swim and a massage, and pick up a pizza afterward for Billy's dinner. She never cooked on Friday nights. If she didn't have a date, she met her friends at the Central for a drink and went out with them for Chinese food and a movie. Friday was her time, her celebration of the week's conclusion. But because of her trial she hadn't done the grocery shopping that week, and if she didn't prepare something for Billy, he'd go to the candy store, buy Doritos and soda pop, and call it supper. Maybe I can have the pizza delivered and not have to stop at home first, she mused as she picked up the telephone to answer the bailiff's summons.

"This is Anne Manning," she said, but it was not the bailiff calling. When the assistant principal of Cascade Middle School identified himself, a spasm of fear gripped Anne. "Yes, Mr. Casey, this is Billy's mother. Is Billy all right? There hasn't been an accident? He's not ill, is he?"

At first Mr. Casey was reassuring. Billy was perfectly safe. No harm had come to him. None of the disasters of which she sometimes dreamed, the carelessness that could cost a limb, or worse, a life, had befallen her son. None of the senseless tragedies, the dread diseases, the awful accidents that made her shudder when she heard of them and then feel guiltily grateful to have been spared, had struck at her or hers. Her fright receded, but as the assistant principal went on speaking it was replaced by the dull throbbing that signaled the beginning of a headache.

As Anne listened, she swiveled her desk chair around to face the office window. She had a strong urge to hold the receiver away from her ear, point it out toward Puget Sound, and let the words float out of the telephone. If she opened the window, a gust of wind would blow them over the water, lift them to the peaks of the mountains beyond, lose them in the mists of the rain forests on the peninsula at the edge of the western horizon.

It was not Anne's first conversation with Mr. Casey; probably, she thought wearily, it would not be her last. As his voice droned on, she grew restless. Her son's physical safety assured, she had only one question in her mind, and she wished the assistant principal would address it directly. What had Billy done now?

While she was listening for the answer, the judge's bailiff called on the other line; the jury was in. Anne tried, first tactfully and then with impatience, to bring the conversation with Mr. Casey to a close. Finally, it was done, and she left her office, running the few short blocks back to the courthouse. Inside, she pushed her way into a crowded elevator, left it on the fourth floor, and hurried down the hall to the assigned courtroom. She took her place next to the defendant. The prosecutor drummed his fingers impatiently on the surface of a table across the aisle from her, and the judge regarded her critically from the bench.

The foreman cleared his throat self-importantly and read the verdict slowly, enunciating each word and pronouncing the final two, the critical ones, with solemn emphasis. Anne permitted herself a brief moment of satisfaction as she heard them. She accepted her client's mumbled thanks and smiled with forbearance as his mother, an elderly black woman whose face was channeled with deep grooves and from whose eyes spilled tears of relief, pumped her arm up and down, up and down. Finally the woman released it, her words trailing off into embarrassed silence.

Anne extricated herself from the courtroom as quickly as she could. Anxious to be done with it, she didn't even bother warning her client to stay out of trouble. She knew his name would show up on the arraignment calendar again soon, probably within days; it was not her client's innocence, but the clumsiness of the arresting officer that had won her case. And when Marty Lehman, whose office in the Public Defender was adjacent to her own, caught up with her as she left the courthouse and congratulated her on the verdict, she told him that.

"So what?" said Marty. "It isn't how you play the game that counts, it's winning, right?" He grinned at her, then struck the pose of a victor, his hands clenched over his head. Like a winning jockey, she thought, for he looked that way, with his small, wiry body. Juries liked Marty; women were reminded of their sons, and men took his side against bigger lawyers, who always looked like they were bullying him.

"I guess," replied Anne halfheartedly.

"You guess? What's the matter, Anna Banana, something wrong?"

She shrugged.

"Got to run," she said. "Later, okay?"

At the office, she stopped at the reception desk for their messages, then passed through the clients' waiting room, full even this late in the afternoon with wary, weary, defeated-looking people; defendants and their kin, spouses, parents, and even children, ready in an instant to proclaim the innocence of their loved ones. The mothers were the saddest, Anne thought; the women like Coralee Washington, whose son Calvin, through Anne's efforts, had just been freed to break, enter, batter, and burgle again, until he was caught again, and again he turned up in her office, protesting the unfairness of the charges against him, railing at the System; cocky, truculent, and, finally, frightened. Every day of Calvin's trial Mrs. Washington had brought Anne something—a bouquet of flowers, a plate of home-baked cookies. "You get my boy out, you set my baby free, Miz Manning, and he won't never be here again," Coralee promised. Anne ached to tell her to let go, give up; that baby of yours will be behind bars again before he's through, she wanted to say, he'll make you cry until the day you die.

But of course she said no such thing. She was too professional. And besides, she was a mother herself.

Back at her desk, she stuffed files and papers into her briefcase. Her next trial was scheduled for Monday morning, and she would have to work over the weekend to prepare for it. On his way out, Marty stopped in the doorway of her office and regarded her sympathetically.

"You look done in," he said. "Defending justice is no easy task, God knows, but you just won a felony trial. Let's go get a beer and celebrate."

She shook her head. "I can't. I've got an appointment at Billy's school."

"Trouble?"

"They don't usually call you in for an emergency conference to tell you your kid is performing brilliantly," she replied.

"You worry too much," said Marty.

"Says who?" she said with a smile. She loved Marty dearly, but there were some things he couldn't understand. No man could, especially a man who had no children.

"Hey, Annie, don't worry, the kid's just being a

kid, that's all. Fourteen's not easy, but he'll live through it."

"I'm not worried about whether he will," she told him as she gathered her coat and purse. "About me, though . . . about me I have some very serious doubts."

"To be perfectly frank with you, Mrs. Manning—"

"It's Ms., not Mrs.," Anne interrupted.

"Yes, of course. As I was saying, to be perfectly frank with you we're in somewhat of a quandary, a bind you might say, about William—"

"Bill, Mr. Casey, he's usually called Bill." Not by her; she couldn't remember not to call him Billy, in spite of his insistence that the diminutive made him sound like a baby. But what did it matter what he was called in this huge, impersonal school where nobody bothered to find out anything about a child, not even his nickname, until he got into trouble?

She hadn't wanted to send Billy here in the first place. The headmaster at the gifted children's school Billy attended before coming to Cascade years had couched his message in diplomatic phrases, but his meaning was clear. "Perhaps Bill needs a more varied peer group," he'd suggested. "Perhaps with youngsters of, umm, less advantaged backgrounds he might do better, have an opportunity to excel . . . you know, they're all very bright here, which makes it hard to stand out."

She'd made inquiries at the other private day schools in the area, but it was late in the year and enrollments were closed. Besides, Billy's record was erratic, so she had settled for public school, and now that wasn't working, either. If they wouldn't have him here, she thought with a stab of apprehension, where could he go?

"Yes, certainly, Bill. Now, Mrs. Manning—"

"Ms., not Mrs.," she corrected him again, and he sighed audibly. She was a contentious bitch; she knew that, but he was criticizing her son.

"Yes, Ms. Manning." He hesitated and then went on. "Ms. Manning, Bill's grades this term are even worse than they were last term, when he passed only two courses out of five. With the lowest possible passing grades, as you know. Certainly I don't have to tell you that your son's grades are no indication of his ability, we know he's a very bright lad . . . I see here he has an I.Q. of 136."

He had that wrong, too, she thought; when Billy was tested for private school his Stanford-Binet score was 143.

"Now, I didn't call you in here to talk about Bill's academic record, although that certainly needs attention, but his behavior in class—"

"Yes?" She felt, briefly, sorry for Casey. Poor guy, she thought, Billy is probably the smartest kid in this school. He doesn't know how to challenge him and Billy is bored, so he acts up. I would, too, if this man is the best they have to offer.

"Bill's algebra teacher, Miss Titus, is quite at the end of her rope," Mr. Casey continued, "and Mr. Grabowski, the physical education instructor, has asked that Bill be dismissed from his class for the rest of the term. There was an incident this afternoon, a fight between Bill and another boy, a Todd Lewis. It was simply the last straw for all Bill's teachers. So I'm afraid I have no choice but to recommend a five-day suspension and hope that—"

"A suspension? Now just a minute, Mr. Casey, I think that's going a bit far, wouldn't you say? After all, what good would that do? It would just give Billy blanket permission to stay home for a week and do

nothing . . . what purpose could that possibly serve?"
Casey held up a hand to stop her, but she rushed on.
"I understand your position, Mr. Casey; you know, I
was a teacher myself once," she said. "Oh, just for a
couple of years, but still, I know how challenging an
extremely bright youngster can be. It seems to me
that some children just need a different approach, a
more supportive environment, a—"

"Yes, Ms. Manning, that's true, but Bill—"

She barely heard the man. Her mind raced ahead,
and she groaned inwardly. She was in trial for the
next ten days at least; what would she do with Billy?
She couldn't stay at home, and if she left him there
alone, he'd sit in front of the television set and vege-
tate. Or, worse, get into more trouble; left unsuper-
vised, there was no telling what he might do. Besides,
he'd lose class credit for those days and fall even further behind in his work.

Mr. Casey was still talking, and she forced herself
to listen.

"Yes, Ms. Manning, support, encouragement,
that's what education is supposed to be about, isn't it?
How does it go, a teacher on one end of a log, a student on the other? But that's not always possible in a
public school. Not when a student disrupts an entire
class time after time . . . and then, of course, there was
the incident last month when Bill stole the basketball
from the gym—"

"You never proved Billy stole that ball! You told
me yourself that you couldn't, that—"

"Well, we never could get Bill to own up to it, but
really, it was in his locker, the evidence was overwhelming—"

"Evidence? What is this, a courtroom?" How dare
this stupid man call her son a thief? That was what
happened when a school levy failed, they let all the

good teachers go, the young, caring, committed ones, and they kept all the dinosaurs like this stoop-shoul-dered, pasty-faced, tired old man, who should have been riffed years ago.

Riffed . . . reduced in force. That was what hap-pened to her when she'd gone back to teaching after the divorce. Gone back for one year, and then, when she was already stretched so thin and tight over her own skeleton, her own nervous system, that one more blow would have shattered her, she had been fired.

She had never wanted to teach. She had wanted to go to law school, but not immediately after finishing college. Instead she took a job in Washington, D.C. It was 1960, the threshold of a glorious era, a time when everything seemed possible, when people her age be-lieved that individuals could make a difference, and she was sure, herself, that she was one who might.

When she married Don and moved to Seattle, the only openings were in teaching, so she got her cer-tification and endured four years of fourth graders until Billy was born, and another after. Then she was left, and then laid off, and only the realization that she would have to support herself and her child snapped her out of her misery. She went east with Billy to visit her parents; her father offered to pay for law school if she still wanted to go. She wanted her husband back and her family together, but since that wasn't to be, she enrolled that September and found that she enjoyed it, was good at it, was good at some-thing again. And now, with the skills she had acquired there and honed in four years of practice, she went on the offensive, not on behalf of one of her indigent defendants but of her sorely misunderstood son.

"I consider it a failure of the school system," she said with indignation, "the system for which, inciden-tally, I pay taxes, when a boy as obviously intelligent as Billy is can't be accommodated simply because the level of education in the public schools of Seattle is geared to the lowest common denominator of—"

"I understand your point, Ms. Manning. We all agree that William is a very capable youngster. We just don't seem to be able to agree on the best way to channel his talents, and frankly, we don't know quite where to go from here. Perhaps a special school, or some outside counseling, might be the answer. We'll be glad to cooperate with whomever you suggest."

"Now just a moment, Mr. Casey! In my judgment there is nothing wrong with Billy except boredom. He's a perfectly sound kid who's encountering the normal problems and mood swings of puberty, and if you'd just be a little more supportive—"

"We've been supportive, and it hasn't helped." Casey leafed through the papers in the file folder on his desk. "Ms. Manning, Bill has had seven referrals to my office this year. He's had numerous opportunities to meet our expectations, which are quite reasonable, I might add. We think he needs some special help, Ms. Manning, some professional attention, and if you could only be more objective about this situation you'd understand . . ."

Objective, sure. Professionals? Sure. This dumb jerk, Anne thought, does he have any idea how many so-called professionals I've dragged Billy to in the last eight years? There was the therapist from the children's mental health center, right after the divorce, when Billy had the terrible nightmares. There was the psychologist to whom they were referred when Billy developed unexplainable rashes and even more mystifying, and frightening, allergic reactions.

And then last year, she'd taken Billy to a psychiatrist, after he'd brought home a new dirt bike, explaining that he'd traded his old bike to a classmate who wanted a ten-speed, even an old, beat-up one, and was willing to swap, straight across. It had sounded fishy, but she'd wanted to believe her son. When she found his old bicycle, shoved way back behind the furnace in the basement, and remembered all the other stories of Billy's she hadn't quite believed, she went to see Dr. Gotenburg, who was recommended by her pediatrician. He saw Billy twice, and then recommended that Billy begin analysis, three hours a week at least, five under ideal circumstances. She couldn't afford it, of course, not without asking her father for the money, and she wouldn't do that. And besides, Billy disliked Dr. Gotenburg and refused to go back after the two evaluation sessions.

Professionals, she thought with annoyance. Everybody's favorite answer, except they didn't know anything and they couldn't do any more than she could. She felt her eyes begin to water and she took a deep breath.

"Mr. Casey, if you insist on a referral to a professional, I will certainly get one, as soon as I can make arrangements. And in the meantime, I'll have a serious discussion with Bill over the weekend, and come to school with him on Monday for a conference with Miss Titus and Mr. Grabowski and you, too, if you like."

Casey looked resigned but not completely defeated. "All right, Ms. Manning, I guess we'll have to go along with you, this one last time."

Thank God, Anne thought, and rose to leave.

It was after four when she left the assistant principal's office. She wanted to head the Vega station wagon back toward downtown. She wanted to buy the first round of drinks for her officemates, traditional when someone won a felony trial. She wanted to gossip with her friend Carol about the new chief attorney in her office, who was sexy, single, and recently arrived from San Francisco. She wanted to eat lemon chicken at Lin Yen, and see a satisfactorily trashy movie afterward. Patrick had called while she was in court and left a message with the receptionist: Mose Allison was playing a late set at Parnell's, and Pat would save her a seat if she wanted to catch up with him at the jazz club. She wanted to do that, too. But instead she turned the car toward home, feeling the last traces of her fine, finished, Friday night feeling leave her, like a lover slipping away without a goodbye.

She passed the pizza parlor and pulled into the Safeway parking lot. Inside the store, she took a cart and pushed it slowly up and down the aisles, reading every word of the unit price tags and examining every label. She deliberated in front of the paper products display until a woman trying to get by her remarked, "It's only toilet paper, lady," so she lingered at the magazine rack and the paperback book display. Finally she bought more than she needed, had her groceries paid for, bagged, and loaded into her car, and there was nowhere to go except home.

She pulled into the driveway and noted that the garbage pails were stacked neatly inside the garage, whose door was slightly ajar. She knew as soon as she let herself into the house that Billy was not home; she could tell from the quality of the silence that she was alone. In the kitchen she found signs of his recent presence—a peanut-butter-smeared knife in the sink, crumbs scattered on the counter next to the breadbox. There was no message from him on the erasable memo board attached by magnets to the refrigerator door.

She was relieved that he was out. Driving away

from the school, she had rehearsed what she would say to him, even though she did not expect him to respond. When Billy talked it was in monosyllables, fragments of sentences. Yeah. No. I guess. Nothing. Or, sometimes, under his breath but still audible, bitch, or shit. Usually she pretended not to hear, but sometimes she could not, and then she yelled at him. When she did, he walked away, and her words followed but did not stop him.

She put away the groceries and started dinner. Then she went upstairs, shucking her work clothes as she went, and stood under the shower until the hot water ran out. Her headache was worse; she took a brown bottle from the medicine cabinet and spilled the contents into her palm. Hadn't there been more codeine tablets than these the last time she'd used them? Yes, she calculated, a dozen at least, and now there were only five—six, counting the one she'd just swallowed. Something else was missing too, up on the top shelf, behind her diaphragm case—the small card of diet pills she almost never used unless she was so tired and dragged out that she couldn't function without the extra edge of energy they provided. The card was gone. Was Billy stealing her pills now?

In her bedroom, she opened the top drawer of the night table, where she kept the flimsy papers and the small film container that held the marijuana Patrick had left the last time he stayed over. The gray and black plastic container was there, but it was almost empty. She knew there had been nearly half an ounce left; she had used it last a week ago. Billy had come into her room before she'd put it away the next morning; she remembered, because after breakfast, when Patrick left, Billy had asked her if he could move his room down to the end of the hall, where she kept her sewing machine and fabric and out-of-season clothes.

She'd been pleased at Billy's suggestion. She was just as glad he wouldn't be right next door to her anymore, where he could overhear her when she confided to a friend on the telephone, or allowed a lover to spend the night with her. Not that that happened often, anymore, but now that Billy was fourteen, she was acutely aware, when it did, that he was nearby.

So she encouraged Billy, took him to the paint store, and allowed him to pick the color for his room; she shuddered at the dreadful parrot-green he chose, but she bought the paint and brushes and rollers and drop cloths. He completed one wall and then lost interest in the project; she cleaned up his spills and painted it herself. She bought bright polished cotton fabric and made curtains and a bedspread. She had finished the room a few days before; today, she saw as she opened his door, it looked as messy and neglected as his other room had.

She felt uneasy about searching his room, but fear stilled her nagging conscience. She was his mother, after all—she had a right to know if her suspicions were true.

She looked in his bureau drawers and under his bed, in his closet and behind his bookcase. Nothing. She stretched out on his bed, considering places she might have overlooked, and her eyes strayed to the ceiling. She noticed a protrusion; one of the suspended acoustical tiles seemed to have come loose. She dragged a desk chair to a spot underneath the tile and reached up, feeling along the wooden beams to which the tiles were attached. She touched something hard and cold, metallic; frowning, she brought it out into the light, into the sunshine that flooded the west-facing room.

She saw what it was and dropped it, horrified. The gun clanked heavily to the floor. It was Don's revolver. It had been locked in a box in the basement, a long, varnished case that smelled of creosote and polish, with her ex-husband's hunting guns. He had taken most of those but left the case, insisting that she keep the revolver for her own protection, and his old shotgun for Billy, when he was old enough to use it. Privately, she thought that would be never, and she had meant to get rid of them for some time. But she hadn't, and here was this squat, ugly, murderous thing.

She lifted it gingerly; she was only slightly relieved to find that it was not loaded. She carried it with her to the basement, where she pushed aside boxes and cartons and suitcases and uncovered the gun box. Its lock had been twisted and bent; she tugged on the handle, and the cover lifted off easily. There was nothing in the dusty green-felt interior except the dismantled shotgun and an empty container that had once held bullets.

A gun, she thought dully. My God, he took a gun.

It was growing dark outside. She slipped on a poncho against the omnipresent drizzle, locked the back door behind her, and made her way through the thicket of pine, fir, and madrona trees that began a few yards beyond her property line. The wooded hillside sloped down to the lake, and when she got there, she swung her arm back and hurled the gun as hard and as far as she could. It hit the water with a satisfying plop, raising ripples in shimmering circles that ceased after a few minutes, leaving the surface glassy and undisturbed once again, except for the drizzle that started, stopped, and started once more as she turned and climbed the hill toward home.

2 The meat loaf was hard and dry, the salad wilted under its dressing, when Billy came home.

"Where have you been?" Anne asked.

"Around here, in and out," he said casually. "Where've you been?"

"Down to the lake."

"Why'd you go there?"

"I needed some exercise."

"Oh. How come you didn't go swimming?"

"I had an appointment this afternoon."

"You coulda gone running. You haven't been running much lately."

"It was raining. I don't like running in the rain."

"But you like to walk in it, huh?"

"Sometimes."

"Oh." He sat down on the other side of the kitchen island where his place was set on the butcherblock counter. She filled his plate with meat and vegetables.

"Please, Ma, I can help myself. Yuk, this milk is warm."

"It was cold when I poured it," she said.

The silence between them lengthened. She chose her words carefully. "Where did you go after school?" she asked finally.

"Over Chris's."

"And?"

He put a large forkful of salad in his mouth. "You told me not to talk with my mouth full." He cut a large slab of butter and slathered it over his potato, mashing it vigorously. "We're building a tree house down in the woods. If you go out later will you get me some nails? I promised Chris I'd get them."

"What's Chris getting?" She didn't especially like Chris; he reminded her of sneaky, obsequious Eddie Haskell on *Leave It to Beaver*. But he was Billy's closest friend, the only boy in the neighborhood his own age.

"Jeez, Ma, why do you always make it sound like Chris is taking advantage of me or something? If you want to know, he's getting the wood. It's from some addition they're building over the garage, I think. So I have to get the nails."

"I see." She didn't know which to tackle first, Billy's problems at school or her missing drugs. The gun was an entirely different matter, and implied difficulties of a much greater magnitude—she needed time to think about that. Bloody, violent images strobed like lightning in her brain, and she willed herself to shut them out, get back to what had to be done first. Some kind of punishment, she guessed, at least for the theft of the drugs and the transgressions at school.

She sighed inwardly. She had never believed in physical punishment, had hardly ever spanked Billy when he was small, and was almost afraid to do it now. She could ground him, she supposed, but then he wouldn't be able to work on the tree house, unless she confined him to only the neighborhood, which was hardly punishment at all. If she restricted him to the house, she'd have to stay home herself all weekend to make sure he obeyed.

Grounding didn't work, anyway. Billy was solitary by nature. He had been a loner until Chris moved in two years before. If she restricted Billy's movements he adopted a detachment so much greater than his habitual aloofness that it was almost palpable and hovered in the space between them even when they were only a few feet apart. When his defiance of her limits was too blatant to ignore and she was forced to do something—limit his movements or cancel his allowance or demand reparations in the form of some task beyond his regular chores—he hardly reacted at all. If she grounded him to the house, he just said okay and closeted himself in his room. If she prohibited him from doing something he enjoyed, he seemed promptly to forget it. He didn't allow anything to matter so much to him that taking it away bothered him, or, if it did, he didn't permit her to see it.

She decided to wait until Sunday to discuss the problems at school. He could spend the day catching up on his incomplete assignments, a list of which she had brought home from her conference with Mr. Casey. As for the drugs—well, perhaps she had made a mistake. Maybe she'd had less than she thought, or used them herself. She was trying to convince herself that she had overlooked some obvious explanation when the telephone rang.

"If that's your grandmother, tell her I'm not here," said Anne. Her mother invariably called on Friday nights, although she knew Anne was rarely at home then. *Doesn't Billy mind being left alone to fend for himself?* she would ask the next time they spoke. *He prefers it,* Anne usually replied. *You only think he does, because it makes life easier for you,* her mother would respond. *What's so terrible about that?* Anne always wondered but she rarely said it.

As she thought, it was her mother calling. "Sure, she's here," said Billy after exchanging pleasantries with his grandmother. "Here she is." He handed her the phone with a sly grin, which widened into a smile when Anne glared at him. She made the conversation as brief as she could.

"Why'd you do that?" she asked when she replaced the receiver on the wall phone.

"You're the one's always telling me about not lying." It wasn't an accusation, only a comment delivered in a flat, noncommittal voice.

"I just didn't feel like talking to her, okay? I had a long, hard day today, I'm not in the mood." She cleared the countertop. "Was dinner all right?"

"Yeah."

"Did you have enough to eat?"

"Uh huh."

"How about dessert?"

"I just told you I had enough to eat."

"Oh. Sure. There's ice cream in the freezer and some brownie mix if you want to make them."

"I'm not hungry, Ma."

He left the kitchen and she watched him go. At least he was a healthy kid. He never got colds, and rarely was sick. Occasionally he had stomachaches, which usually preceded her discovery of some small crime or misdemeanor. At nine, he'd developed an allergy that manifested itself the first time with a skin rash. When she replaced his wool sweaters with synthetic garments, it seemed to go away. Then one day it struck with terrifying intensity, in big red welts that seemed to jump out on his body before her very eyes. In moments the soft tissue and membranes around his gums and nostrils began to swell; she was afraid he would choke, unable to take in air, and she rushed to the hospital with him. They injected him with epinephrine, and almost immediately the symptoms disappeared. In the next month she had him tested for every possible allergy, but the tests showed no unusual sensitivity to any identifiable substance. The doctor gave Billy an emergency kit and taught him how to inject himself if it became necessary; he was going to camp, where there would be overnight hikes, times and places when a doctor might not be immediately available. Billy brought the kit back from camp unused, and it was still in the medicine cabinet. She had wondered if she could ever bring herself to pierce his skin with the needle, even to save his life.

The pediatric allergist thought the rash might be psychosomatic, although every doctor, she thought, said that about any problem that did not easily yield an etiology. Pressed by the specialist for information about anything out of the ordinary that had preceded the attack, she remarked that it had occurred a week after a visit from Billy's father, who had moved to California after their divorce. For the first couple of years he had come to see Billy at Christmas, always laden with extravagant gifts. Between visits he rarely had any contact with him. The child psychologist to whom the allergist referred them thought there was a connection between Billy's allergies and his father's sporadic appearances. "Billy's paying the bill for parental inconsistency," she told Anne. "Ideally, his father would maintain a regular presence in his life, be someone he could count on. Between visits, for instance, he would call, write, keep in touch with Billy, reinforcing the relationship in spite of the physical distance between them. I think Billy needs to be protected from his father's capriciousness. Every time he disappoints Billy by not showing up when he's promised to, it's a gestalt of the divorce all over again for the boy. I wouldn't allow that to continue."

Anne wrote a carefully phrased letter to Don in California. "You always told me how you hated your own father for doing what you're doing to Billy . . . disappearing for months at a time and then coming back after he's gotten used to your absence," she wrote. "If you're willing to be in Billy's life on a regular, consistent basis, even if it's mostly letters and phone calls, fine. If you're not, stay away." She explained to Billy, "Daddy's a good person, but he isn't very good at some things, like keeping promises. Sometimes he forgets he made them, even to people he loves. And then those people get their feelings hurt. I'm not going to let Daddy hurt your feelings again."

Anne never received a response to her letter, but the next time Don called, Billy refused to talk to him, and Anne didn't force the issue. I'm sorry, she told Don, that's just the way he feels, and you have to respect his feelings.

"Hey, Ma?" It was Billy, calling her from his room. "Can Chris spend the night tonight? We want to start on the tree house first thing in the morning."

Wearily, she agreed, and went out to buy the nails.

3 His mother was humming to herself while she stirred the spaghetti sauce, her thick, shiny hair hanging like a curtain in front of her face as she bent over the stove. "You going out tonight?" Bill asked.

"Mmm hmm," she nodded. "To the movies, with Carol. Want to come?"

"I don't have any money. You said I couldn't get any allowance this week," he replied.

"You didn't do your chores."

"I took out the garbage."

"Once. You didn't clean the basement, you didn't rake the lawn, and I found the clean clothes I asked you to fold and put away stuck back in the laundry chute, all mixed up with the dirty ones. If you spent as much time doing what you're supposed to as you do figuring out a way to avoid it, you'd get your allowance more than once a month."

"It doesn't make any difference, you'd take it away for something else. You always do."

"You give me reason to. Have you done your homework?"

"I did it in study hall."

"All of it?"

"Yeah."

"In every one of your subjects?"

"We didn't have any in math or social studies."

"Since when?"

"I dunno, maybe the teachers are tired of correct-ing it."

"Billy, are you telling me the truth?"

"Why should I lie? That's dumb, you'd find out about it."

"I probably would. Right after you flunked math and social studies."

"I told you I did it."

"Where is it?"

"I handed it in before I came home."

She sighed, the way she always did when she wasn't sure whether she believed him. Actually, he'd done his assignments, sort of. But after study hall he'd made a paper airplane out of his science paper, which had flown for several minutes before landing in a puddle in the schoolyard. And he'd started to write a book report for English, but the book he was supposed to read was so dumb he couldn't finish it, so he'd written one on *Dove* instead. His last three book reports had been on *Dove;* he got an A on the first one, a C on the second, and no credit for the last one. But there was a substitute in English this week, so maybe he'd get away with it. *Dove* was his favorite book. He often imagined he was in the tiny craft with Robin, the eighteen-year-old skipper who had sailed around the world by himself.

His mother looked up from the stove. "If you want to go to the movies I'll advance you something on next week's allowance. If you fold the clothes that are in the dryer and put them away and take out all the garbage and finish the lawn."

"I think I'll go over to Chris's."

He went to his room and lay on his bed, bouncing a tennis ball idly against the wall. His mother called to him from the living room below. "Billy, what's that noise? What are you doing?"

"Nothing." He continued bouncing the ball.

"Billy? What's that noise?"

"Nothing." He missed it that time; the ball rolled under his bed and he left it there. A few minutes later, he went back downstairs. He folded the clothes, leaving them on top of the dryer, and emptied the waste baskets into the garbage pails in the garage. Then he raked most of the leaves on the front lawn into a pile and swept them across the sidewalk and into the gutter, from where the wind blew them into their neighbor's driveway. He left the rake leaning against the side of the house and went back inside. "I did my chores. Can I have that advance?"

"I thought you said you were going to Chris's."

"I am."

"Then why do you need money?"

"Oh, forget it," he said impatiently, turning to leave the room.

"No, wait. I really want to know," she said.

"Does it matter? It's my allowance, I earned it, right?"

"If you mean, you did one day's chores, therefore earning around a dollar forty, I suppose you did."

"Then give me the dollar forty."

"What for? You can't do anything with that little money except blow it at the store on junk. Why don't you wait till you've accumulated a little more, and you can go to Skate King or buy that Iron Maiden tape you want."

"Look, if it's my allowance I can do whatever I want with it, right? Well? Is it? Because if it's not, forget it, you can do the chores yourself and keep the lousy money." He turned on his heel and left, ignoring her request to stay and "resolve the issue." Resolve, shit. They never resolved anything. She yada-yada-yadaed—communicating, she called it, or having a dialogue. Which meant that she criticized or complained or repeated the same dumb things; do this, Billy, why don't you do that, Billy, don't you think we should talk about your lousy grades or the chores you didn't do or why do you have to play that music so loud or how can you live in such a pigsty, if the board of health saw it they'd quarantine it. That was her idea of communicating.

A lot of the time she made absolutely no sense at all. It was his room, he could live in it just fine, and there was no way to play heavy metal except loud, everybody knew that. Sometimes she'd say something one time and then completely reverse herself the next time. You can have your allowance if you do the fucking chores, but then you do them and she gives you a hard time. Or, you can't have your allowance, you didn't do what you were supposed to do, and then, five minutes later, if you want to go to the movies with me I'll give you an advance. No dice if you wanted to spend it on something she thought was stupid, like video games or Doritos.

As a matter of fact, he did want to go to the movies, but not with her and her girlfriend Carol. Not on a weekend night in December, when everybody was downtown shopping for Christmas and might see you hanging out in public with your old lady. There was a dance at school; if he told his mother, she'd give him money for that. She thought school functions were "appropriate." Dumb, that's what they were, with assholes like Todd Lewis coming up to you and brushing imaginary crud off you and trying to be cool—"Evening, Manning, my man, and who is this exquisite creature gracing insignificant little you with her presence on this glorious occasion?" when it was only old Clary Redman who he, Todd, had lived next door to since he was practically born.

Little you, that's what he said, the creep. Next to him, maybe, but Todd was practically six feet tall, a fucking fourteen-year-old giant, and he, Billy, was barely an inch taller than Clary, who was not exactly your large economy size. In his own room, he studied his reflection in the mirror. Straight brown hair, which his mother was always nagging him to get cut. Brown eyes, nothing special but they worked—he could see, couldn't he? A straightforward nose; when they studied ancient Greece in social studies, Clary showed him a picture of a young Greek athlete from Sparta, with a nose she said was just like Billy's—classic, she called it, a classic profile. His mouth was okay, but when he smiled all you could see were teeth, he musta got a few extra, like some kind of a mutant. He had a couple of zits on his face, but he could probably cover them up with that stuff of his mother's if he was going to a dance or someplace like that. Not that he was, of course.

He turned on the TV and stretched out on his bed. *Hogan's Heroes*—an old rerun, he'd seen it at least twice before. Klemper was a dumb-looking bozo; he reminded Bill of that fat shrink she took him to last year. Gotenburg. What a prick. Always pushing him, prodding him. Always wanting him to talk about his father.

He didn't remember his father very clearly, not how he looked. Just that he was big—fucking enormous. There was an old jacket that he had left behind; when Bill put it on the sleeves hung down practically a foot beyond his own thin wrists, and the shoulders sloped almost to his elbows. He wondered if he'd ever get that big. Probably not; with his luck, he'd take after his mother, who was barely five three. He was only an inch taller than her himself. He didn't seem to have grown much lately; she hadn't had to let down his jeans for a few months. He couldn't understand it. He'd started out regular size, just like everyone else. Around sixth grade he seemed to have stopped growing. Chris was eight months younger than him and a full head taller. Todd Lewis had shoulders like Steve Zohrn, and he wasn't even fourteen yet. Shit.

The jacket was the only thing he had left of his father's. That, and the gun. Only he didn't have the gun anymore. He'd known right away that she'd found it a month before; she hadn't replaced the ceiling tile right. She hadn't said anything about it yet; he twisted uncomfortably on the bed, wondering when or if she ever would. Not that he minded her taking it especially. He didn't particularly want the thing. He must have when he took it, a couple of years ago; he remembered thinking it would be handy to have around in case somebody broke into the house, since there wasn't anybody around except his mother, and she wasn't very strong.

He couldn't seem to get comfortable; he got off the bed and stretched out on the floor. Right after he'd taken the gun, he put it in his old toy box, down at the bottom, under a bunch of junk. He hadn't hidden it exactly, but it wasn't out in plain view, either. When he moved to the spare room and got rid of the toy box, he hid the gun in the ceiling, on the beam above the tiles. He must have not put them back right, and she noticed. Or maybe she'd been searching his room for something else.

Sometimes when he appropriated things from somewhere in the house, she took them from his room and put them back where they belonged and never mentioned it. A lamp he liberated from the family room—she never used it anyway. A flour sifter from the kitchen—lucky for him he'd cleaned all traces of weed out of it after he used it to sift the stuff he'd traded some kid in school for that card of diet pills he found in the medicine cabinet.

He still didn't know what she'd done with the gun. He'd looked in her room—it wasn't there. He found some other things he'd taken from her, but not the gun. Not that it was hers to begin with. Any more than that picture was, that picture of his old man in the little silver frame. He'd found that in her drawer a long time ago and taken it. In the picture his old man, big and grinning, held a small bundle tucked underneath his arm. The bundle was him. Unless, of course, there was another kid somewhere.

That was a thought. Another kid. Maybe he had a brother somewhere, or a sister. Maybe it died after it was born, or maybe they gave it away because it was crippled or deformed or something. Maybe he could find it and go see it and visit it. Maybe it was somewhere nearby, in the neighborhood even, only he didn't know about it.

Except that was crap and he knew it. There wasn't any other kid. There was just him, the kid in the picture, the bundle. How many times had he heard her dumb story about how much she wanted a baby except they thought she couldn't have one, and then, all of a sudden, there he was, growing in her stomach. Bluh, what a thought, coming out between her legs, all bloody and slimy. He'd seen a movie about babies being born in ninth grade sex ed. Yuk.

He stood up and chinned himself on his closet bar. No, it was him in that picture all right. A goddamn miracle, like she said. Too bad his old man didn't think he was such a miracle, not enough to stick around and find out anyway.

He didn't know where that old picture was now. Once after he came home from an appointment with old Gotenburg he'd thrown it against the wall and broken the glass frame into little pieces, which he left on the floor. She must have cleaned them up because the next morning the picture was gone, as if it had never existed. As if he'd never been that little red, wrinkled baby being held securely under the arm of a big, smiling stranger.

He hadn't heard anything from or about his old man in a year or so. Not since that Friday night he was home alone, watching *Night of the Living Dead* on TV. His mother had only recently stopped getting him baby-sitters—Christ, he was nearly thirteen then. Still, when the phone rang it startled him. Sometimes it was creepy in the house by himself, especially if the wind was blowing. It made the tree outside his window sway, the one with the iron bar bolted to it that had once held a swing and was still connected to the side of the house with another bolt. When the wind blew hard, the tree creaked with a sort of low, rumbly sound.

But the sound that startled him wasn't the wind, it was the phone. At first he didn't recognize the voice. It was sort of blurry, the way Chris's father sounded when he drank too many beers.

"Bill?"

"Yeah?"

"This is Don." Pause. "Your father."

"Oh, yeah. Hi."

"How're you doing, son?" Like it had only been a few days. Like his mother hadn't told him not to bother them anymore. To protect him, she'd said, like his old man was some kind of virus or something.

"Okay I guess."

"That's good. Still skiing?"

"Not yet. It hasn't snowed in the mountains."

"Oh, sure. I forgot. How are you doing in school, fella?"

"Fine. Okay."

"Good, good, that's great. Keeping your grades up, that's important."

"You want to talk to Mom? She's not here now."

"No, no, that's fine. I just wanted to . . . to say hello, that's all."

"Well, hello."

His father laughed, a funny-sounding laugh. "Hello yourself," he said. Then there was a clumsy silence again until his father broke it. "Well, I'd better go, this is long distance. Say, Billy . . ." His voice trailed off.

"Yeah?"

"Take care of yourself."

"Yeah, I will."

That was the last time he'd looked in his mother's drawer for the picture, but it wasn't there. He knew where there was another picture, though, in his baby book, in the hall closet, way up high, in the same box where she kept papers and letters and his old report cards and locks of his baby hair and stuff. After his father's call, he rummaged through the box until he found another picture like the one he'd thrown away, and he put it in his room, tacked it right up on his bulletin board, and she never said a word about it.

After that weird call from the old man, he took dope from his mother's stash for the first time. He got Chris to come over and keep him company and they got stoned and split their sides laughing over that dumb movie, which didn't seem so scary anymore. When his mother came home he didn't tell her about the telephone call. His father hadn't called to talk to *her*.

He put some music on his tape deck and stretched out on the bed again. She came into his room—God, couldn't she ever learn to knock? What if he was beating off or something?

"Would you mind knocking on the door before you come busting in?" he said irritably.

"Excuse me." She stepped back into the hall and tapped on the door.

"Yeah, come in."

"Thanks a lot. When are you going to Chris's?"

"I dunno. Later."

"How much later?"

"Later, that's all. After he does his homework."

"I want you home from Chris's by ten."

"Eleven."

"Ten."

"Ten thirty."

"Okay." Usually he could beat her down on things like that if he kept at it.

"I'll see you later then," she said.

"S'long."

"Is that all? Just so long?"

Dutifully he raised himself off the bed on one arm and pecked her on the cheek. She leaned over and put her arms around him. He could smell the perfume she always wore. She hugged him; he could feel her chest squashed against him.

"How much do I love you?" she asked, and he responded dutifully.

"As much as the world and more."

"That's right," she smiled, and ruffled his hair. "Well, good night, then."

"Night."

After she left his eyes felt all itchy, like he was getting an allergy or something. He was jumpy; he could feel his muscles quiver underneath his skin, and practically see the pulse beat in his wrist. He rubbed his eyes until the itchy feeling went away and then he stood up and pulled his mattress away from the box springs on his bed. In a hiding place between the springs, where the fabric stretched over them was torn, he had secreted a tiny pipe. He shoved the mattress back in place and went to another of his caches, a loose baseboard that gave way when he tugged at it and revealed a large space between the bottom of the plaster wall and the edge of the floor. He took out a small piece of aluminum foil folded several times over a bud of dope he'd taken from her room. He tapped the dope into the pipe and lit up, settling back on his bed, watching the prisoners outfox the stupid Nazi camp leader. He waited for the dope to make the itchy feeling go away. But it just seemed to make him jumpier, so he poured a little vodka from the bottle she kept in the freezer, added water to the bottle to replace what he had taken, and swallowed what he had poured for himself. It tasted like hell going down, but it made his skin feel warmer. He went back to his room, switched on the Sonics game, and was asleep before the first quarter ended.

4 Anne rounded the last curve before home at the best moment of her run, when her stride and her breathing were perfectly synchronized, when her feet rose effortlessly off the packed dirt path and seemed barely to touch it when they landed. A few yards farther on, she slowed and ran in place, stopping to marvel at her neighbor's camellia tree, which seemed to have blossomed overnight. She bent to sniff the delicately layered, velvety white flowers; they had no fragrance, but their moisture was cool and fresh against her face. Thank you anyway, she told the tree silently—just putting out flowers in February is enough. She loved the way spring came in the Northwest, sneaking in disguised as the end of winter, until the omnipresent drizzle warmed slightly, and on the snowy ridges of the mountains, east and west, the dark rivulets appeared, which meant the thaw had begun.

Billy was in the kitchen, tinkering with the toaster. "I got it fixed," he told her. "The thing was, the cord was frayed and it was shorting out all the time. I put a new plug on, too. Want me to make you some toast?"

"No thanks," she panted, collapsing heavily on a kitchen stool. "A little water though, I could use that."

"I'll squeeze you some orange juice. I fixed the juicer, too. Same problem. You're tough on appliance cords, you shouldn't yank them around like you do."

Anne was pleased with Billy's initiative. She could not fix even the simplest household appliances, or keep up the maintenance her seventy-five-year-old house seemed constantly to require. When a closet door stuck or a window hasp broke or a doorknob came off in her hands, she was helpless, and when something went wrong with the plumbing, the electricity, or the antiquated heating system, she was totally at the mercy of repairmen. Her house, she often thought, was the living example of entropy.

"I didn't even ask you to fix those things . . . thanks a lot," she said. "I'll tell you what, I'll pay you for fixing them, five dollars each. It would have cost me more than that to take them into the shop."

"You don't have to pay me."

"I know I don't have to. I want to."

"That's okay, forget it."

"No, really—"

"I said forget it, Ma, I like to fix stuff."

"You ought to put a notice up at the hardware store in Madison Park, offering house to house service," she said. "You could use the extra money to support your heavy metal habit."

"Yeah, I guess."

"Why don't you make out an index card with your name and phone number and ride down to the hardware store and put it on the bulletin board?"

"I don't feel like it."

She sighed. "Never mind. Anyway, thank you for fixing the toaster and the juicer. I appreciate it."

"That's okay," he said. "How far'd you run?"

"Three miles. Down to the hydroplane pits and back. Not bad for an old lady, huh?"

"You're not so old."

"Thanks for the vote of confidence. Are you stay-ing over at Chris's tonight?"

"Yeah, he and I want to work on the tree house first thing in the morning. You going out with Patrick?"

"Mmm hmm." Mentally she revised her evening plans. Since Billy would be out, she and Patrick would come home after dinner. A delicious tingle rippled through her body as she anticipated the sensual plea-sure of being casually, carelessly naked within her house, of leaving doors ajar, letting the sounds of lovemaking echo through them.

"What about dinner?" she asked.

"I just made a humongous sandwich, don't fix anything." He stood in back of her, and massaged her shoulders.

"Mmm, that's terrific," she said, as Billy kneaded her shoulders firmly and then rubbed her back more gently in a slow, circular motion. She felt vaguely un-comfortable; there was something almost sexual about his touch. She spun around on the kitchen stool and stood up briskly, ruffling his hair. "Thanks, that felt good," she said. "I'd better hit the shower, Pat-rick's picking me up in half an hour."

"I'm going down to Chris's then," he said. "Have a good time tonight. And don't do anything I wouldn't do, but if you do—"

"I know, name it after you." She giggled. "Then I'd have two kids with the same name."

"Yeah, well life's a bitch, but it won't matter in six hundred years."

"A comforting thought," she said, as he pecked her on the cheek. She closed the front door behind him and went upstairs, her step light, her mind on the evening to come.

"Where's the boy wonder tonight?" Patrick asked as they lingered over dessert and coffee at the Brasserie.

"Spending the night with a friend."

"We have the house to ourselves?"

She nodded.

"Then why are we sitting here?"

"Beats the hell out of me," she smiled, and he signaled the waiter. She didn't think she loved Patrick—his politics were impossibly conservative and his air of arrogance, which attracted her, sometimes became a smugness, which did not. But they laughed easily together, shared an appreciation for reading Dickens aloud, and were relaxed in each other's company. Like her, he had been married once; like her, he had been in therapy after his divorce. It gave them not only a common experience but a mutual expectation that they would behave honestly and decently toward one another. Which might not be as heady as infatuation, she thought, but was much more reliable and less potentially painful. They were well matched sexually, too; he was taut and wiry, with a well-muscled body which pleased her, and in the car on the way back to her house he stroked her thigh underneath her skirt, slowly and teasingly. By the time they arrived she was eager to be naked next to him, stretched across her big brass bed, to have him inside her.

She put her key in the front door, but it did not turn in its tumblers; it was already unlocked, and she could hear the television from Billy's room. She frowned. "He must have forgotten to turn it off, and forgotten to lock the door, too. Sometimes he is such a space cadet it drives me nuts. Go put some music on, I'll check upstairs."

Billy was in bed—underneath the covers, she noticed, wearing pajamas and a wool bathrobe. The only light in the room came from the flickering of the television set.

"I thought you were spending the night at Chris's."

"I didn't feel good, so I came home."

She bent over him and touched his forehead with her lips. "You don't seem to have any fever," she said. "What hurts you?"

"My stomach."

"Did you eat something at Chris's?"

"We went to Gag in the Bag for burgers. Probably from that."

"You went where?"

"Gag in the Bag. You know, Jack in the Box."

"Oh. Sure."

"I feel better now. You know, in my own room."

She stifled the quick stab of resentment she felt. It's his house too, of course he can come home if he wants to. Just because his mother wants to scream her head off when she fucks is no reason to push him out. Not much of one, anyway.

"You feel well enough to go back to Chris's? It's not even ten o'clock yet." God, that certainly sounded loving and caring, didn't it? "I mean, if you want to, of course. You said you wanted to get an early start on the tree house."

"Nah. I might feel sick again. I barfed once tonight, wouldn't want to do that in a strange place."

Chris's house is hardly a strange place, she countered silently, then caught herself—stop that, she thought, what kind of a mother are you, anyway?

"Sure. Well, I'll be downstairs if you need me."

"Yeah. You have a good time tonight?"

"Mmm hmm."

"Pat staying over?"

"Yes."

"Oh. Good. I mean, if that's what you want. Hey, Ma?"

"Mmm?"

"I love you."

"Me too you. Night, honey."

"Night."

She and Patrick were curled together on the rug in front of the fire, teasing each other playfully, lingeringly—Anne wanted to wait until Billy was asleep before they went upstairs to bed. A flame licked at the bark of a cedar log, igniting it with a sharp crack, and a second later the doorbell chimed. Patrick looked at her questioningly, and she shrugged. "It must be one of the kids in the neighborhood," she said, getting up and rearranging her clothes with automatic gestures. "Probably Chris coming to check on Billy, I'll send him home and be back in a minute."

It was not Chris but his father whose bulk filled Anne's doorway. He had a bull neck on thickly muscled shoulders, and he towered over her by nearly a foot. She invited him inside but he shook his head and stood there under the porch light. "Your son and my boy, they was together tonight. Earlier." It was a statement, not a question, and he went on without waiting for her to confirm it. "They broke into the Lawlor house down the street—you know that?"

She shook her head dumbly—what was he talking about?

"They go out to the drive-in for hamburgers, the wife's got to go to the Safeway anyway, she takes 'em in the station wagon. I sit down to read my paper, I hear they left the damn record player going, and I can't concentrate with that loud noise, so I go down to Chris's room to turn it off. Then I see all this stuff spread out on the bed like they didn't have time to put it away before they left. A camera. A hunting knife. A wristwatch. And some dirty pictures."

"Billy has a camera. And he and Chris both have knives, you must have seen them before. As for the pictures—well, teenage boys, you know—I wouldn't get too upset about that."

"You wouldn't, huh?" The man leaned toward her, and she moved back, feeling trapped and confused. "Your kid have a four-hundred-dollar Pentax? He got a forged-steel hunting knife in a leather sheath with the initials J.S.L. burned into it? I been hunting elk and deer over to eastern Washington for years with Joe Lawlor now, I seen that knife plenty. It ain't your kid's. And I seen them pictures, too, what Joe got in Korea in the war."

She shook her head. No, it wasn't Billy, couldn't have been Billy. It was Chris, it must have been Chris, he did it and was showing off in front of his friend.

"Sorriest day of my life, I got to take my worthless kid over Joe Lawlor's house and say here, this is my kid, he broke in through your basement window while you and Terry was down to the mall at Southcenter, and my kid he took your camera you bought when you went to Japan with the Jaycees and your knife and your watch and your pictures of them Oriental girls screwing, pardon my French, lady. Same Joe Lawlor, never said beans when your kid took a half dozen good cedar boards from out behind his garage where he's building himself an addition. He paid good money for them boards."

"Boards? What are you talking about?"

"Just what I said, where'd ya think they got the lumber for that damn tree house? From the lumberyard? You got any idea how much cedar costs a running foot these days?"

"Billy said . . . I thought it was wood scraps left

over from some project, I thought you were doing it, but maybe I misunderstood . . ."

"Leftover, huh? I see Joe hauling more boards in the other day, I say, hey, Joe, you count wrong the first time? And he says hell no, I counted right, some kids musta took a few of them boards. And Chris says Billy told him Lawlor says he could have some scraps, so I go down them woods before I come here tonight and I take a look at the tree house and they ain't no scraps, that's Joe Lawlor's lumber in that tree house. And Chris says hell, he don't know, Bill says they was scraps and he don't work in no lumberyard, how's he supposed to know?" He cleared his throat and shook his fist in the air between them. "Listen, Miz Manning, I ain't telling you no lie. I asked 'em, they come home from the drive-in, they admit it. Chris does, your boy don't say nothing. I take Chris and the stuff they took over Lawlor's house, and Chris, he gives it back and he apologizes. He's gonna be paintin' Joe Lawlor's house this summer soon as school gets out, 'stead of going up to the camp up there in the islands with your kid like they planned. And then I take my boy home and I whomp his ass. Same's I suggest you do your kid. And I don't want to see Bill around my house no more. Not till he's learned his lesson."

The man turned on his heel and left as quickly as he had come, and Anne stood in the semidark of the front hall for a few moments, trying to order her careening thoughts, which fastened fleetingly on what Chris's father had said about the summer. If Billy didn't go to camp—if Billy stayed home that summer, with no school, no structure, no friends, even, if Chris's father meant what he said—she'd go crazy. But if Billy had done what Chris's father said, she couldn't simply overlook it. She would have to do something that would deprive Billy equally of his va-

cation . . . wouldn't she? And why was she being punished? She hadn't broken into someone's house, taken
their things, invaded their privacy, ignored their
locked doors and . . .

"Hey, Anne, what's going on?" Patrick asked. Almost without acknowledging his presence, except to
push past him, she started for the stairs.

She didn't knock on Billy's door—she pushed it
open, snapped on the light, and confronted her son.
"Did you break into Mr. Lawlor's house tonight?" she
demanded.

Billy said nothing, just scooted backward on his
bed as she advanced on him. Her voice increased in
volume with each forward step. "Well, did you? Did
you? Answer me, William Manning, answer me right
this minute! And you'd better tell the truth, goddamn
it!"

Billy raised his arm in front of his face, shielding
himself from her, and she grabbed him by the elbow
and yanked it away so she could see what was in his
eyes. She read only defiance—not guilt or fear, just a
cool show of bravado.

"Well? Are you going to answer me?" she shouted.
"No? You goddamn will or I'll break your neck, I'll
beat it out of you, I'll . . . I'll . . ." She grabbed his thin
body by the shoulders and shook him hard, again and
again, as if to expel every lie, every bit of dishonesty
and cowardice.

"It's not the way you think, Ma," he began, but she
did not listen.

"What the hell are you trying to tell me, Billy Manning? Do you just want to go to jail like a common
thief? Is that why you lie and steal and break into people's houses? Is it? Is it?"

"I don't do that, I'm not a thief, I *don't* always do
those things—"

"Well, what do you call it then?" She was shouting again, she could not control herself, she couldn't even try to. "Borrowing, is that what you call it? Did you borrow Mr. Lawlor's camera and his watch the way you borrowed his lumber? Don't you know the difference between borrowing and stealing, for Christ's sake? Don't you? Didn't I teach you anything? Why don't we just put an end to this stupid game of yours once and for all? Why don't you get in the car and I'll drive you right down to Juvenile Hall? That's where you'll end up anyway, on the way to the reformatory!"

"Lawlor's not going to call the cops," Billy said sullenly. "He said we could paint his house this summer, pay him back. Besides, if I wanted to go to jail I'd of busted the Bon Marche."

She didn't understand. "Then why? Why did you break into his house? He's our neighbor, he's lived here since before we moved in, he's always been nice to you, hasn't he?"

"Yeah, he's okay."

"Then why? I don't understand, Billy, make me understand. Don't you have a watch and a camera? Isn't it a good enough camera? And a knife . . . don't you have a Swiss Army knife, didn't I buy you one last Christmas?"

"I got a camera, it's okay. I got a knife."

"Then why? WHY?" Her anger returned, stronger this time, overwhelming her, and she grabbed him by the arm and dragged his body across the bed toward her. "WHY IS MY SON A THIEF?" she shouted, as he recoiled from her wildly striking fists.

"Hey, what's going on in here?" Patrick asked, entering the room. "What are you doing . . . Anne, quit that, lay off, you're hurting him—"

She wheeled to face Patrick, her face red and an-

gry. "Get out of here! Leave me alone! Leave us alone
. . . he's my son, not yours," she shouted. "He's my
problem, just go away!" Hot tears of anger and humiliation coursed down her cheeks. "Really, we're
fine now," she said. "I think you'd better go . . . I'm
sorry, I'll call you tomorrow . . . no, please, it's over
now, we're fine . . . please, would you go now?"

"You sure you're all right?"

"I'm sure, really I am, we're okay, we're fine." She
composed herself, smoothed her hair back from her
face, wiped the streaks of tears with the back of her
hand.

"You want me to talk to him? Sometimes a boy
needs a guy around, a man, you know—"

Angrily, she pushed him away. "You think that's
the answer for everything, don't you? A boy needs a
man, a son needs a father, that's it, right? Well, he
doesn't have a father, all he's got is a mother, all he's
got is me, and all I've got is him and it's just going to
have to do, that's all there is to it. Oh, Pat, just go
away, can't you?"

"Sure, sure, that's the way you feel, okay." Patrick
backed away from her, from them, out of the room,
out of their lives.

That's the end of him, she thought dully. It's true
now. All I've got is Billy. He's all I've got, he's all I'll
ever have.

5 Anne finally fell into a restless sleep just before dawn. When she woke up, near noon, she was disoriented; it was not until she heard the bells from the church up on the crest of the hill, several blocks away, that she realized it was Sunday and she had not overslept, missing a client or a court appearance. Then she remembered the night before, and Billy. But if it was Sunday it was his ski lesson day, and she hadn't made his lunch or checked his gear to ensure that he'd taken an extra sweater or a pair of dry socks. Nor had she made sure he was up in time for the ski bus; Billy could sleep through any alarm clock, he was probably still in bed, and she was out twenty dollars, which was the prorated cost of each lesson and lift ticket. On the other hand, she thought as she put the filter paper in the coffee maker, he doesn't deserve to go skiing after what he did. Tough luck if he overslept, he can just stay here and deal with it.

Except he hadn't. He was not in his room, and a cursory check told her his skis, boots, and pack were gone. So he'd sneaked out. Well, to be fair, he'd gone ahead and gone, the way he was supposed to, since she hadn't told him he couldn't.

She took her coffee and the newspaper back to bed and thought about what she would tell him he couldn't do, how she would punish him for his crime, the larger implications of which she wasn't ready, herself, to deal with. Anne buried her face in her pillow and pulled the covers over her head. She didn't want to think about it. She couldn't sleep it away, though. Billy would be home that evening, and she had to know what to do. What to think. What to say to her son, and how to say it. With Billy's actions the previous day, he had escalated the conflict between them into a different kind of struggle. He wasn't just acting out against her now. He was taking on the world, and she was suddenly as frightened for him as she was sorry for herself.

She picked Billy up at the ski bus. He was mostly silent on the way home; they ate dinner with a minimum of conversation, and she had to remind him to do the dishes. He left the job half done. He certainly isn't trying to win me over, she thought. She rinsed the dishcloth and went into his room without knocking.

"I want you to see a psychiatrist," she told him.

He sighed heavily.

"Look, Bill, it's gone beyond the petty little crap around here—taking my dope, telling me lies, not doing your chores. And it's gone beyond the things at school, too. At first I thought you were just messing up to get at me. But not this. What you did to Mr. Lawlor—you could get in real trouble for that. Trouble I can't get you out of."

"Who says I was getting at you? Why do you always have to take everything so personally, for crying out loud?"

"Well, if it's not at me I don't know who you're mad at."

"Who says I'm mad at anyone?"

"If you're not, then something else is eating at you."

"Nothing's eating at me."

"Then why did you break into Mr. Lawlor's house?"

He didn't answer, and the silence between them lengthened. Finally he said, "You always think shrinks are the answer to everything. Forget Gotenburg, the creep, I ain't going to him."

"Aren't," she corrected automatically.

"All right, I aren't going back to that creep."

"What if I make you?"

"Why would you do a dumb thing like that?"

"Because this behavior has got to stop. I don't want to see you end up dead in an alley from a drug overdose or getting shot by someone when you burgle his house."

"For pete's sake, Ma, I'm not going to OD on drugs. You think because I smoke a little marijuana now and then I'm gonna be a junkie, don't you? Then how come you're not a junkie, huh? You smoke it, too."

"I'm older than you are."

"Oh, shit, that's what you always tell me. I'm still not going to turn into a junkie, don't worry. And I'm not going to burgle any houses."

"Do I have your promise on that?"

"Yeah, you got my promise. Now will you leave me alone?"

"No, I will not. We still haven't settled on how you're going to be punished for what you did yesterday, and how you're going to pay Mr. Lawlor back for it."

"You can ask Gotenburg, he's got all the answers. But I'm not going there. If you drag me there and force me to sit there for his lousy hour and beat me if I don't, I'll go. But I won't talk."

"Beat you? When did I ever beat you?"

"Last night. Look, my arm's all black and blue." He pushed his pajama sleeve up and it was true, his arm was swollen and angry looking. She flinched and looked away.

"That was different. I lost my temper. I didn't beat you, I shook you."

"You hit me."

"You provoked me."

"I'm not going to Gotenburg."

"I'll find someone else."

"Some other creep. Go ahead. It's your money, you want to waste it."

"I want to waste it."

Billy went off to school the next morning without incident. At the office, Anne looked up a number in her Rolodex and called Dan Jarvis, a psychiatrist whose expert testimony she had often relied upon in her criminal practice. "Can I buy an hour of your time and pick your brain on a personal matter?" she asked him. "Not my own," she added. "Well, not exactly."

"Yeah, I know, you've got a friend who," he said good-naturedly. "You can't buy my advice, but you can pick up the tab at lunch. You want to do it today?"

"That would be wonderful," she told him. "At McRory's, at noon?"

"You're on."

He was waiting for her in the restaurant foyer, a slim and neatly tailored man with lively blue eyes, a carefully trimmed, red-blond mustache and goatee, and oddly pointed ears who looked, she thought, like Reynard the Fox. Over oysters and beer she explained the problem. "Lately, Billy's been pushing the limits. Trouble with me, trouble at school, and now he's on a tear. If you were testifying in court about him, I guess you'd call him predelinquent," she said.

"You think he should see a psychiatrist." It was not a question, and she nodded.

"What about something like the Big Brother program? They have good luck with kids like that. Boys need a man, someone to identify with, a role model."

"That's simplistic," she said. "Give a troubled kid someone to look up to, and everything else goes away, right?"

"No," said Dan, "it doesn't go away. Sometimes what's troubling him goes underground for a while, though, and just the passage of time makes things easier. Why are you set on a shrink?"

"Because I think Billy's problems go deeper than just needing a male role model in his life. There are plenty of kids without fathers who do fine and don't get into this kind of trouble."

"But Billy's not one of them, and you think he's sick, right?"

She recoiled. "I didn't say sick."

"That's what you're implying. That he's sick and a man in a white coat with a couch in his office instead of an examining table can make him well again."

"Not well. Just happy, that's all. He's not a very happy person."

"That's a big order. Psychiatrists, as a rule, don't have much luck with adolescents. Kids that age don't want to be close to an adult, they don't want to talk about their feelings. They can't—even the smart ones, like your boy, have no emotional vocabulary. They couldn't describe or explain their feelings if they had to—all they know is, they're overwhelmed, with fear or love or shame or lust—that's a big one with teenage boys, lust—and they have to do something to discharge it. Billy probably couldn't make a connection between how he feels and what he does. It's not the action itself that's important, it's the discharge that it provides, the getting rid of feelings by stuffing them back inside with dope or superimposing another feeling, like excitement, the fear of getting caught, on the ones that are churning in him but he can't give a name to."

"Then what else can I do? I can't give Billy a man, that's not in my power. I try to provide constructive opportunities for him to work out his feelings, but he chooses the destructive ones." She stirred her coffee.

"I think he needs something I can't give him," she said. "I want the name of the best child psychiatrist in town."

"Have you ever been in therapy?"

"Yes. I see someone now, occasionally. Maintenance, he calls it. I was in his group for a year or so."

"Why don't you ask him for a referral?"

"Because he's an M.S.W., not an analyst. He's good, don't get me wrong, but I think his referrals would be to the same kind of therapists he is."

"Did he help you?"

"Yes, but that's not the point. I want Billy to see a real doctor. Like David Gotenburg, but not him. Billy's seen him, and he won't go back to him."

"You have a lot of faith in the power of credentials, don't you?"

Anne colored. "What do you mean by that?"

"Oh, nothing. Tell me, except for Billy, and expert witnesses, have you had much to do with psychiatrists?"

"I have a brother who spent several years of his life at the Menninger Clinic."

"Where is he now?"

She laughed. "Playing the sitar in Nepal, I suppose. The doctors at the Clinic told my parents to let him go. He did a lot of acid in the sixties, dropped out of college, sat in his room for weeks on end. Then they took him to Topeka, and after a while they said he's never going to adjust to life in this culture, let him do what he wants. If you try to force him to conform, he'll probably kill himself. So my father supports him, which is very inexpensive in Nepal, and once a year or so he comes home and my mother feeds him and my father asks him if he wouldn't like to go back to college, and he leaves. He lives with a Swedish woman there."

"Do you think the doctors gave your parents the right advice?"

"Who knows?" Her face darkened. "He had tried suicide once. Unsuccessfully, thank God. Sometimes I think . . . maybe Billy . . . maybe it's a genetic thing . . ." She wiped the corner of her eyes with a napkin, and Dan offered his handkerchief, which she declined. "No, thanks. I'm okay. It's just that sometimes I . . ."

"Sometimes you want a doctor with diplomas on his wall and a reassuring manner to tell you your son isn't going to end up playing the sitar ten thousand miles away."

"I guess," she said. "When I went into therapy, it was just . . . situational. After a divorce. So a social worker was fine. The group was very supportive. I got better—the passage of time, as you said. But Billy . . . I don't think he has that time. He'll end up in real trouble first."

"Here's a name for you," said Dan, scribbling some words on a card. "He's a honcho in the child psychoanalytic institute in town. Credentialed up the wazoo. And a very nice, very decent guy. Kids seem to like him. Give him a call, use my name. He'll work you in."

"You know him well?"

"He's my brother-in-law. That's his home phone, you'll never get past the office nurse, he's booked solid, isn't taking on any new patients. But he'll see Billy. I'll call him this afternoon."

Dr. Wilson's office was a suite in a small, two-story brick building on Capitol Hill on a quiet street in a mostly residential neighborhood. The waiting room was tastefully furnished with comfortable chairs and current issues of magazines—she noticed *Skiing* and *Outdoors* and wondered if they reflected the psychiatrist's interests or those of his clientele. His own, she thought, when he appeared and led her into his office; he was a tall, ruddy-faced man with a powerful body, and she could imagine him schussing down a slope or climbing a mountain peak. He welcomed her with appropriate words, and then asked her to tell him about herself, about Billy and their family.

"He says shrinks are dumb," she reported to him. "He says if it makes me feel better, I should go, but he doesn't need to."

"At fourteen it's hard to get them into therapy," said Dr. Wilson, echoing what Dan Jarvis had told her. "But I don't think that's all there is to it. I suspect that Bill may be frightened of men."

"Why? No man has ever mistreated him. Not physically, anyway."

"No, but one—his father—has hurt him just the same. And if Billy would let himself feel, he would be feeling very, very angry. At his father for leaving him. At you because he needs you. At his teachers because they can't control him. But he's so frightened of the potential power of his anger to harm—himself, other people—that he can't let it out. Won't accept it. Will do anything to avoid it."

"I've always encouraged him to express his feelings. To face them, not judge them."

"Ah, but that's your way, don't you see? You're an adult. You know that feelings can't kill, maim, send away those you love. You've been in therapy, you're somewhat knowledgeable about psychiatry . . . those things make it possible for you to accept your feelings. Although I think if we probed a little more, we'd find out that you are, in fact, judging them. Judging yourself for being mad at your son, for losing your temper, for feeling frustrated and unable to cope. Maybe you could use a little help yourself."

"Would you see me?" She liked this doctor. She liked his frankness, his intelligence, and she felt comforted by him.

"I'd see you with Billy, as part of his therapy. I'd only see you separately if he agreed, or if it was in response to something he'd done, and only with his knowledge. He has to feel that he can trust me."

"How, if he won't even see you?"

"Tell him he doesn't have any choice. He comes, whether he likes it or not. End of discussion. That's it. Drive him here yourself if you have to."

"He'll just sit here and won't say anything."

"He doesn't have to say anything. He just has to sit here. Sometimes the presence of an authority can be reassuring to a boy his age. He can feel as though someone is setting limits. Up to now, he's been acting out in very safe ways—lying to you, stealing from you, getting in dutch at school. He's not refusing to do his schoolwork because he doesn't want to, by the way—he can't."

"Of course he can. He's twice as smart as anyone in his class."

"Sure he is. But he has a work inhibition. It's probably damn near impossible for him to study or concentrate, he's so busy corking up his emotions. If they ever got out, he'd explode . . . that's probably what he thinks. If he thinks. Kids that age don't, much. Mostly, they feel. They're one big bundle of neurons, and life is a struggle to stay in control. It doesn't leave much energy for anything else, including school."

"So it's safe to do things to me, and his teachers?"

"That's right. You're not going to hurt him. You're not going to put him in jail. And, it seems to me, you're not going to say either abide by my rules, by school rules, by society's rules, or get out."

"Where would he go? He's only fourteen."

"That's right. Some parents would say that to a fourteen-year-old and mean it. You won't, and Billy knows that. I think he does, anyway. Let's make an appointment for him to see me—I can tell you better after that."

"And if he won't?"

"You make sure that he does."

When she brought Bill to Dr. Wilson's office a few days later, the doctor said, "I think I'd like to see Bill alone, at least at first. Why don't you wait in the other room, and we'll talk after Bill and I have had a chance to get acquainted."

While she waited for Dr. Wilson to call for her, she studied the other people in the waiting room, those who came out of other offices and some who entered from the street. There was a mother and her daughter; the girl sat a studied distance from the older woman, who read a magazine, biting a fingernail each time she turned a page. A young boy of about seven ran down the hall noisily, sliding to a stop at the nurse's desk and looking around in confusion. "Your mother called, she'll be a few minutes late, Davey," the nurse told him, and he chewed his lower lip, considering what to do with the information. Anne gave him a friendly smile, but he ignored her and busied himself in a corner of the room with a matchbox car he dug out of his pocket. A young man in a business suit, carrying a briefcase, sat down and drummed his fingers on his knees, then stopped abruptly and folded his hands firmly. After a few minutes he got up and carefully inspected each of the botanical prints hung in a neat series on the wall opposite Anne.

Finally Dr. Wilson came out of his office, and beckoned Anne into the room. Billy sat on a leather couch in one corner, the doctor leaned casually against his desk in another, and he gestured her to a chair at the third angle of the triangle formed by the furniture. Billy looked away, out of the window that faced on the wide avenue where she had parked her car.

"Well," Dr. Wilson began, "it seems like you and Bill are having a hard time of it these days. I think Bill ought to see me on a regular basis."

"How regular?"

"I think two or three times a week, for a while, at least. But Bill doesn't want to. He says he's got a lot to do, with school and all. So we made a deal. He stays out of trouble, he only sees me once a week. He screws up, he sees me more. That agreeable with you?"

She nodded.

"Good," he said. "I've got a free hour on Wednesday mornings."

"But he's in school then."

"I'll give him a note. His school is only a few blocks away. He can walk here and back. He'll miss one class and lunch. He can handle that if he wants to—he's a smart kid, he can get by once a week without lunch." He waited, as if for a laugh, and when he did not get it, he rubbed his hands briskly together. "That's it, then. See the nurse for an appointment card on the way out. And oh, yes—Bill and I have another meeting this week, tomorrow after school. We're going down to Juvenile Hall to have a look around there."

"What for?" she asked, alarmed.

The doctor was casual. "It'll be easier for Bill the first time they take him there if he knows what to expect. It can be frightening, being thrown in there and not knowing how to act."

"What are you talking about?" she demanded. "He's not going to Juvenile Hall. Mr. Lawlor isn't pressing charges."

"No, and that's fortunate," said Dr. Wilson thoughtfully. "But sooner or later, if he keeps stealing, Bill's going to end up there. I think we ought to make it easier for him, if we can. Right, Bill?"

Bill nodded, and the doctor rubbed his hands together again. "Fine. I'll pick you up at three fifteen tomorrow, Bill." He went to the door and held it open for them; Billy went out, into the hall, but Anne remained behind. "I think we ought to talk about this first," she said. "Juvenile Hall, I mean."

"Fine," said Doctor Wilson. "Hey, Bill, will you come back here a minute?"

"Alone, I mean," Anne said.

"No reason for that now," Dr. Wilson replied. "It's nothing Bill doesn't know. But perhaps we'd better go over it together." He ushered them back into the room, and they took the same seats.

"It sounds to me as though you're just assuming

that Billy's going to end up in jail, and that's not why he's coming here, so he can get comfortable with that possibility," Anne said.

"Not possibility, probability," said Dr. Wilson. "Billy's been stealing for a long time. Not just from you, either."

"From whom?" Anne demanded.

"Doesn't matter." The doctor, who had been filling a pipe as they spoke, made a vague gesture with it. "Now he's heading for more serious trouble. Kids like Bill, they start shoplifting, then usually stealing cars. A kid's a thief, he ends up in the joint, sooner or later."

"But Billy's not a thief!" she protested.

"Sure he is," Dr. Wilson said, calmly. "The question is, can he stop?"

"Well, can he? Can you?" she demanded of her son, who was staring out of the window once more. He said nothing, and the psychiatrist went on.

"Maybe, maybe not," he said. "We'll just have to see. Meanwhile, I have to see another patient." With that, he held open the office door again, and, minutes later, closed it behind them.

On the way home, she searched for a safe topic of conversation, but could find none. Finally she said what was on her mind. "How did you feel when Dr. Wilson called you a thief?" she asked.

Billy shrugged. "It's okay," he said noncommittally.

She was aghast. "Okay?" she echoed. "Is that who you are, a thief? Is that what you think when you think of the future, of who you're going to be when you're eighteen, or twenty, or fifty, for God's sake? A thief?"

"I don't think much about that."

"Well maybe you should!" she said indignantly.

"Look, you said I had to see the guy, I'm seeing him, aren't I? Why don't you let me think about what I want to think about, 'stead of telling me what I should think."

"It's not what you should think, but how you should feel," she argued. "If you feel like a . . . a thief, say . . . you'll act like one. That's not a very good self-image."

"Don't worry about my self-image, it's—hey, there's Chris, stop the car, okay?" She slowed down and pulled over to the curb. They were two blocks from home. "I thought Chris's father didn't want you around," she said.

"I ain't going to be around, we're going down to the lake," he said.

"But that's not what his father meant," she began, but Billy was already out of the car. She gave up, and drove slowly, thoughtfully, home.

6 "I know you'd rather be somewhere else, but that was the deal we made—the more you get in trouble, the more times you have to come. Until you stop getting in trouble—then you only have to come once a week," said Dr. Wilson.

Yeah, and then I get to sit here and stare at your stupid face for an hour, listen to your crap when I could be doing something else, Bill thought.

"Let's talk about breaking into your neighbor's house," the doctor went on.

Bill said nothing. I'm not talking to you, asshole, he addressed the psychiatrist silently. She can make me come here but she can't make me talk. She can't make me say shit if I don't want to.

After a few minutes the doctor sighed. "Well, since you seem to be in a reflective mood, let's play a little chess."

Bill grunted, and moved wordlessly to the chess table set up beneath the office window. Even playing chess with Wilson beat sitting around staring at his bald head. I wonder what it'd be like to be bald? I wonder if he knows how dumb he looks, all bald?

"I'll move first."

It's your game, dumbo, go ahead. Oh . . . that one, huh? I could take this game in five moves if you do that one.

They played without speaking for a while. Then the doctor said, "Things getting pretty tough at home, hmm?"

"They're not so bad," he said. He didn't want to talk at all, but it was hard just sitting there watching Wilson throw the game away. "Look, Doc, you coulda saved your game if you moved here, and there."

"I guess I could have. Anything you want to talk about?"

"Not especially. You want to play another game, long as I got to sit here?"

"Might as well," the doctor said.

"Might as."

"Bill . . . hey, Bill, wait up!" Clary Redman tugged at his shirt sleeve as he was about to cross the street in front of school. She was always following him around, since the time her dog Daisy got hit by a car. Dumb Daisy who followed her mistress to school every day and waited for her until the dismissal bell rang. Until one day Daisy got creamed by a dude in a fancy pimp car who didn't even slow down when he hit her. Daisy lay there in the middle of the street twitching and everybody hollered but nobody did anything, until finally Bill went and picked up the yelping, bloody dog. He wrapped it in his gym towel and carried it half a mile to the veterinary hospital, even though he knew it was probably hopeless. The vet took one look at Daisy and shook his head, which made Clary cry uncontrollably, until finally Bill himself called Mrs. Redman, who came and comforted Clary. Ever since that time, Clary had acted like Bill was practically God or something. Clary wasn't really bad looking, he thought. At least she was shorter than him, and it seemed like she'd done something different to her hair, too—it curved around her face in a new, soft way, like wings, he thought, when a bird folds them close to its body. Bill looked around for Todd Lewis, who was always hanging around Clary, but he was nowhere around.

"Guess what?" said Clary. "I finally decided what to call my new puppy. Her name is Mudge."

"That's a dumb name for a . . ." he began, but for once he shut his mouth before he said something stupid. "For a person," he finished lamely, "but for a dog I guess it's okay."

"Want to walk home with me and meet her?"

"I can't," he said. "I've got an appointment."

"With the dentist?"

"Uh . . . that's right." Dr. Wilson had changed his appointment schedule; there'd been an after-school opening that his mother had insisted he take, since he was doing even worse at school than usual. He did his homework but he didn't turn it in; he couldn't seem to stay awake in class, and when he could, he couldn't concentrate. Old Casey was the only one at school who knew where he'd really been on Wednesday mornings for the past few weeks. He hadn't meant to keep it a secret—it wasn't any big deal—but since he'd gotten braces around the same time he started seeing Dr. Wilson, people just assumed he was seeing an orthodontist, and he didn't figure there was any reason to set them right. He wasn't ashamed of seeing a shrink, but he could just imagine what someone like Todd Lewis would say if he found out. "Hey, Crazy Billy, how long before they take you away to the funny farm and put you in a sport jacket that buttons up the back?" Billy didn't figure it was a great idea to give a creep like Todd any more advantages than he already had, like being tall and being able to catch practically any pass you could throw at him and having girls hanging on him like he was a movie star or something.

"You could come see Mudge Thursday. After school, I mean. My mother has a meeting, she doesn't like me to come home when there's nobody else there, so she said I could ask a friend over. She won't be home for a long time . . . till supper practically."

"Uh . . . yeah. I guess that would be okay." Was she saying what he thought she was saying? He'd been at Clary's house a couple of times after school. He'd managed to kiss her a few times, and once she'd let him French her, but every time things started getting good her mother'd interrupt them. "Clary, Billy, what are you doing in there?" she'd holler when they were tussling around in Clary's bedroom. "There's milk and cookies, come on down!" It wasn't milk and cookies he wanted, it was a chance to get a handful of Clary's tit.

That wasn't all, of course. Besides being not too hard on the old eyeballs, she was smart and sometimes she was so funny she broke him up, especially when she did her imitation of Miss Titus swinging her boobs around and getting all the guys hot and bothered. When Clary found out he liked *Dove* she gave him a copy of a book about Sir Francis Chichester, who'd sailed around the world by himself in a small boat, and then she found these nautical charts in the library and Xeroxed them when she was supposed to be copying some test papers for Titus, because he'd told her one time he was going to sail around the world himself when he got older.

"Thursday after school . . . yeah, I guess I could do that," he said casually. She smiled, and he thought he saw something different in her expression, like she knew something he didn't. He could feel his rod stiffening, and he turned away in case she could see it. "Well, I got to go to the doctor now, I'll see you tomorrow."

"The dentist, you mean."

"Yeah, the dentist. See ya."

"See you."

"Your mother tells me you stole her car last weekend," the psychiatrist said.

"I didn't steal it, I moved it. She told me to wash it and it was too far away for the hose to reach."

"You were gone three hours. It must have been frightening, driving around wondering if you'd be caught, or get into an accident."

"It wasn't."

"Did you think she wouldn't notice you were gone?"

"Sometimes she doesn't."

"You mean, other times you've gone joyriding with her car and she hasn't noticed?"

Old fart thought he was pretty smart, trying to trap Bill into admitting he'd been taking his mother's car whenever he got the chance. Sure, it was scary, sort of, wondering if the pigs would stop you. That time the guy in the pickup ran the stop sign and nearly careened into him, he practically pissed in his pants. Chris had, but he hadn't. And that time his mother went out and just left the car keys on the kitchen counter, that time was scary, too, 'cause he was really stoned and went cruising around down by Seward Park and got up to eighty-five before he knew it, practically creamed a big madrona tree when he came into the curve just before the boat basin.

"You just gonna sit here and yak or am I going to beat you at chess again?" Bill asked.

The doctor sighed. "If you want to."

"I don't, particularly, but we got another half hour, might as well."

"Might as well."

All during study hall he stared at Clary Redman's butt, curved over the seat of her chair. He went to the bathroom three times during the hour—once to take a leak, another time to pat on some shaving lotion he helped himself to from Todd Lewis's locker, a third time to put Clearasil on a zit that had sprung up overnight right on the end of his nose. If he kept his face turned away from Clary, he figured, she might not notice it.

After class, Chris caught up with him. "You want to go to Goldie's and play Space Invaders?" Chris asked. "We got a substitute in math today, subs never take roll call."

"You oughta go to math class, you flunk it one more time and they'll hold you back another year." Chris wasn't dumb, exactly, but he couldn't seem to get the hang of algebra, or science, or even English. Sometimes Bill did Chris's math homework for him, and he always got an A on it, which was sort of a laugh since, he, Bill, was pulling D's and never did his own homework unless his old lady really stood on him.

"Yeah. Well, I'm gonna cut and go to Goldie's. Besides, I still got some of that dope you gave me. You got any more of that, by the way?"

"Nah. I'm out until Jiggs gets some more. He owed me for those pills of my old lady's I got him. Dumb asshole. Maybe nobody ever told him speed kills."

"Your mom takes it, doesn't she?"

"Practically never, those pills were there for a couple of years before I scored 'em. The date on the card's been expired for ages, they're probably not even any good anymore. 'Cept for trading."

"Yeah. Well, how about it? Want to cut class and go over to Goldie's?"

"Yeah, might as well."

"Billy?"

"Yeah?"

"This is Clary."

"Oh. Hi."

"I thought you were coming over to see Mudge this afternoon."

"Oh, yeah. I must've spaced it. Hey, look, my mother's callin' me, I got to go. See you in school. Maybe I'll come see Mudge tomorrow."

"My mother will be home tomorrow."

"Yeah, right, I'll see you then."

He sat on his bed after he hung up the phone, tossing a baseball back and forth between his palms. Boy, was he dumb. He hadn't spaced the date with Clary, he'd just felt funny about it. Not scared or anything, just funny. Probably it wouldn't have been such a big deal anyway. Probably her mother would have been home, or she wouldn't let him do anything, or she hadn't meant to let him in the first place. Or maybe she would have let him, except he wouldn't have been able to. He might have even got into her pants, and at the critical moment he wouldn't be able to find his way in there even with a flashlight and a set of directions. Just thinking about it made him hard, but then his mother really did call him, so he put Clary out of his mind and went downstairs for supper.

"Why didn't you keep your date with that girl?" Dr. Wilson asked. Bill had made the dumb mistake of mentioning Clary's invitation to Old Baldy, just to have something to do besides take him at chess, and now the guy wouldn't shut up about it.

"Didn't want to, that's all," he muttered.

"Sometimes you can get so keyed up by something like that that it's very painful to actually follow through. Sometimes even physically painful. All your systems are operating in high gear, fantasizing, anticipating, expecting whatever it is you're expecting. Like your skin is too tight and your body wants to jump right out of it."

"Look, I just didn't want to go."

"Did you get stoned with Chris?"

"Yeah."

"I see."

Shit, he was doing it again. "What? What the fuck do you see, anyway?"

"The grass makes the excitement go away, doesn't it? Makes your system settle down, gets you in control again."

"Sort of."

"The feelings you're having about girls these days are pretty exciting, aren't they?"

"You could say that."

"And the grass kind of puts a lid on that excitement, doesn't it?"

"A little."

"You're going to have stronger feelings as you get older, Bill. One joint isn't going to make them go away. What are you going to do then?"

"I dunno."

"I do."

"Yeah?"

"Yeah. You're going to smoke another. And another. Until one of these days a couple of joints doesn't do it, doesn't make the feelings go away, and you'll turn to something harder."

"You sound just like my old lady. She thinks I'm going to end up a junkie."

"She could be right. That's how addicts get to be addicts—not just drug addicts, but food and alcohol addicts. Anything that stuffs the feelings down, way down where they can't get you excited, scared, turned on."

"Who says I don't want to get turned on?"

"I do."

"Why do you say that?"

"You're a smart kid, Bill. Why don't you think about that and we'll talk about that next time, okay? Our hour's just about up."

"Yeah."

He had to take a leak before he left, so he used the doctor's bathroom, which was just outside the office. He washed his hands and felt the sting of a hangnail that pulled off when he dried them, so he opened the medicine cabinet, hoping to find a scissors to trim around the sore, reddened skin. They were there, in a flat little manicure kit. On an impulse, he pocketed the kit. Then he flushed the toilet an extra time, tucked his shirt in his pants, and left, whistling the theme from *The Empire Strikes Back* as he closed the bathroom door behind him.

7 On April Fool's Day, Anne's birthday, Marty brought her the first
tulips of the season and a bagel the
size of a pizza, filled with cream cheese and piled high
with Port Chatham smoked salmon. He lit the candle
in the center of the bagel, and placed it on her desk.
"Make a wish," he commanded.

"On a bagel?" she laughed. "What kind of wish do
you make on a bagel?"

"For a good Jewish husband, of course," he said.

"I'll blow to that," she said.

"I figured, turning forty and all, you'd be giving
up girlish passions like chocolate," Marty commented.

"Why, do I need to?"

He inspected her critically. "Not so you'd notice.
You're aging well."

"Maybe on the outside."

"What's the matter, the kid getting to you again?"

"No," she said thoughtfully, "not especially. He
seems happier these days. Maybe the shrink is doing
him some good."

"What's it doing for you?"

"Making me feel like someone's in control." She
hadn't been to Dr. Wilson's office for over a month,

but she spoke to him once a week, or more frequently if she needed to. "When Bill messes up, I want you to tell me about it, but don't do anything about it," he'd advised her after he'd seen Billy several times.

"You mean, I'm not supposed to punish him? Even when he goes joyriding in my car, or lies, or takes something that doesn't belong to him?" she asked. "That's right," he replied calmly. "Your punishments haven't worked, so give it a rest. Leave it between Bill and me." "I don't feel completely comfortable about that," she said. "I'm sure you don't," Dr. Wilson agreed, "but if you want to come in and talk about it, I'll ask Bill at our next meeting if that's okay."

"You're in control, Annie Banana, you're bigger than Billy. And meaner," Marty added, helping himself to another piece of the bagel. "You wiped the floor with that prosecutor yesterday, and you got Freddie the Fifth Avenue Finger Fucker into the funny farm instead of Walla Walla. I hear your name bandied about in high places for the chief trial attorney slot."

"Like where?"

"The men's room on the top floor of the courthouse," he said, and she spun him around and headed him toward the door.

"Out," she said, "I've got two motions to write by noon, and then Carol's taking me out to lunch. Thanks for the bagel, it's the biggest birthday cake I ever had."

"The best?"

"Definitely the most unique," she smiled. "Now get out of here and go to work."

"You sound like management already," he said, and left her office.

Anne waited for Carol at a table by the window in

a restaurant in the Public Market. Green and white ferries, chunky little tugboats, a Japanese freighter, and a couple of graceful sailboats shared the sun-tipped waters of Elliott Bay; it was the kind of day that made her wonder why anyone would choose to live anywhere but Seattle.

"Sorry I'm late, a client stood me up." Carol swooped down on her, planting a kiss on her cheek and a huge box in her lap. The spicy fragrance of carnations from Carol's perfume filled the space between them; an expensive Italian knit suit clung to her curvy body, and a soft cashmere cloche covered her chestnut curls.

"You ought to bill him for the time anyway, like psychiatrists and dentists do," said Anne.

"When I've got enough lawyers in my little office to fill a letterhead and a secretary to do the billing, I will," her friend promised. Carol had left the Public Defender a year before and opened her own practice. She wanted Anne to come with her, and had tried, was still trying, to talk her into it. Carol could take that risk—her husband was an investment banker, and they could easily afford to provide Mark, their only child, with every advantage. When Anne's spirits were low—when she had what Billy called "the dwindles"—she envied her friend her secure, worry-free life. When she was severely depressed, however, it was almost physically painful to hear about Carol's son, admittedly a brilliant, talented, and genuinely nice kid who had never, to Anne's knowledge, given his parents any trouble at all.

"That's one advantage of working for clients who can't afford a lawyer—they hardly ever stand you up."

"They can't, most of them are in jail," Carol replied.

The waiter took their order for cold cracked Dungeness crab and a bottle of champagne. Anne opened the brown-and-silver box from Magnin's and held up a beautiful silk nightgown trimmed with lace.

"Elegant and decadent, my favorite combination," she said. "You shouldn't have."

"Sure I should've, you're only forty once," said Carol. "What you need now is a man deserving of that negligee. What's going on with you and Patrick, by the way?"

Anne refolded the gown and replaced it in the box. "Not much," she admitted. "I went bonkers about Billy one night when he was there, and I think it scared him. God knows it scared me," she added. "Men without kids—they just don't understand what it's like. Or maybe they do, and that's why they don't stick around."

"Maybe. Or maybe you don't encourage them to."

"I didn't push Patrick away," Anne said.

"No, but you didn't encourage him to come any closer, either. Or the fellow before Patrick, or the one before that. Sometimes I wonder if you really want to be in a relationship."

"Sometimes I do, too," Anne admitted. "Let's face it, my most significant male relationship is with my son, and that takes all the energy I've got. That, and the job . . . say, did I tell you what Marty told me about the chief attorney's job?" She changed the subject as deftly as she could. Much as she loved Carol, she could not tolerate it when her friend probed as deeply, and perceptively, as she sometimes did.

Their lives had been similar in many ways. Anne came from Westport, Carol from Greenwich; Anne had gone to Wellesley, Carol to Smith. They had both come to Seattle with their husbands and had sons of the same age; they met while taking the bar review course and again when they found themselves shar-

ing an office at the Defender. They were lucky to find
each other, they agreed, and their only disappointment was that their children were not equally fast
friends. Anne had heard Billy describe Mark as a
preppie creep; Mark probably had equally uncompli-
mentary things to say about Billy, she thought.

They finished their lunch leisurely, and it was
nearly two by the time the bottle of champagne was
empty. "What's on your agenda for the rest of the
day?" Carol asked. "Are you going back to the office?"

"I have to, I'm up to my eyeballs in work. I've got
two trials next week and I have to write my opening
statement for the first one, at least. I'll stay downtown
till six, then I have a conference with Billy's doctor—I
told you that, didn't I, when you wanted to take me
out to dinner?"

"Mmm hmm. And how are you celebrating
tonight?"

"No special plans. It's just another Friday night."

"Maybe so, maybe not," said Carol. "Anything can
happen when it's your birthday."

"Sure, and if you kiss enough frogs, someday
you'll find your prince," Anne said. "Thanks for
lunch, and the nightgown."

She walked slowly back to the office, thinking
about Carol and her perfect life. That's what yours
could have been, she told herself silently. If you'd
married Peter Greenspan when you were a senior,
the way your parents wanted, you'd have a life like
that. A solid, reliable husband, a maid twice a week, a
son who's first in his class at the best private school in
town, a pair of diamond earrings on your fortieth
birthday. The same man to wake up next to every
single morning, the same warm, known, loved body
close to yours at night. A career you could take seriously if you wanted to, and walk away from if you

didn't. Someone to tighten the loose doorknobs and fill up the empty spaces—the other half of the closet, the other half of your life. She brushed a tear away from the corner of her eye. You should never drink in the afternoon, even champagne, she told herself. After forty years, you still can't hold your liquor.

"I think Billy's doing better," she said. "No incidents for nearly a month in school, unless he's signing my name to referral slips."

"He's not," said Dr. Wilson. "I talked to Mr. Casey this week. Billy's doing okay in school. Not great, but okay. And at home? Has he stolen anything from you lately?"

"I don't think so."

"You ought to be sure. Did you put the locks on your closet door and put your valuables inside?"

"Not yet."

"Why not?"

She squirmed in her chair. "I don't want to turn my home into a locked fortress. I want to be able to trust Billy."

"But you can't," the doctor said flatly. "He's a thief."

Her cheeks flushed hotly. "I wish you'd stop saying that."

"But it's true. Billy steals from you, therefore he's a thief. And therefore you have to protect him by locking your things up."

"Protect me, you mean."

"No, protect Billy. You have to protect him from his impulse to steal from you. You can't leave your purse around for him to rifle, your grass out for him to steal—"

"I don't keep it in the house anymore," she interrupted, "it's not worth the hassle."

"That doesn't mean he'll stop using it, you know," said the doctor, "it just means he'll get it somewhere else. But it's just as well that you stopped keeping it around, there's no sense setting him up any more than you already do."

"Doing what to him?"

"Setting him up."

"I'm not setting him up, I'm trying to instill a conscience in him, some sense of morality."

The doctor tapped his pipe on the edge of a heavy crystal ashtray. "Waste of time," he said. "He knows the difference between right and wrong already. He doesn't feel it, though—he doesn't feel shame or embarrassment when he does the wrong thing, not if he can manage to avoid feeling it."

"When is that going to change? Or is it?"

"I don't know," said the doctor. "With some kids, never. Others respond to treatment, learn to handle their anger, or their guilt, or their fear, and then they can feel their conscience, keep a rein on their instincts."

"Well, what are you doing with him, then?"

"Not much," the doctor admitted. "Listening when he talks, which isn't often. Letting him know someone's here. With teenagers, that's usually all you can do—provide a safe place, a sense of comfort, an idea of limits, a ray of hope that there's somebody around who won't let you go crazy, won't let you hurt yourself. That may not be enough for Bill, though."

"It seems to be working. He's much more relaxed these days."

"Temporarily," Dr. Wilson pronounced. "It's symptomatic relief, but it won't last. Soon he's going to have to confront feelings that he can't keep a lid on, and then the same things will happen again. The bad behavior has just gone underground for a while. It will be back."

"What are you saying? Are you telling me my son is just going down the tube, going to end up in jail or hooked on drugs or, or, I don't know, living in Nepal or something, and I am powerless to stop it?"

"Who lives in Nepal?"

"My crazy brother," she said, and briefly told him about Jeff.

"How do you feel about your brother now?"

"Sad, mostly. He had everything going for him— looks, brains, talent. I see it as a tragic waste."

"Not angry? You don't feel anger at your brother?"

"What for? He couldn't help being sick."

"Couldn't he?"

She thought about that for a while. "Maybe he could. Maybe he didn't have any other way to avoid following the scenario my parents laid out for him— the right college, the right medical school, the right wife . . . all that."

"So he got away by getting sick. How did you get away?"

"I married a man they totally disapproved of," she said ruefully. "And you know, they were right. He was everything they worried about—immature, unstable, unsuitable."

"Then why are you smiling?"

"Am I?"

"Yes."

"I don't know . . . look, I'm more interested in Billy's psyche than mine."

"So am I. But you didn't create a style of parenting out of nowhere, you know. You learned those kinds of attitudes from your own parents, which is why it's sometimes helpful to examine how and why you act toward them as you do."

"If it will help Billy, I'll do it. I'll do anything to help him."

"Anything?"

"Anything."

"Even let him go?"

"What do you mean?" She sat up straighter in the chair. "Let him go where?"

The doctor leaned back in his own chair and made a tent of his long, bony fingers. "Bill is going to run. Soon. He has to break his ties to you. They're too strong—you're too dependent on one another. What scares him even more than becoming a man is being hooked on his mother. You're a strong woman—he has to best you to claim his manhood."

"Where would you suggest I let him go to? Boarding school?"

"Most places you'd like him to be at wouldn't take him. Places with treatment options—that's a different story."

"Treatment options . . . you're talking about a mental hospital, aren't you?"

"Bill isn't sick enough for a place like that. Not now, anyway. No, what I had in mind was a foster home. Or something along those lines."

"No." She was emphatic. "I've seen the kind of foster homes available around here, when I worked in the Juvenile Office. They're for delinquents, battered kids, wards of the court, kids nobody wants. People take them in just for the welfare money. No. Not a foster home. Not for Billy."

"There are group homes for kids with problems like Bill's. Places he could live during the week, and come home from on weekends."

Her eyes watered, and she reached for a tissue from the box on the table at her elbow.

"I know it sounds tough, but it's what he needs."

"An institution? You're saying Billy needs to be institutionalized?"

"I'm saying your boy needs some limits. Some help, of a kind you can't give him. There's a group home about twenty miles away from here I think Bill would like. I think you should make an appointment with the director and take Bill to visit. Let him see what that might be like."

She knew what it would be like. Thin cots in cramped rooms, showers that smelled of Lysol, and walls. Walls to keep Billy in and her out. "I can't," she said. "I can't . . . let him go. To a place like that." She shook her head. "My son is not sick and I won't have him in one of those snake pits."

"Anne, you're not being rational. You're talking about hospitals for severely disturbed, significantly impaired children."

"But you're saying that," she sobbed. "Isn't that what you're saying, isn't he disturbed?"

Dr. Wilson waited until she stopped crying. "Anne, you're not hearing me. Just go take a look at that group home, won't you? It's not what you think."

"I don't need to look at it. Just tell me what to do, how I can help Billy. At home. In his own house."

Dr. Wilson relit his pipe methodically, tamping the tobacco into the bowl with measured beats, sucking on it until he produced a cloud of smoke in the air above his head.

"You think I should have raised him with more rules, is that it?" she asked.

"I think you did the best you knew how, Anne. Certainly you've loved him—too much, perhaps. Too much to let go of him, and that's what he needs now. Think about that group home, Anne. Just think about it."

She was thinking about it when she let herself into

the house. Remembering how Billy had seemed to go away from her when he was a small boy, six or seven. When she'd talk to him and know that he wasn't hearing her words. "Where do you go when you pull the shutters down over your eyes like that and close me out?" she'd asked him. "To a place in my head where I'm always right," he replied. She had been delighted with his answer, believing that it indicated his intelligence, his creativity, his adaptability. She'd repeated it to his teacher at the school for the gifted, and the teacher frowned. "That's the way schizophrenia manifests," she said, and Anne dismissed her as an idiot— one course in elementary psychology and the woman thinks she's a shrink, she'd told herself.

Talking about institutions and treatment centers and group homes had brought that memory back, and she was flooded with others. Visiting Jeff at a mental hospital . . . her own brother locked up with men and women with vacant faces and unseeing eyes who brushed along the corridors in felt slippers, spoke aloud to unseen presences. She remembered feeling so relieved to leave, and hearing her mother cry in the car on the way home.

She shuddered. By then Jeff was a victim of institutionalitis—a need for walls, a fear of living in the world. Her brother had traded the walls of a mental institution for the cliffs of the Himalayas, but he was locked in just the same. Safe, that was how he had described it: Nothing can touch me here, he told her.

She was inside her own front door, finally—she willed the memories away. She had to, before she could face her son.

She heard a sound from the living room, and then a loud chorus of voices. "Surprise!" "Happy birthday!" "Did you think you were getting away without a party?" She was surrounded by friends—people from her office, Carol and her husband, Marty and a woman she didn't know. Someone put a party hat on her head, and someone else handed her a glass of wine, and Carol led her into the living room, where an enormous chocolate cake with forty lighted candles awaited her.

"Where's Billy?" she said, and he appeared, with a gaily wrapped box and a welcoming smile. He gave her a hug, and she hugged him back fiercely.

"Hey, watch it, you'll bruise the merchandise," he said, but his eyes were warm, and he was smiling. "Are you surprised? Are you really surprised?" he asked.

"Completely," she said. "Did you do all this?"

"Carol did most of it, but I helped some. I cleaned the house before everyone got here."

"And a very good job, too," she said. "Oh, Billy, this is terrific, I love it, where did you get it?" It was a jewelry case, teak and cherry wood laminated in alternating strips. The outside of the case was polished to a soft gleam, the inside carefully lined in dark green felt.

"I made it in shop. It's not finished yet, I have to solder the clasp on, but I can do that next week in class."

"I thought you forgot my birthday," she said, ashamed of having doubted him.

"I don't forget it," he said. "Sometimes I don't do anything about it, but I never forget it. Hey, you going to cut that cake pretty soon? I'm starving!"

Everyone agreed that it was a great party. There were huge quantities of wine, plenty of cake, and later, around midnight, Carol's husband, Ted, made his special omelets for the whole crowd. Anne gave him a warm hug as they said goodnight. "Are there any more out there like you?" she asked.

"I'll look around the bank and see," Ted said.

"Come over for brunch tomorrow morning, I'm making something special."

"So am I, if I can ever drag him out of here," said Carol, taking his arm. She kissed Anne. "Billy said he'd clean up tomorrow morning, so just come over around eleven, and we'll see how much more mileage we can get out of this momentous occasion, okay?"

"Okay," said Anne. "And Carol . . . thank you."

"My pleasure," her friend said. "See you tomorrow."

There was something funny about Carol the next morning, Anne thought.

"You've been scrubbing that frying pan for ten minutes and it's perfectly clean," Anne said. "What's going on?" She was concerned; usually Carol didn't hold back when she had something to say, she came right out with it. "Is everything okay with you and Ted? Or Mark . . . it's not Mark, is it?"

Carol sat down and lit a cigarette. "No, it's not Mark," she said, "or Ted, either."

"Then what is it? Carol . . . what is it?"

"Fifty dollars."

"What's fifty dollars?"

"The money that was taken from my purse yesterday afternoon. At your house. When Billy and I were setting things up for the party. I'd cashed a check just before I came over. Marty picked up the cake I'd ordered from Frederick's—when I went to pay him, the money was gone."

"Who else was in the house?"

"Just me and Billy. And his friend Chris, he came over. But that was after Marty arrived with the cake."

"You think Billy took it." It was a statement, not a question.

"I don't know what else to think," Carol said. "I

didn't want to think it—not about Billy. Why, he's practically a second son to me. I know you said he's been doing some acting out against you, and you mentioned that he'd taken a few things from you, but me? I don't understand it. I couldn't believe it. I wasn't going to say anything to you about it, but Ted said—"

"Ted? You told Ted about this? How could you?"

"He's my husband, of course I told him. And he's your friend, too—and Billy's. We all love Billy, and we thought he loved us, too. That's why this is so difficult to understand. Oh, Anne . . . I'm sorry."

"So am I," said Anne quietly. "I'm very sorry . . . and I'm very embarrassed. I'll pay you back, of course . . . here, I'll write you a check."

Carol stayed her hand. "Don't be ridiculous, the money's not important. And there's nothing to be embarrassed about, you didn't steal it. I mean . . ."

Anne covered her face to hide her shame. "Oh, Jesus . . . Carol, what can I say? I'm sorry . . . I'll make it right . . . I don't . . . I . . ."

"Stop apologizing, Anne. It's not up to you to make it right, it's up to Billy. Ted and I agreed that I should talk to him about it. I was going to do that anyway, not even tell you, but Ted thought I should."

"Oh, don't, Carol . . . don't talk to Billy. Not yet, anyway . . . not until I talk to Dr. Wilson about it."

"He didn't take it from him, he took it from me."

"What do you want, an eye for an eye?" Anne's temper flared, and she was immediately apologetic. "I'm sorry, Carol, I didn't mean that. I know you have Billy's best interests at heart . . . just let me handle this, okay?"

"No, it's not okay. Billy has got to start being accountable for his actions sometime."

"Let's just see what Dr. Wilson says, okay? He may

think it's a good idea for you to confront Billy, but I want to discuss it with him first."

"You're not going to be able to hold the world away from Billy much longer, sweetie." Carol was sympathetic but determined.

"I'm not doing so great at it now, am I?"

"Oh, shit, I wish I'd never brought this up. I told Ted, I said, fifty bucks isn't worth it, it's not worth my friendship with Anne."

"No it isn't, and it's not going to come between us, I promise. But if you don't mind . . . I think I'd like to go home now." She felt her cheeks flame with humiliation, and the more tolerant and understanding her friend was, the more desperately she wanted to escape. Finally she extricated herself, promising to call Carol as soon as she reached Dr. Wilson.

"I'll do whatever he thinks is best," Carol said. "If he says, confront Billy, I will—if he says drop it, forget it, I'll do that. You just tell me what you want, and I'll do it."

"I know you will, and I love you for it. But meanwhile, he's my son, and I'm responsible for what he does, so please . . . take this check."

"I'd rather not," said Carol. "I'd rather Billy gave me back the money himself."

"I'd rather, too, but I don't think he will. If he does, you can tear up the check. But if he doesn't . . . we're even."

"Even without this, we're even. You know that, don't you?" Anne's face crumpled, and Carol embraced her. "We love each other, right?"

Anne nodded against Carol's shoulder. "Then we're already even," Carol whispered to her, and they stood there, in Carol's kitchen door, holding each other for what seemed to Anne like a very long time. Then Anne got into her car, drove home, and cried the warm, rainy afternoon away in the locked, darkened privacy of her own room.

8 They turned off the main road at the bus shelter; there was no gate, but a sign at the turnoff pointed the way to the Evergreen Home. A few yards beyond, at the crest of a smallish hill, Anne parked the car in front of a cluster of houses, sheathed by narrow clapboards, cedar aged to a silvery gray. The shutters on all were freshly painted dark green; the roofs of each house were shingled in natural cedar. Beyond the complex of houses were some outbuildings, one of which looked like it had once been a barn.

"Looks pretty neat," Bill commented as they entered the largest house, in the middle of the cluster. On one side of the entrance hall was a living room dominated by a scarred upright piano and a line of benches arranged around it; on the other there was a reception desk, a battered Naugahyde couch, and two plastic chairs separated by a small table that held some old issues of the *National Geographic*, a Gideon Bible, and the current *Rolling Stone*.

A tall, sad-faced man arrived a few moments after the elderly woman at the reception desk took their names. "Bill? Mrs. Manning? I'm Mike Parker, the assistant director here. Rob Wilson said you'd be coming this afternoon to take a look around." He held out his hand, and Bill shook it. "I've arranged for one of the boys in Bill's class to show you the layout here," he said. "After you've had the grand tour, I'll be in my office to answer any questions either of you might have."

"Class? Do the boys go to school here?" Anne asked.

"Only if they can't manage in the local public schools. There's a good junior high a few miles from here; the bus stops right down at the road, where you turned off."

"What about the . . . others?"

"Some of them are tutored here, by special-education teachers. There's an extra fee for that, but the state reimburses us if the family has no available resources."

"Do you get most of your support from the state?" Anne was just being polite, waiting for their guide to arrive. She knew she couldn't send Billy here. He would be stamped, labeled, identified, as a problem like most of the boys who came here. Despite what Dr. Wilson said, she knew the majority had been referred by the juvenile justice system, the courts, the welfare people. It wasn't reform school, but it wasn't Exeter, or even Seattle Country Day.

"Not enough," replied Mike Parker. "The most severely troubled boys—classes two and three—are usually wards of the state. If their families can pay, they're charged according to a sliding scale based on financial need."

Classes two and three. What had the psychiatrist said? "Bill is class one—not sick enough for a residential treatment center, what you would call a mental hospital. Or class two, emotionally impaired or developmentally disabled. Or class three, actively hostile and potentially violent."

The boy who eventually appeared to show them around was sixteen, two years older than Bill, but in ninth grade; he said he had dropped out of school for a while, "when I was living around, you know, on the street." He led them first to the barnlike building whose musty odors, even overlaid by the powerful smell of Lysol and the even more pungent odor of dried perspiration, did not conceal its origins. The barn had been converted into a gymnasium, and on a bumpily uneven court, four black youths and two white ones were engaged in a desultory basketball game.

"Hey, honky, you gonna live here, is dat alligator on yo' shirt gone eat us niggers up, huh?" said one of the boys.

Anne colored in embarrassment for her son. She'd made him change his clothes before they came, take off his too-short tee shirt that crept up over his rib cage, change his torn jeans for clean corduroys.

Bill did not seem perturbed. "Yeah, man, gonna eat you alive," he responded, and they laughed and tossed him the ball. He dribbled it between his legs and then sank it into the basket from where he stood. His prowess surprised her and provided the first good feeling she'd had all day.

"You ain't bad for a honky kid. You come, you kin be our water boy, hear?"

"I hear you, man," said Billy, and they left the gym. In another building, one of the small houses, they inspected the bedrooms.

"Mostly doubles and trips," their guide said in response to Anne's question.

"No singles?" asked Bill, peering into one.

It was practically indistinguishable from his room

at home, Anne thought. Clothes, books, and sports equipment were piled on all available surfaces and spilled over onto the floor. The music of Pink Floyd blared from a record player.

"Not unless you get too many demerits," the boy answered. "Then you have to move down to solitary, right next to the dorm head."

The dorm head. It could have been an exclusive prep school, if she closed her eyes. Oh, Billy, when you went away to school I didn't want it to be somewhere like this, she thought.

"How do you get demerits?" That was Billy, more inquisitive than usual.

"Lip off to Mike Parker or one of the other staff members. Get caught with booze or drugs. Flunk inspection. Take off without a pass."

"Pass?"

"Yeah. You got to earn your weekends home. You get demerits, you stay here."

"You go to school right here?"

"Nah, I go to the high school over near Boeing. They pick you up, bring you back."

Anne was nauseated—she couldn't take any more. "Billy, you look around a little longer. I need some air. I'll see you at the car after you're done." She had no questions to ask of Mike Parker; she had seen enough, she thought.

She left them and made her way outside, where she leaned against the side of her car in the weak, late afternoon May sun, and let the tears roll down her face. A woman close to her own age passed by, heavily made up, wearing a short jacket of some long-haired synthetic fur, tottering on very high heels. She gave Anne a sympathetic look, then stopped and touched her arm.

"You have a boy here?" she asked.

"No. Yes. Not really. I mean, we're looking at it." Anne wiped her face and looked away, hoping the woman would get the idea and go on about her business.

"I remember when I brought Tommy here, the first time. I thought it was an awful place. I couldn't bring him back. I made his father do it."

"How long has he been here?" Despite her embarrassment, Anne wanted to know—no one, not even Dr. Wilson, had said how long Bill might have to stay. If he came, of course, and she was certain he would not. Dr. Wilson had suggested it to scare him into behaving, like the visit to Juvenile Hall.

"A year."

A year? How could she stand it? On the drive to the home, Anne had thought, maybe for a few weeks. Just until the end of school. Then he'll go to camp for a month, and to her parents in Westport for his annual visit. If they could just get to the end of the school year, it would be almost normal.

The woman went on talking. "It's done my boy a lot of good. He used to be . . . well, the judge said he was incorrigible, and gave Tommy a choice—here or jail. Course, they don't call it jail, not for kids. But that's what it is, you know."

What's the difference between the Evergreen Home and jail? Anne wondered, and felt sick to her stomach.

"It's not so bad, really it isn't," the woman said, her voice softening. "You'll see . . . a year or two here, he'll be a different boy."

Billy appeared and she studied him as he walked to the car to meet her. He was the source of her strongest, deepest feelings; he was the sharpest pain, the sweetest joy, the greatest frustration. She would manage, she thought; somehow, she would cope. And she would never, ever, send him away in anger.

"Well, what did you think?" She would stop for ice cream on the way home, she decided. Billy loved ice cream.

"It looked okay."

"But you wouldn't want to stay there, would you?" You wouldn't want to leave your own house and your own room and your clothes and skis and television set. You wouldn't want to leave your school and friends and your . . . Her fingers tightened on the steering wheel, and she forced her attention back to the highway.

"Yeah, I might."

She pulled back into her own lane after passing a semi, cutting it close.

"Hey, watch it, you almost creamed us."

"What do you mean, you might?"

"I might want to go there. I gotta be someplace."

"Have to," she corrected automatically, "but you don't. Have to be someplace. You have a place, at home."

"Yeah. Well that doesn't seem to be working so hot, does it?"

But it could, she thought. If you tried, it could work. If you could just love yourself more, love me more, it could work. She remembered that she'd said those words to his father, years before. *If you really loved me, it could work.* And she recalled his reply. *I could do it for a while, maybe. Go through the motions. Pretend it was working. Except it won't. It hasn't. Not for a long time now. It hasn't been working.*

"The only thing I don't like is no single rooms." Billy brought her back to the present with a start.

"That's the only thing you don't like?" She kept her voice as even as she could, but Billy knew. He had a remarkable ability to hear between her lines.

"You want me to hate it, don't you?" he said. "Then why'd we bother going out there, anyway?"

To show you how awful it is, she answered him silently. To show you living at home isn't so terrible. Wouldn't be so terrible, if you'd only try, if you'd only—

"Hey, Ma, you almost rammed that bus, watch it!" Billy was annoyed. "You want to kill yourself, go ahead, but leave me out of it, okay?"

And let you kill yourself, right? The image of the squat, black, ugly gun swam into her head, and she knew with a certainty that she was going to be sick to her stomach. She pulled the car off the highway as fast as she dared and just managed to get out of it before she threw up.

Billy got out, too, and began to curse in a low, steady voice. "Shit. Piss. Goddamnit. Ma, don't get sick. I'm sorry, I'm really sorry, actually I hated that place, it was awful, I don't really want to live there. I'll be good, I promise . . . Mommy, don't be sick any-more!" He was frightened, and the panic in his voice stopped her gagging, controlled her nausea.

"It's okay, Bill, I ate something that didn't agree with me, I'll be okay, don't worry." She got back into the car and started the ignition. Her mouth tasted awful, but her spirits were lighter, somehow, her determination stronger.

He was really frightened when he thought I was sick, she thought. He loves me. He doesn't want to leave me.

9 Anne put the Evergreen visit out of her mind, and for a few weeks so, apparently, did Billy. Neither of them mentioned it; Billy went to his regular appointments with Dr. Wilson with only a little grumbling, and life seemed almost normal to Anne again. She put off talking to Billy about Carol's missing fifty dollars, and she did not discuss it with Dr. Wilson, either, during the weekly phone calls that were the only direct contact between them. Somehow she felt that would be betraying Billy, who seemed sobered by the Evergreen visit and was behaving pretty well. Although she had not confronted him about the missing money, she had, she thought, laid down the law to him.

"It's up to you," she'd said. "You can either shape up or ship out. If you can't live by my rules, you can live by someone else's. Or by some institution's." Billy had begun to help Chris prep Mr. Lawlor's house for painting, and his teachers reported that he seemed more attentive in school.

She reported that to Dr. Wilson, who said, "He's even less talkative than usual. I don't know how much longer you can make him keep coming here."

"Did he tell you I told him he had to live by my rules, or he'd have to live elsewhere?" Anne asked.

"Yes. And he also said you don't mean it."

He was right, Anne thought. The memory of the group home remained clear in her mind: she would not, could not send Billy there. Besides, it was less than a month until the end of the school year. A few weeks more and he'd be at camp. He always did well at camp.

Anne began to look forward to the summer, her only respite from single parenthood, with anticipation. She would paint her room and fix up the house while he was away. She would give a party. She would cut her hair, buy some new clothes, and put some energy into finding a man. Not for Billy, she cautioned herself; he was too old for a father, or even a father figure. A new man in his mother's life might be a friend, even a close friend, but he wouldn't be a father. So be it, she thought. But it would be nice to have someone to love her, someone to turn to when she needed him. When Billy went to camp, she'd look around. Romance was definitely in the air, even if it was damp and chilly most of the time. In Freeway Park, where she took a sandwich and an apple one day at lunch, couples nuzzled each other without embarrassment, and two dogs rolled on the grass together. Her peonies bloomed in the garden, and she was arranging some of the fragrant flowers in a tall vase one Saturday morning when the policeman came to talk to her.

"Is your son William Manning?" he asked.

Anne panicked, but only for a moment. She knew policemen—in her work, she dealt with them every day. She knew, too, that Billy had not been injured in any kind of accident; he was painting at the Lawlor house, she had seen him there when she went out to cut the flowers.

"Your son has been implicated in some drug dealing, Mrs. Manning," the policeman told her. He looked uncomfortable; he was very young, Anne realized. She invited him to come in, and he looked around the living room, with its low leather couches, Oriental rugs, framed O'Keeffe prints, and vases of peonies. "Kids these days, from all kind of families . . . mind if I have a look at your son's room?"

"Of course I mind," she said indignantly. "Do you have a warrant?"

"No, I don't. Most parents don't care about search warrants—they just want to be sure their kids aren't involved with drugs."

"Most parents aren't lawyers, which I am," she told him tartly. "And Billy's not involved with drugs." Except a little marijuana, she thought to herself, but they weren't arresting for simple possession these days. "Where did you get your information, anyway? Who implicated my son, as you put it?"

"We picked up an older student we know has been passing a lot of drugs at junior highs in the neighborhood. Little stuff, mostly. But these days there's an epidemic of amphetamines even in the lower grades—speed."

"Billy's never had any amphetamines. He has no access to them. Besides, he doesn't have any money, except his allowance. You've got the wrong boy, officer." She thought about the diet pills, but just for a moment. Ridiculous, those were just a little Preludin, not speed. After all, the doctor had prescribed them.

The policeman left a pamphlet with her. The cover read "How to Know When Your Child Is a Substance Abuser," and inside there were horrible pictures of skinny children injecting themselves with needles. Ugh. She'd seen Billy's arms—they were clean. He hated injections—he'd never do anything like that to himself, she was certain. Still, she searched his room again, very carefully. She had found the loose baseboard and was feeling around inside the wall behind it when Billy came into his room and found here there, on her knees.

"Well? Find anything?" There was an odd little half-smile on his face, almost a smirk. "Why are you sneaking around my room, anyway?"

"I'm not sneaking, I was going to tell you I'd been in here. A policeman was here a little while ago."

He looked nervous, or was that her imagination? "Yeah. What did the pigs want?"

"To know if you were dealing drugs," she replied. "I said you weren't."

"But you weren't sure, were you?" He was taunting her, and she could feel her control begin to slip away.

"No, I wasn't," she said testily.

"Well, look all you want. You won't find anything."

"Why? Did you get rid of it? Sell it?"

"Sell what?"

"That marijuana you took from me a couple of months ago. Or my diet pills. Since you ask."

"Don't be dumb. Your dope is lousy, you couldn't get five bucks for it." He did not, she noticed, refer to the pills. "Look, am I entitled to my privacy or aren't I? You got a lock on your door . . . how come I can't have one on mine?"

"Because you can't."

His face darkened. "Shit. I can't have anything I want, can I?"

That did it—the last vestiges of control disappeared, leaving a white hot anger in their stead. "You can have my fucking blood," she shouted, "that's what you want, isn't it? You can have it all . . . my house, my job, my friends, my friends' money, my happiness, my whole goddamned life! Go ahead, kid . . . take it all!"

"What are you talking about, your friends' money?" he said.

"You know exactly what I mean, Billy Manning. The money you took from Carol the night of my birthday party, the fifty dollars that disappeared from her wallet."

"I don't know what you're talking about," said Billy sullenly. "Why would I want to take money from your creepy friend? Christ, her old man's loaded, anyway, if somebody took her money she can afford it."

"So you did take it?"

"I didn't say that."

"You did!"

"I didn't."

"You're lying to me, Billy."

"I am not lying." As if dismissing her, he turned and began to walk away.

Anne exploded. Grabbing him by the sleeve, she spun him around to face her. "What I give you isn't enough, is that it?" she yelled, her face inches from his own. "Then take it all, Billy . . . take my entire life! Maybe then you'll be satisfied!"

"I don't want your fucking life!" Billy wrenched his arm away from her grasp. "I don't want anything! I hate this lousy house, I hate that fucking shrink, I can't stand your fucking job and your fucking friends and your headaches and your crying and your everything! Get out of here . . . get out of my room!" He pushed her roughly out and slammed the door behind her. She tried to open it, pushing against it, but he held it closed, and she heard him drag his desk chair up and jam it beneath his doorknob.

"Open that door!" She pounded on it with her fists. "Open that door or, I swear, I'll kick it in!"

"Go fuck yourself!" he hollered. "Just get out of here and leave me the fuck alone!" He yanked the door open, almost sending her sprawling, and stood there glowering at her. His face was red with rage, and he held his Swiss Army knife in his right hand.

"What are you going to do with that knife?" she demanded. "Cut me with it? Is that what you're going to do? You're going to carve a hole in my heart, is that it? Is that what you want?"

"Shit, I'm not gonna do that. I'm not gonna cut you. But if you don't go away . . . if you take one step in here I'll . . . I'll—"

"You'll what?" She reached for the knife but he held it away, beyond her reach, pushing her with his free hand, shoving her out of his room, into the hall.

"I'll cut myself, that's what I'll do!" He slammed the door in her face again, pulling the chair back up to wedge it closed against her.

Oh my God, thought Anne, he's going to kill himself. "Billy, don't! Billy, open the door, please . . . Billy give me the knife, I promise I won't . . . Billy, open the door!"

But it remained shut despite her efforts to push it open, and Billy did not answer her cries. She ran for the telephone. "This is Anne Manning," she told the receptionist, "I need to talk to Dr. Wilson right away. It's an emergency."

"I'm sorry, doctor is with a patient right now. If you'd like to leave your number, he'll get back to you when he's free."

"I can't wait, tell him my son is trying to kill himself, I have to speak to him now!" While the receptionist put her on hold, she shouted to her son. "Billy? Billy? Billy, are you okay?"

The psychiatrist got on the line. "Just a minute, he's not answering me, I'll be back in a second," she said, and let the receiver clatter on the floor. She ran back down the hall to his room and pounded on the door. "Billy? Are you all right? Billy, please open the door!"

He opened it easily; his face was composed, and there was no sign of the knife. "Yeah, I'm fine. Just lay off me, will you? Just lay off!" He closed the door with an emphatic thud, and she went back to the telephone, explaining to the psychiatrist what had happened, beginning with the visit from the policeman and finishing with Billy's threat to cut himself.

"He's not going to do that, Anne, and he's not going to cut you, either. He's just threatening, but he doesn't mean it. He's not suicidal, not at all."

"Are you sure? You said he was depressed. Withdrawn, you said, he has no affect, he's angry but he's keeping it inside. It's not inside right now . . . how do you know he's not going to hurt himself?"

"Because I say so," Dr. Wilson repeated firmly. "That's not what he wants. He'll be okay. I'll see you both in my office in an hour."

"What if he refuses to come?"

"Then pick him up and drag him to the car, or call the police and tell them you need help getting him in to see me."

"Are you sure?"

"I'm sure. He'll come. We have a deal. He gets in trouble, he has to come see me. Tell him that. Tell him he's in trouble."

For the next hour, she knocked at his door every ten minutes until she heard his muttered, "Yeah, Ma, I'm okay." When it was time to go to the psychiatrist's office, she demanded that he open it and talk to her.

"What do you want?" He was sullen, but not any longer in a rage.

"I want you to get in the car. Now. We have an appointment with Dr. Wilson."

"I don't want to." He tried to close the door, but she jammed her foot in it.

"I don't care what you want. You have no choice. Get in the car or I'll drag you there myself."

"Okay." She was surprised at how easily he capitulated.

Neither of them said a word on the way to the office. Billy remained silent while she recapped the events of the previous two hours for the analyst, who regarded them calmly and fiddled with his pipe.

"What do you have to say about this, Bill?" he asked. Bill did not answer; he sat coiled within himself, saying nothing at all, refusing to meet her eyes.

"Bill, why don't you talk to Dr. Wilson? Why don't you answer him?" Anne said.

"I'm not talkin' with you here."

At Dr. Wilson's gesture Anne left the office and took her accustomed seat in the waiting room. She leafed through a magazine, trying with little success to concentrate on what she read. After a brief interval, Dr. Wilson came into the waiting room and asked her to join them. She followed him back inside, and sat down across the room from Billy.

"Bill says you told him if he couldn't live by your rules at home he'd have to live somewhere else. Right?"

"Yes." She hadn't wanted to say that, but Dr. Wilson had insisted. *This time, you have to mean it,* he'd warned her.

"Bill feels he cannot continue to live at home." She looked at Billy, who said nothing, but nodded almost imperceptibly.

"He'll be in camp in a month," she said. "School's out in a few weeks."

"He can't wait that long."

"Is he going to . . . that place?" It had all been decided between them, she realized. This doctor, this psychiatrist, this man she had trusted, was going to have Billy sent away from her.

"No, he can't," said Dr. Wilson. "I've just spoken with Mike Parker. There's no room for him there now."

She thought for a moment. "He could go to my mother's," she said.

"No way," Billy interjected. "Grandma's worse than you. She's always on my case, she never leaves me alone. She always asks me if I moved my bowels yet."

"I don't think your mother's is a good idea, Anne," said Dr. Wilson. "After all, that's where you learned how to be a mother . . . Bill can't handle that now."

"My friend Carol would take him. She and Billy get along—well, they used to, anyway. He could stay there until school's over."

"No," said Billy, "not on your life. She's a jerk, your friend Carol. Her and her dumb husband and her dumb perfect Marky baby. I won't go there."

Anne was at the end of her patience. "No?" she shouted. She advanced on Billy and yelled in his face: "Where the hell do you think you're going?"

Dr. Wilson took her by the arm and led her back to her chair, like a referee separating two boxers. "Stop it, Anne, that won't do any good."

"What will?" she asked, burying her face in her hands, beginning to cry.

Billy snorted in disgust. "She's turning on the faucets again," he said to Dr. Wilson, "trying to make me feel guilty."

"I am not!" she shouted at him. "I'm not trying to make you feel guilty!" That was what Don had accused her of—attempting to manipulate him with guilt. It wasn't true then, and it wasn't true now, either.

"Please, Anne, settle down. We're not talking about guilt here, we're talking about solutions. Now, I've called the youth center downtown, and they—"

"You mean Juvenile Hall? You called the juvenile authorities and turned Billy in without consulting me? How dare you? What gave you the right? How could you?" She was horrified; Billy's own psychiatrist was delivering him into the hands of the police. He couldn't . . . there was no evidence. He hadn't been charged with a crime. Not that that was necessary, she recalled—the youth center also had what they called "holding facilities," as Dr. Wilson tried to explain.

"Anne, I'm not turning Billy in. The youth center isn't just for delinquents. It's a receiving home, a temporary solution until they can locate a good foster placement, a—"

"Foster placement? Oh, no. Did you see the story in the paper last week about foster homes in Texas? How they take kids, orphans, abused kids, kids whose parents can't care for them, and then use the money to buy things for themselves while they starve the kids and beat them and—"

"Oh, shit, she's not gonna listen, it's no use, don't waste your breath, man," said Billy disgustedly. "Never mind, Ma, let's go home. Forget it. Just forget it."

"Bill, step outside for a few minutes, will you? I want to talk to your mother alone."

"Yeah, okay."

He went out, leaving Anne still sobbing. It was a while before she could pull herself together and listen to Dr. Wilson.

"Anne, you've got to let him go. If you love him, you have to. For your good as much as for his."

"For my good?" She raised her tear-stained face. "It's for my good you want to put him in some awful place, send him to jail, make him—"

"Yes!" The doctor spoke with uncharacteristic force. "Anne, you're letting Billy destroy you. I've watched you closely for the last three months, watched how you're falling apart . . . you're running on fumes, Anne, that's all."

"I don't care! I don't care if he destroys me . . . he won't! I'm tough, I can take it. I'll watch him carefully, I won't let him out of my sight, won't let him hurt himself. You said he's not suicidal, it'll be okay—"

"No, Anne, it will not be okay. No, Billy won't hurt himself—not the way you fear. You don't do that when you're angry, in a rage. You hurt others. Not physically, maybe, but every other way. You hurt the ones you love, the way Billy's hurting you. You aren't that tough, Anne—very few parents are. You'll fall apart, and he'll have that on his conscience, too. Don't do that to yourself. Or to Bill."

"What am I supposed to do? Send him to the youth center, let them put him in some sleazy foster home? No . . . I can't. I can't do that."

"Then he'll run, and you may lose him for good. I guarantee it, he'll run. Not today, maybe not tomorrow . . . but very soon. He can't keep the lid on anymore. He has to break away from you. This is your last chance. If you don't want him to be glad when you're dead, let him go."

"No—he won't. I won't let him. I'll stay home, I'll quit my job, watch him . . . he won't run."

The doctor sighed. "It's your decision, of course, but I think you're making a mistake."

"Then it's my mistake," she said defiantly. "I'll take the consequences."

Later that day, Anne made some telephone calls. Dan Jarvis. A social worker she knew from juvenile court. The director of a residential treatment program she had met years before. Carol. Marty. A friend whose son was in military school in Florida. No one had any answers, and finally, at dinner time, she gave up, exhausted. She made supper for herself and Billy. The phone rang while they were eating. "Can I go to Skate King with Clary Redman?" he asked. "Her father said he'd drive us and pick us up."

"Sure, go," she said absently. Her conversations that afternoon had turned up one slim lead, a special camp, beyond the Cascades, in the eastern part of the state. The director said he could take Billy early—as soon as school was out. He could stay there for two weeks, until his regular camp began. It was expensive, a thousand dollars for ten days. She didn't know where she'd find the money, but if the place would take him, she'd find it somehow. She could always call her parents. They'd give her the money, but they would worry. A special camp, round-the-clock psychiatrists . . . it sounded like the places they'd considered for Jeff, and she didn't want to open that wound in them again. Her father had an ailing heart, and her mother was worried about him . . . no, she wouldn't ask them. There was only one other call she could make, and as soon as Billy left, she decided, she would make it.

Clary's father honked the horn a half hour later. "You have money?" Anne asked Billy.

"I still have some allowance left."

She gave him an extra two dollars. "In case you want to buy Clary a soda or something," she said.

"Ma," Billy began, "I'm sorry about what happened today. I don't hate you. I love you. I just got to get away, that's all."

"Yes," she said. "I know. We'll talk about it tomorrow. Have a good time at the rink. Be nice to Clary. She likes you a lot. She's a good girl."

"Yeah, she's okay. Hey, Ma?"

"Yes?"

"You love me?"

She hugged him fiercely. "Of course I do, Billy. As much as the world, and more."

10 On a cloudless May afternoon, Don Manning rounded the point and dropped sail on *Windsong*. The momentum carried him past the breakwater and into the small harbor that curved east until it almost touched the old highway, the King's Road between Long Beach and San Diego. He steered the boat neatly into its slip, and his passengers jumped out onto the dock almost before he had the mooring ropes in his hand. The man did not look down at Don but seemed to be addressing the expanse of the Pacific before him.

"To tell you the truth, fella, I think me 'n' my old lady, we've changed our minds. We're not really in the market for a sailboat. We were thinking of something with a little more pizzazz. You know. Something fast. Sorry we took so much of your time, guy, but that's the way it is. Thanks for the sail, it was great. We'll get back to you."

Not likely, Don thought. Punk kid. He probably wants a souped-up stinkpot so he can run a few kilos in from Baja. I wonder how long it's been since he had a shower—God, even out on the clean, fresh water he stank. And that broad with him . . . you could see everything she had under that shirt. No bra for sure, no panties either by the look of it.

Stop it, Don, he told himself. That's all you need, messing around with some cokehead's woman. You could tell what he was by his eyes; they bugged out of his head like those rubber glasses you saw in trick stores. The constant sniffing and swallowing was a dead giveaway too. But that broad . . . she kept rubbing up against him every chance she got, leaning into him when he brought the thirty-footer about. He'd taken them out past the breakwater and caught the westerly breeze just right, feeling the boat move with him, under him, up and down the ropy muscles of his legs, in his toes curled under inside his Top-Siders as they heeled. On a good day he didn't know where he left off and a fine old boat like *Windsong* began—there was just him and it and the wind and the water, all moving together as one. In harmony— enough to ignore the punk. He'd figured him right from the beginning, known he wasn't a serious buyer. But what the hell. It was a beautiful day, there was no traffic in the marina, and why not?

The sun was beginning to set over the horizon. He checked the mooring ropes on *Windsong*, locked the cockpit, and patted its gleaming, varnished teak. He snapped the sail cover down over the boom—no sense putting the sheets in the locker, I've got to show this one in the morning, he thought. He clicked the guardrail closed and stepped onto the dock.

In the small bathroom behind the showroom he rinsed his hands and face, inspecting himself critically in the mirror above the sink. You could do with a shave, he told himself, and ran an electric razor over his face, erasing the dark shadows on his jaw, across the top of his upper lip, under and up to the sideburns. You could use a haircut, too, you're getting a little shaggy around the edges, he told his reflection. His hair was longer than he'd worn it in the Navy, but not by very much. His face was creased and seamed from long exposure to wind and water; the sun had burnished it to a dark mahogany color. His eyes were set deep under thick brows, and his broad cheek-bones tapered down to a strong, square chin. He was a handsome man, rugged-looking, though at the corners of his eyes there were age lines that fanned out to his temples, and his hair was thinning on top.

There was an impatient rat-tat-tat on the door. "Right out," he called.

"Hi, Don, I saw you bringing in the *Windsong*. They goin' to buy it, you think?"

"Doubtful, Trav."

The little towheaded kid lived with his mother on the thirty-six-foot yawl tied up at the overnight guest dock. It wasn't legal, of course; the sign on the marina's office door said it, Sunset Yachts, Sales and Service, and if you let them stay longer than three days, you had hassles with the port inspectors, trouble with the tony yacht club down the beach, difficulties with the health department. *Pandora* had tied up a couple of months ago, making it into the marina just ahead of a bad squall that had raised whitecaps up and down the coast from Crescent City to La Jolla. When Peggy McCarthy came into the office to request moorage that first night, her eyes were red and puffy, and her voice had something in it that was almost but not quite a quaver. Nice-looking woman, small and neat and muscular, but not mannish; nothing, not even the wiry strands of gray in her short, thick, coppery hair could make Peggy McCarthy look anything but female. Not smooth and succulent, like the overripe California women who frequented beach towns like this one, but female like a woman ought to be, strong and graceful and seasoned, with faint grooves at the corner of her upturned mouth that told him she must be close to his own age. She paid him in advance for three nights, nodding her head when he told her she couldn't stay any longer. Unless, of course, she needed service.

She didn't really need service—the *Pandora* was in perfect condition. But after the three days had passed, she asked him to check out the engines, and when Ricco, the yard manager, reported that the diesels were in excellent shape, she asked Don about a haul-out. He quoted her a price and she flinched; instead she ordered a new stove, which would take at least a week to order and install. She might be going on a long cruise, she said; the propane-fueled stove she already had wasn't as sensible for that as one that could run off the battery.

In the week before the work on the stove was completed, she kept mostly to herself. It didn't strike him as odd; people who sail blue water aren't usually gregarious. Hell, that's why they packed it in for a boat. There were too many people ashore, too many punks and crumb bums and just plain bodies. You had to like being alone to live aboard, and clearly she did. Of course, she wasn't completely alone—she had her eight-year-old son, who filled Don in on the facts of their lives.

"We live in Sausalito, but we're thinking of living somewhere else," her boy told Don. "We used to live in a house till we got divorced and then we bought *Pandora*. Mom's an accountant, she works in the cabin when I'm at school. I'm on spring vacation right now. Did I tell you I'm in the fourth grade?"

"I believe you did." He was a cute little tyke, polite and well brought up—Don could see that. When his mother called him he hotfooted it over there, and in the mornings Don watched him polishing the brightwork, helping his mother keep *Pandora* shipshape and beautiful, the way a great old wooden boat like that should be kept. It was a Garden design, a little beamier than he personally liked them, but solid and comfortable, good for living aboard.

"All my friends at school think it's neat that I get to live on a boat," Travis told him proudly.

"Yeah? How do you feel about it?"

"Well . . ." He stretched the word out as he dug his toe into the dirt and pushed the gravel around. "Well, I like it kinda okay, except I had to give most of my toys away when we moved on it. There's not much room for a lot of stuff, and you can't put a basketball hoop on a boat, you know. Say, were you ever a basketball player? You sure are big . . . how big are you, anyway?"

"About six four, last I checked. You like basketball, huh?"

"Sure do. I'm going to play for the Blazers when I grow up. My dad used to play for them, and the Knicks, too. He was a forward. He retired, though—his knees went bad, he had to have a whole bunch of operations. You know my dad? Nat McCarthy? Number 17?"

"Yeah. I know about him, saw him play a few times. Great forward, too. Too bad about his knees."

"Yeah, it was. Say, does that Coke machine work?"

"It does if you've got two bits."

"Oh."

Don grinned in spite of himself and put some coins in the machine. "If I drink the whole thing I'll likely belch in front of a customer," he said, taking a swallow of the drink. "Want the rest?"

The boy's eyes brightened. "Sure do . . . sir."

That was why the woman had looked familiar to him; he'd seen a picture of her in the paper, when the Blazers, led by her husband, won the championship a few years back. Now he was the spokesman for some sporting goods company; Don had seen him pitching the firm's products on television. So this was the wife and kid he'd dumped along the way. A dumb move—anybody could see that Peggy McCarthy was quality goods.

A few nights later she waylaid Don in the yard, just as he was leaving the marina. She came right to the point. "I'm looking for a place to live. Aboard," she added pointedly. He said nothing, and she went on. "Look, we won't be in the way. You'll hardly even know we're here. You're gone at night, and there's nobody here unless the guest slip is occupied. You have expensive inventory around here—someone could break in and do a lot of damage."

He was amused. "You want a job as a security guard?" he asked. "You and your boy?"

She colored. "Not exactly. But I could keep an eye on things, make the place look occupied. That would keep the riffraff away."

"What if the riffraff wanted more than the inventory?"

She fixed him with a steady gaze. "I'm not some dumb boat bunny, you know. I have a gun and I know how to use it. I was brought up on a ranch in Nevada. Plenty of snakes in Nevada. You learn to get them before they get you." She wrinkled her nose, and her freckles danced across the bridge. "Different kind of snakes around here, maybe."

He laughed. "And what about your boy? He going to pull guard duty, too, hang around here all day?"

"Of course not. He'll be in school. I enrolled him today, in the elementary school down the beach."

"Pretty sure of my answer, weren't you?"

"No," she said. Her shoulders sagged slightly, and she looked defeated. Then she straightened up and returned his lazy grin with a smile of her own. "Not sure. Hopeful, maybe, but not sure."

Desperate, too, he thought, but he did not say that. He liked Peggy McCarthy's forthright manner, her green eyes that met his confidently. She didn't make unnecessary conversation, and she kept her boat nicely, moving around it with a deft surefootedness that pleased him. And her son tickled him, too—in the mornings, when the two of them were polishing the brightwork, he liked to hear the kid's thin, childish voice in counterpoint to her deep, husky one, singing folk songs like "The City of New Orleans" and "Red River Valley."

Why not? he thought. The port authority people hardly ever came around now that the financing for the marina improvements had fallen through; he'd had to withdraw the drawings, the permit applications, when that happened. If they came around, he could handle them. And he could handle the extra money from Peggy McCarthy, too.

The marina had barely broken even since he'd taken over the lease from the widow of its previous operator. She'd wanted him along with the deal, but he'd found a few dollars to buy out her interest and he was not beholden to her. He sold used boats—only wood ones, old, graceful yawls and scarred, weather-beaten ketches, and a cutter that had been built in a yard in Glasgow nearly a century before. He refinished and rebuilt them, and then sold them—he did haul-outs and survey work and some engine repair to get by between sales, which were few and infrequent.

He had a buddy, Karl, who was a naval architect and signed off on Don's inspections, trusting him to spot the flaws, the rot, the problems. Don had wanted to be a naval architect himself, once—he'd tried going back to school for his degree, right after he and Anne got married, but he couldn't hack the math. Night school was hard when he tried it later, especially after Billy came, and yowled when he was trying to study.

So he quoted Peggy McCarthy a moorage fee and she paid him for four months in advance. Then she flew north with her son to pick up some things from storage in Sausalito, including her car.

"Thanks a lot," she told him before she left. "We won't be any trouble."

You just might be, he told her retreating backside—her neat, tight little butt and sturdy legs. You just might be a great deal of trouble, but I'll take my chances.

To his surprise, he liked having the McCarthys at the marina. Travis had usually left for school by the time he arrived in the mornings, but every afternoon at three thirty he rode his shiny red bicycle into the yard, raising a rooster tail of dust that settled back onto the dry scrub and gravel like a sudden fog on the ocean. It got so that Don could set his watch by the boy's arrival; when Travis was late, Don's stomach tensed and stayed that way until he saw the boy with the shaggy white-blond hair and the Blazer tee shirt.

As soon as the kid reported in to his mother and changed into cutoffs, he was back at Don's side, chattering on and on. He told stories about his school, his teachers, his class gerbil project, a heron he'd seen when he rode down to the marshes. He was always asking questions: Does an explosion in space make noise like it does on the machines at the video arcade? Do lobsters feel pain when you boil them alive? Did Ricco really get that scar on the side of his jaw from a shark, like he said he had?

"I hope Trav isn't being a pain in the neck," Peggy

said to him that day when she came to take Travis shopping. He was busy playing pirate, climbing on and off the old Morgan that was pulled up in the yard awaiting a part from an eastern distributor. The boy had tied a long stick to his belt and wore a red kerchief around his neck. He leaped around the boat, brandishing the make-believe sword.

"Mom, do I have to go? Can't I just stay here? Ricco and Don said it was okay if I played around here as long as I don't get in the way. I'm not in the way, am I, Don?"

He shook his head; no, Travis wasn't in the way. It was kind of nice having him around. Natural. And of course he'd rather stay here than go to the shopping mall at the other end of town on a hot day like this one. "Sure, let him stay," he told Peggy.

When she came back to the marina, dusk had lengthened the shadows in the yard to near-darkness, and Travis was stretched out on his stomach in the office, reading old issues of *Sail* and *Yachting*. "Sorry I'm late," she said, "I forgot about rush-hour traffic. I hope the groceries didn't spoil in the heat. If you feel like it, we'd be glad to have you join us for supper."

"Yeah, Don, that's a terrific idea, my mom's a great cook. Yeah, Don, come to supper, huh, please?"

He wanted to say sure, I'd like that. But he couldn't. Barbaralee was waiting for him, in her condo in Del Rey. He considered calling Barbaralee and breaking their date, but he hesitated too long.

Peggy said brightly, "Don't pester Don, Trav, I'm sure he has other plans."

"That's right," he said quickly. "A customer for the big ketch on the far dock wants to talk about financing, he's bringing his partner to dinner . . ." It was a weak excuse. Anne used to say he was a terrible liar, and she was right. He wanted to say yes to

Peggy's invitation—he realized that he did not want to leave her here and go to Marina Del Rey.

"Some other time," Peggy said, in a deliberately casual voice. Her son's face fell, and their disappointment, mother's and son's, resonated in him and made him briefly angry. He was gruffer than he meant to be, and all the way to Barbaralee's he berated himself for his stupidity. He'd hurt a few too many people in his lifetime, and he had enough tears on his conscience to float that Morgan in the yard right out to the Pacific and over the edge of the world. He didn't need any more.

Barbaralee was waiting for him over in her all-white apartment in Marina Del Rey, the apartment with the hidden lights and the stereo speakers in every room and the big circular bed. Barbaralee, with her long silver fingernails, nails that dug into his back when she came in long, bucking, noisy spasms. She loved to screw, Barbaralee did, and she was good, even with those kinky sex toys she was so fond of. Sometimes screwing Barbaralee was like playing pinball; here, there, there, here, oops, tilt, not there. He wasn't crazy about the toys and games and routines; even the velvet ropes that hung over the bed made him uneasy. He'd always thought of himself as pretty good in the rack—at least, no woman had ever complained or needed gadgets like those to enjoy herself in bed with him. When he complained about them Barbaralee just laughed and said, we've got to keep up with the times, got to keep abreast of technology.

She was a stewardess, but she was no airhead. There were plenty of guys sniffing around her in that overpriced singles condo that was her home between flights. She was funny and quick, and she carried her miles well. She planned to give the friendly skies another year or two before she grounded herself, married some rich man from the front of the plane—not a pilot, she said, she'd had enough of those, but some passenger from up where the seats were wider and the drinks were free.

Meanwhile, she called him whenever she had a layover, and even if it was mostly sex between them, it was comfortable, affectionate, friendly sex. What the hell, he was pushing forty-five, he wasn't a kid anymore. Not like the times when he could get it up a dozen times a night and keep it up, and still be horny as a goat the next morning. Maybe women slowed down that way, too, maybe they needed all the help they got from the gadgets. People said women in their thirties and forties were in their prime. Maybe, but they were also exhausted from keeping their boobs from sagging and their miles from showing and their cellulite from puckering. It was amazing what some of them went through just to keep a man, any man, as long as he came across with whatever it was they wanted from him—money, clothes, jewels, sex, even a mortgage and a house and a kid.

He wondered what Peggy McCarthy had gone through to keep Nat McCarthy. Who left her anyway, when all was said and done. Somehow he didn't think she'd gone through as much with her husband as Anne had with him. The thought made him uncomfortable. That night, none of Barbaralee's toys had the desired effect on him, and it took considerable effort on his part to satisfy her; enough, at least, so that she finally fell into a restless sleep beside him in the round bed. Unable to sleep himself, he poured some brandy over ice cubes, thought about adding water, said the hell with it and added more booze instead.

He took his drink out onto the lanai, a three-by-six

rectangle overlooking the pool. There was a couple in the water, and he could hear them laughing in the quiet night. He felt memory and desire stir in him, mix in his gut like hot peppers with warm beer. Finally the pair quieted down and moved into the shadows, near the oleander bushes that edged the patio. He knew that if he listened he would hear a woman's sharp cry in the darkness, a man's labored exhalation of breath, and the rubbery slap of body against body. He did not want to hear, so he got up and refilled his glass and put a Moody Blues tape in the deck.

He settled down on the white velvet couch, swirling his brandy around in the glass, watching the crystal catch the light from the red power switch on the tape deck and refract it into thousands of tiny rainbows, like an oil slick on a puddle after a rainstorm.

Christ, he had screwed it up—Peggy, Anne, Barbaralee, all the others. It was probably just as well to keep it casual with Peggy. Peggy McCarthy, he thought, would make a better friend than a lover. They couldn't be both—few men and women could manage that. Even Barbaralee was a pain in the ass sometimes, especially when he didn't really want to screw her, like tonight. Peggy might be a good friend to have, if she trusted you. More than a few women had, he reflected, and just as many hadn't—it all worked out the same anyway, lousy.

Pussy whipped, his old man used to call him, "You get led around by your dick, or whatever it is women go for," his father said. "I give you every advantage and you throw 'em all away just for pussy. Better learn to keep your dick under control, 'fore you use up all the chances I bust my ass to give you."

Yeah, every advantage, and he had to admit it, he hadn't done a hell of a lot with them. He'd gotten himself kicked out of a few schools, never for anything really terrible except lousy grades and a bad attitude. It was Culver Academy that bounced him junior year for bad attitude. Which really meant getting caught laying the commandant's daughter behind the field house—what was her name? Sandy, that was it, Sandy Rexall, like the drugstore. Her father caught them at it and it was wham, bam, out of here, man. His father had him enrolled at public school in Groton forty-eight hours later. Grounded him for three months and made him dig out the basement and make a family room down there. All those warm spring nights, digging, when the street was so quiet you could hear a snatch of melody from a convertible pulling up to the corner stop sign, then speeding off, leaving him sweating and shoveling, feeling his life and his youth race away with the car.

He put in his time and waited, hating his rigid, granite-faced father, who ran his family the way he ran his ship and never gave him any slack, never any at all. So he quit school the day he turned eighteen and joined the Navy as an ordinary swabbie, which infuriated the old man, who'd been trying to wangle him an appointment to the Academy. So he, too, could spend his life kissing the ass of any bozo who had one more stripe than he did.

Instead, he did his tour, four years; made a rating, lost it for cutting loose on liberty in Wellington after wintering over for five months at the Pole. Earned it back and lost it again for a bar brawl in Pago Pago. And then it was over and he was out, ready to do something with his life. His father was dead by then, and he no longer had to prove anything to anyone. He got in just under the deadline for veteran's benefits and rode the G.I. Bill through to a few credits short of graduation. Then he just didn't give a shit any longer; he needed to get out to sea, where he could think. He packed his clothes and his drafting kit, and signed on with Sun Oil, making the coastwise runs between east coast refineries and Venezuela, putting in at Port Aransas and Brownsville and Sparrows Point and Perth Amboy, holes gritty with the smell of unwashed bodies and creosote and dead low tide, and when he pulled the dog watch, late at night, he'd sit with a graph pad on his lap, tracing designs for the boats he'd build someday.

He sat for his first mate's license and shipped out for two or three weeks at a time. He was making good money and developing a taste for good Scotch and bench-made clothes tailored to fit his big frame, the body that began with wide shoulders and tapered to a waist so narrow that his clothes had to be made for him or they bunched up around his middle and bagged in the ass. He bought himself a twenty-eight-foot sloop, one of the last ones built by old Tom Varney down on the Chesapeake, in the yard that had been turning them out, handcrafted and balanced as sweet as they come, for half a century. He kept it down on the Eastern Shore, where his father's people came from. He had inherited a little property there when the old man died. It wasn't much—one of the little offshore islands without a name, mostly scrub and marsh, a waist-high walk from the mainland at low tide. It was populated with small game, birds and waterfowl, and occasionally white-tailed deer. Long before he was born, his father had built a shack on it. When he was about the age Travis was now, his father had taken him there, shown him how to handle a gun, gut a fish, tell the poisonous shrubs and berries from the ones you could eat. After Billy was born, at Anne's insistence Don made a will. He set up a conservancy trust with a wildlife society, giving Bill the use of the island in his own lifetime, and resolved some day to take his son there, teach him what his old man had taught him. How old was Billy now? Don counted back to the year of his birth . . . hell, the kid was probably a teenager; he'd probably think the island was a drag.

He got up and made himself another drink, thinking that it was the kind of night when old ghosts escaped, the same ones that kept him from sleeping, that made him remember the island. And Billy. And Anne, and his old man, and even Sandy Rexall. And the brandy dropped lower and lower in the bottle until it was empty.

After a couple years at sea, he'd conquered it again, that need to place himself on the bow of a boat, a ship, anything that could float. Somewhere he could look into the waves until his eyes blurred, search the sea for answers to questions he couldn't even put into words, then. The answers never came; the sea did not give anything up. When he realized that, he knew it was time to put into port again.

He studied the want ads and put on his sincere suit and saw executive recruiters up and down the eastern seaboard. Finally he signed with a search firm—they wanted him to use his old man's connections and his Navy junior ties to find the right desk-bound captain, the one who'd been passed over too many times for promotion but could still be useful to a defense contractor. He was good at the job; he earned regular bonuses and he found a decent apartment near Foggy Bottom in Washington, and occupied his nights entertaining old salts and occasionally—hell, regularly—one of the girls who flocked to the nation's capital every year, looking for life but finally settling for whatever she found. He wasn't thirty yet, and he was earning more money in one year than his old man had in any three—his old man, who had died one stripe short of flag rank.

Then he met Anne, and she was so goddamned cool and intelligent and earnest and innocent, all at the same time. She looked at him with those enormous eyes of hers and stopped his easy, lazy lines before he spoke them. There was something different about her; not just that she played hard to get at first, and not just that he knew she wanted him, that it was just a game like the games he'd played so often. For months after they met, he'd leave her at the door of her apartment and go home bent over with lover's nuts like a goddamned teenager. He'd stop at a bar for a quick one and some broad would give him the eye, and he'd ache so much he'd follow her home. Then the next morning he'd wake in a strange apartment, unable to recall the name of the woman next to him in bed. So he'd stumble out before she woke, go home to shower and shave and eat a handful of aspirin for his hangover and from still wanting Anne so goddamn much.

She didn't trust him at first. She didn't put him down, didn't call him on the numbers he ran on her. Not that she didn't notice. She noticed, all right, and the more she did, the more elusive she was, the more he wanted her. Then they offered him a transfer to Seattle. Boeing and Lockheed wanted someone closer than Washington, and Seattle looked like a good place for a new branch of the search firm. They gave him stock options and talked about a partnership. Don was ready to cast off. Half jokingly he suggested that Anne come with him, and that night, when she walked through her apartment door, poured him a drink, and went into her bedroom, he wasn't sure what to do. But then she turned and looked over her shoulder at him with those big Bambi eyes, not saying a word, and he knew.

They were married two weeks later. Her parents didn't like him; he knew that immediately, although he tried his best to make them warm to him. He answered their questions about his background without embarrassment; he came from good people, had nothing to be ashamed of. There was nothing he could do about the fact that he was not Jewish, as they and Anne were, but she told him it wasn't important, they were not observant. He didn't meet her brother Jeff then; he was in a sanitarium in Kansas. And he never met her grandmother, who sat *shiva* for Anne when she married a Gentile in Westport City Hall, with words spoken over her by a justice of the peace. After the wedding he looked away while Anne's father kissed her and said, "Here's some money so you can come home when it's over."

He wondered if she had ever used that money. He tried to remember, but the sun had come up and turned the light in Barbaralee's white living room the color of aluminum, and the glass in his hand was empty. On the way home he shared the freeway with truckers and early-morning commuters. And as he let himself into his own apartment on the beach, a few miles from the marina, he wondered why and how he knew that he had closed the door on a place, and a woman, to whom he would not be returning.

11 "There, that ought to do it," Peggy said, placing a sheaf of papers on the desk in front of him. "The financial statement, the P&L, the copy of the port lease, the preliminary construction estimate, and the tax records. It's an attractive investment for the right people."

"Here's hoping the right people are the ones I'm seeing in L.A. next week," said Don. "A little infusion of capital would do a hell of a lot for this place. Thanks for your help."

"Anytime," Peggy said. "The marina's books, though, are in terrible shape, and if your people are interested they're going to give them a pretty thorough going-over. I'd be glad to get them in shape for you. My business is always slow for a few weeks after April fifteenth. And I know you're itching to get your hands on that boat you took in on consignment yesterday . . . go ahead, I'll work here and keep an eye on things."

"You sure you don't mind?"

"I'm sure . . . go on."

Peggy McCarthy was one helluva woman, he reflected as he headed for the far dock where the fifty-foot *Monk* was berthed. He'd dropped by the *Pandora* as casually as he could manage the day after he'd declined her invitation to supper, and asked her and Travis to come out for an evening sail on *Windsong*. He'd stocked the galley and the ice chest, and they sailed out around the point and dropped anchor. The sun made its leisurely way down over the horizon, and they picnicked on the deck until the moon came up, then caught a night breeze back to the marina. Travis was asleep by the time they'd dropped sails and tied the boat down; Don picked him up easily, carried him to the *Pandora*, laid him down on his bunk, and covered him. Peggy made coffee, laced it with rum, and they sat in companionable silence for a while.

He wanted to kiss her but did not; it was too soon, so he said good night and went home, whistling happily as he let himself into the apartment. The next day, stopping in at the office to pick up her mail, she found him bent over his desk, adding and subtracting, tapping out figures on a calculator, trying to make the numbers reflect the potential he knew was in the marina. He explained the new financing plan, the upcoming presentation to the money men, and she looked over what he'd done, chewed the end of a pencil, and offered her help—"I'm an accountant, you're a visionary," she said, "you need me."

I certainly do, he thought, but lady, probably you do not need me. Probably you have no need at all of this aging, ass-chasing dreamer who never did a hell of a lot with all that potential everyone always said he had, who drinks too much and is losing his hair, who never could stick with anything long enough to make a go of it. Who'd start out with the best intentions, the right instincts, and end up making you miserable. If you were really smart you'd raise sail and get out of here, and if I were the kind of guy you seem to think I am, I'd tell you to. Maybe I will, he thought. But not just yet.

He was checking the twin diesels on the *Monk* when Anne called. Peggy hollered at him from the door of the office; there was a strong wind blowing from the channel, and he could hardly hear her. "Long distance," she shouted. "From Seattle."

Anne never called him here; when she communicated with him, which she did infrequently, it was via impersonally typed letters, having to do with the absence of support checks. Christ, he was barely keeping his own head above water these days, and it wasn't as if she really needed it. She must be raking it in with her law degree, and her parents were loaded, they were always sending the kid expensive presents and plane tickets and buying him skis and paying for those fancy schools Anne sent him to. If he thought the kid really needed anything, he'd have tried to keep up the support payments, but he knew Anne could always ask her father for money.

He picked up the telephone, prepared to tell her he was tapped out and listen to the inevitable guilt trip, but he could barely hear her at first. Her voice was muffled like she had a cold, and then he realized that she was crying. His stomach turned over—had something happened to the kid?

"Billy's not . . . he isn't . . . physically he's okay, but . . . he's not doing so well these days," she said. "He has to go somewhere. To a . . . a special school."

"He went to a special school, didn't he? For gifted children, or something?"

"I took him out of there almost two years ago, I told you that. He's at public school. But it's . . . not right for him," she replied.

"So you're going to yank him out of there now,

and send him to another one? Can't you let him finish the year there?" She must have found someplace that would guarantee the kid would get into Harvard or something—she'd been talking about sending him there since before he was born. Her old man had gone to Harvard, and her crazy brother, too.

"This isn't exactly a school. It costs a hundred dollars a day. He needs to go there until camp starts in July," she told him.

"A hundred dollars a day?" He exploded. "What for?"

"Doctors. Treatment. Round-the-clock attention."

"What kind of doctors? What treatment? Why does he need attention round the clock? What the hell is going on, anyway? Is Bill sick?"

"Yes. No. Not physically, I mean. Don, you've got to understand, he's a very troubled boy. The psychiatrist says . . ." She was crying, and he was having trouble following her.

"What psychiatrist? What do you mean, troubled?" She believed in psychiatry with a strength that approached faith. It never made sense to him, seeing that all those shrinks they'd taken her brother to hadn't done him any appreciable good. She'd made Don go to see one when he told her he wanted a divorce—a marriage counselor. He'd gone along with her, not because he thought there was any hope of things getting better between them but because he hoped it might help her see that his decision was final.

"It's very hard to explain if you haven't . . . if you don't . . . Billy and I seem to have come to the end of our rope. Together, I mean. He's been going through a . . . well, he's been in trouble. Not seriously—not with the police, I mean—but that's probably coming next. He's practically been expelled from school twice this year. He's not doing well there, academically or any other way. He's been lying, stealing, taking my car . . . he broke into a house in the neighborhood a couple of months ago."

"He did what?" Jesus, what had she done to the kid? What had he, Don, done?

"He's threatened to run away. He's only fourteen and he can't . . . He doesn't want to live here anymore, Don. With me, I mean. And I . . . I . . ." She was sobbing now, and he waited, not sure of what to say. When she continued, her voice was tremulous.

"Today he had a knife and I thought he was going to . . . never mind, that's not important. I guess what I'm saying is, I can't handle him anymore. There's this place in eastern Washington, it's a kind of crisis-intervention place, short-term placement only, a few weeks. There's a psychologist who runs it, it's very intensive diagnosis and evaluation, and they help the person sort out his options, and set goals and recommend a long-term solution, a special school, maybe . . . he could go there now and finish the school year by correspondence, and then at the end of the six weeks he'll go to camp, and then to Westport. Then in September . . . well, this place will help me find the right school for him next year, and if I can get him in, I'll ask my parents for help with the tuition. I don't want to ask them for this . . . it's too much like what they went through with Jeff, I can't put them through that again. I can't . . . Billy can't make it here until July, Don. I'm afraid he'll do something to himself, or get in big trouble, or split and go live on the streets, you know, be a runaway, and . . . and . . . I can't take that, Don, I just can't take that."

She was crying in big, gulping sobs now; Christ, he'd never heard her like this, not since the day he moved out. She'd used the same words, too . . . "I can't take that, Don, I just can't take that." While her sobs subsided, he tried to think. Seven hundred dollars a week. Breaking into someone's house. A knife. "Anne, I can't put my hands on that kind of money . . . maybe a couple of hundred sometime around the first of the month, but . . . look, I know this is going to sound stupid, but why don't you send him to me?"

There was silence on the wire; in the stillness of the moment, he heard the office door close and felt grateful to Peggy for leaving.

"Anne? Anne? Are you still there?" he said.

"Yes, I'm still here," she said softly. Then he heard her sigh. "Look, Don, that's not why I called. Eight years ago you made it very clear that you didn't want the responsibility of fatherhood. I just thought, given the situation, you might be willing to help out. That's all."

"What the hell do you think I'm trying to do, lady?" She could really piss him off sometimes—always had, always could, he supposed. She had one thing in her head, couldn't hear anything else. "I'm trying to help out, the only way I can," he said. "Billy doesn't need a place like that. Doctors. Round-the-clock supervision. He needs something else."

"A father, I suppose? Have you come to the conclusion after all these years that your son needs a father? Is that something that just occurred to you, or have you been thinkng about it for a long time?"

Shit, now she was sticking it to him. "Look, Anne, I'm just trying to do what I can. You want to fight about history, or do you want to solve this problem?" he asked. Her problem. His problem, too. Billy—their problem.

"Oh, I'm sorry, Don, I didn't mean that. Perhaps a short vacation with you wouldn't be a bad idea. It's been a long time, after all . . . he's grown, you wouldn't recognize him. It wouldn't hurt him to leave school now—it's only a month to the end of the year, maybe he could take his exams later, before he goes to camp. Yes, it might be good for him to spend a few weeks with you, and then he'll come back and—"

"Nothing doing," he said. "You send him down here and he goes to school until it lets out for the summer and then I put him to work around here. Not summer camp. Boot camp is more like it." Stealing, joyriding, housebreaking . . . had his kid turned into a punk? If he had, he'd knock it out of him.

"You don't understand, Don. He's not used to that kind of thing," Anne protested. "He's a very sensitive boy. The psychiatrist said—".

"Don't tell me what the psychiatrist said. You sound like your folks talking about Jeff. Billy's not crazy, he's not sick. He's feeling his oats—that's the age. He needs discipline." You've spoiled him, he thought but didn't say. You always spoiled him, even when he was a baby. You have to be firm with a kid, set limits, make him toe the mark.

"Discipline?" she said. "The kind of discipline your father gave you?"

She still knew how to get to him, knew exactly how to make him feel stupid and guilty. He wondered if that was what she did to Bill. "Not exactly," he said. "My old man would've thrown me across a room, I gave him lip or broke into somebody's house. I won't beat up on the kid." Not if he's fast, he thought. I was pretty fast when I was a kid, outran the old man most of the time.

"Oh, God, Don, I don't know . . ." Her voice trailed off. "Why this big father routine all of a sudden? Why, after all these years, are you suddenly riding to the rescue?"

After all the times you ignored him—he could hear her thinking it. Well, what if she was? She was right, wasn't she? She was always right, he thought wearily, and tried another approach. "Anne, have you changed any since we got divorced? I mean, have you grown up any?" That was a touchy one—he hoped she'd understand what he meant, wouldn't get on her high horse.

"I think I have," she said, and he heard the coolness in her tone.

"Well, then, give me credit for having done some growing up of my own," he told her. "You never asked me for anything for Bill before—nothing I could give you, anyway. And I don't have all that much now. An apartment, a lease on a marina that's a few bucks from folding . . . don't worry, I've got enough to feed him. Nothing fancy, but I can manage that."

"And what else?" she asked quietly. "What else can you give him?"

He tamped down a cigarette on the desk's surface and spoke into the phone, as quietly as she had spoken. "Whatever I have, Anne," he said. "Whatever I have."

They were both silent for a long few moments. Then she said, "I still don't understand, Don. Why? Why now? After all these years . . . why?"

He took a deep drag on the cigarette. "Why don't we just say I guess it's time I paid my dues, Anne, and leave it at that?"

12 His father. Jesus fucking Christ. He still couldn't believe it, thought Bill, as he cleared out his locker. One day your old lady says you want to go live with your father, and just for the hell of it you say yes, and that's it, wham, bam, thank you ma'am, I'll be hitting the road now.

He hadn't thought he'd heard right when she asked him—he thought it was some kind of weird joke. So he said sure, why not, that'll shut her up, if she thinks I'd rather live with him than her maybe she'll lay off me a little.

"Okay, then," she'd said.

"Whaddya mean, okay?" he'd asked.

"Okay, you can go live with your father. Just for the summer. You'll come back in September . . . maybe we can get along better then."

"Just like that?" he'd asked. "You going to send me down there with a ribbon wrapped around me, C.O.D.?" He thought that was pretty funny, actually, but Jesus, she was acting weird. Then she told him about that place east of the mountains and how she'd called his old man to hit him up for money to pay for it, and he'd said send him to me. Just like that.

"Yeah, it's probably cheaper to have me down there, I can do a lot of shitwork around the marina, he'll get off a lot easier than paying for that place," he'd said. "To which I'm not going, by the way, it sounds to me like a fucking mental hospital."

"For what you do that passes for work, he'd be better off hiring somebody that knows the meaning of the word," his mother had said, raising her eyebrows in that way she did when she was making a wisecrack, only she really meant it. "No," she'd said, "that's not it, he wants you. He loves you, you know."

Since when, Bill wondered. Since fucking when? Where did that come from after all those years? It musta been the best kept secret of the century. Then Clary Redman appeared at his elbow and he put it out of his mind.

"You sure have a lot of stuff in your locker. How are you going to get it all home?" Clary asked.

"I dunno. I guess I'll leave most of it here. They probably have different books in California." It was amazing how much crap you collected over a school year, Bill thought. Most of a year, he corrected himself. All the lockers were probably taken in the school he'd be going to for the next month.

"Aren't you going to take that down vest, and your skateboard, and your shop project? Come on, I'll help you carry it."

"Yeah, well . . . uh, sure, thanks." It was a quarter of an hour after the dismissal bell; they'd probably be the only ones on the last bus. They left the school, and he sort of wanted to turn around and look at it one last time. There was a funny lump in his throat. He couldn't quite swallow, his mouth was too dry, and he shrugged, adjusting his pack, and walked away. Clary had to take a bunch of short quick steps to match his longer, more determined stride. When he noticed it, he slowed down a little.

"I think you should take your skateboard. When I go to my cousin's house in La Jolla, we skateboard everywhere," Clary said.

"Yeah, I guess they do where my—where I'm going, too. It's on the beach, there's a big boardwalk there." He had only a vague recollection of the place his father lived in; he'd gone there once, when he was eight years old, and mostly they'd gone to the movies and to Sea World and Disneyland, stuff like that.

"I'll bet you get to go surfing. Are you going to have a surfboard? God, it sounds neat. I always wanted to live in California, it doesn't rain all the time there like it does here. You're so lucky!" Clary chattered.

"Yeah." Maybe he was, maybe he wasn't. It hadda be better than here. No more scenes with his old lady. No more having to paint Joe Lawlor's house. Course, he'd help out Chris that afternoon, he wouldn't get to see him after that. Shit. He'd got used to Chris, living so close all this time. He'd miss Chris. But at least he wouldn't have to see Wilson anymore, or any other shrink. That was the deal. His father made his mother promise. She told him how his old man said if Bill was coming to live with him, they'd try it his way for a change.

He wondered what that meant. He didn't know, but it sounded vaguely threatening. He'd had this strange feeling of things happening to someone else lately, someone who looked like him and talked like him but wasn't him. It must have been the business with the knife, he thought. Jesus, he'd just been using the opener to pry the cap off a bottle of beer he had stashed in his room when she got all weirded out about that, thought he was going to cut himself or something. He got really pissed at her sometimes, but not enough to do anything that stupid. He ever wanted to kill himself, he'd drown, out in the middle of the ocean somewhere, so nobody could ever point to the spot where he was and say there, that's Bill Manning, that's where his body is.

It all happened so fast, from the time his mother told him he was going to live with his father till now, since Monday and it was only Friday, and he was almost all packed and was leaving the next day. His mother'd taken him shopping, made him get some new clothes—"Your father is going to want to see you in something decent, he's very straight about things like that, and you'd better get a haircut while you're at it." She wouldn't let him take his old jeans, that he'd written on the leg of and let the knees wear out in, that were broken in just right, but he'd wadded them up in a ball and stuck them in his duffel anyway. It was like she was polishing him up, getting him all shiny and new for his old man, in case she was worried that he wasn't good enough the way he was.

"Here's the bus," Clary said, "looks like we're the only ones on it."

"Yeah, I figured." They took the big seat all the way in the back. "I really appreciate it, you helping me with the stuff and junk and all," he said awkwardly as the bus neared his stop.

"Oh, sure, no problem," Clary said. "I hope you have a good time in California, and come back real soon."

"I'm just going till the end of summer, probably," he said. "I'll see you in September—are you going to Ingraham next year?"

"I guess so," she said. "Well, anyway, write me a letter sometime, will you?"

"I might do that," he answered. "Well, here's where I get off." He picked up his pack and adjusted it on his back, and she put the things she had carried in his arms. "See you."

"See you." When he crossed the street in front of the school bus and it started up again, he looked at Clary, waving to him from the window, and kind of nodded his head. Then he shouldered his burdens and walked up the steep hill to his house.

He was dumping all the stuff in his room when the phone rang, and he went into his mother's bedroom to answer it. "Bill?"

It was his father; he hadn't spoken to him in a long time, but he remembered the voice. It was a big voice, not loud but thick somehow, and deep. Now it sounded hesitant.

"Uh, yes, sir?" His father was big on manners, and being polite, saying sir and ma'am and standing up straight and looking people right in the eye when you talked to them.

"It occurs to me that a whole bunch of other people are deciding your future for you and you might want a chance to put your two cents' worth in," his father said. "So I figured I'd better ask you before it's done—do you want to come down here and try it with me?"

"That might be okay," he replied, hesitant himself. Was his father having second thoughts? Maybe he didn't really want him there at all, maybe it was just cheaper than sending him to that loony bin east of the mountains his mother'd told him about.

"I thought you ought to know, it's not going to be like the last time you were here," his father said. "I've got this marina to run, I can't just leave it and take you to Disneyland."

"Disneyland's for kids," he answered. "I don't need to go to Disneyland."

"You're going to be too busy anyway," his old man

said. "I'm going to work your tail off. There's plenty to do around here. You like boats?"

"Yeah, I like boats okay . . . I mean, sure, sir." He'd never been on one, except once when he was little, before his father left, and he didn't remember that very well. He'd been on ferries plenty of times, of course, and in rowboats and canoes, but that was different. He hoped he wouldn't get seasick, something stupid like that.

"Good," said the man with the strange, deep, powerful voice. It sounded different now, a little softer, sort of. "I'll see you tomorrow."

"This time tomorrow, you'll probably be on the beach in sunny Californ-i-yay, 'stead of scraping paint off in the rain," Chris said.

It wasn't really raining, just kind of heavy misting, and actually he liked it, it was nice and cool—scraping paint was hot, dirty work, but what the hell, it was only one more day. And he sort of owed Chris—he'd been the one who'd really gotten him into the mess with his old man, it'd been his idea to bust into Joe Lawlor's house. Just to have something to do, get rid of that antsy feeling he had so often these days.

"Probably will," he replied. "I'm going to get me a surfboard, first thing. There's great surfing where my old man lives, I read this article in *Outside* about it."

"Yeah," said Chris. "I really envy you. God, I'd sure like to get the hell out of this place and go somewhere else, like California. You suppose they got skiing there? I mean, considering it's hot down there most of the time."

"There are mountains, but I think they're pretty far away and anyway, by the time ski season starts again I'll be back here and we'll go up to Rainier and ski Paradise."

"Sure," said Chris, and they scraped paint in silence for a while. "You really think you're gonna come back, huh?"

"Course I am, shithead, I'm just goin' for a visit, not forever or anything. I mean, I live here, don't I?"

"Yeah, I guess," Chris replied. "But goin' to school down there and stuff—that's not like a visit."

"It's only till the end of this year, so's I can get my credits and all. I'll be going to Ingraham with you in the fall, just like we planned."

"Sure, I guess," Chris said, not sounding as if he believed it.

"Hey, listen, I got an idea," Bill said. Maybe you can save up enough money to come down and visit me this summer. After school's out, I mean. We could go surfing and everything . . . maybe my father'd let us use one of his boats."

"I got to paint this damn house this summer, remember? I ain't even going to camp."

Billy felt a stab of guilt. "Well, listen, I'm gonna write you letters, and you write me, okay? And maybe your father'll feel sorry for you, missing camp and everything, and after you finish the house you can come down to California."

"Fat fucking chance," Chris said. "But maybe . . . you never can tell."

"Never can," Bill agreed, and they worked on the house until it was time to go home for supper, and considering everything, he thought, they had a pretty good time.

13 The night before Billy left, Anne occupied herself with the small but chilling tasks of his imminent departure. She packed a small carry-on bag; in it she put his transcripts from school and his medical records, and the emergency epinephrine kit with the disposable needles and the Benadryl tablet the allergist had given her years ago. She put in his rain gear, and new tubes of toothpaste and shampoo; she added a stray pair of socks she found in the back seat of the car and the clothes he had worn that day, freshly washed and still warm from the dryer. She added a paperback book she'd picked up that afternoon, *The Man Who Skied Down Everest*, and hesitated over some stamps and envelopes. It wasn't like getting him ready for camp; this was different. Her son was going to live with his father.

She went to bed, finally, but could not sleep. The next day Billy would fly away from her to a man he hardly knew, a stranger who had his last name. A fantasy he had put away a long time ago, along with the lacing shoe and the picture books and the outgrown clothes. She had put that fantasy away, too, and in the darkness she tried to call it up again, tried to remember the man who had become a stranger to her and to their son—a man whose ways were different, whose life had taken turns unknown to her. A man who shared her memories, her history of time and space, her geography of place and event. There was no one she saw now who had known him; she had created a new life for herself and Billy with the leftovers of her marriage, erasing enough of the traces so that, were it not for her son, she could almost think it had never happened, she had never fallen in love with that stranger, married him, lived with him. She had been lonely at first, having no one to share her memories; after a time, it made it easier to forget them.

She met him in a taxicab that stopped to pick her up in front of her apartment building on Connecticut Avenue the night before John Kennedy was sworn in as President. A thick snowfall crippled the capital that night; she was on her way to an inaugural gala at the Armory, the tickets a gift of her employer, a congressman. There was already someone in the cab, but it was usual then in Washington for several passengers to share a taxi headed in the same direction.

She hesitated for a moment, and a darkly attractive man stepped out of the interior of the cab and held the door open for her to enter. His bulk dwarfed her; when she looked up, the first thing she noticed were his eyes, deep set and sparkling as though lit from behind. He helped her into the cab, gravely and politely, as if she were a valuable, delicate package, and once inside, made easy conversation about the havoc the weather was undoubtedly wreaking on the plans for the inauguration; perhaps Jack should make Teddy the weatherman in Camelot, he suggested.

The snow was approaching blizzard proportions;

each block took them deeper into a city that seemed almost paralyzed. It took nearly three hours to get to the Armory, and by that time she had forgotten the gala completely. She was dizzy with excitement, completely and totally charmed by this handsome, well-spoken, smart, compellingly confident, sexy man. He was not glib, as so many of the men she saw in those days were; he did not have that ivy-encrusted snootiness, that air of belonging as if by divine right to a privileged elite, that was characteristic of most of the men she had known since college. When they arrived at the Armory—his destination, too, as it happened—he said, "If we give up this taxi, we'll never get another. They'll find us when the thaw sets in, frozen, standing straight up on the curb, pleading for someone to stop for us." She agreed completely, and grinned with delight when he gave the driver a handful of bills and told him to take the slow way home.

He courted her for five months. Winter ripened into spring, and they went down to the shore and sailed his sloop on the Chesapeake, and ate lobster in Annapolis and drank Courvoisier in the smart new nightclubs of Georgetown. They went to Winchester for the apple blossom festival and had picnics in Rock Creek Park. They watched the tourists watching the White House, hoping to catch a glimpse of Jackie. At the National Zoo he showed her the penguins he had helped trap and capture in the Antarctic. He filled her apartment with roses, and held her close against him when they danced at the Shoreham.

She thought only once, in the very beginning, of resisting him. Of not allowing herself to fall in love with him. She fell asleep considering it, and when she woke the next morning she felt bereft, as though someone had died while she slept. It was an awful loneliness, which frightened her until she thought of him, and then, as suddenly as it had come, it disappeared. But by then it was too late. She knew that he had her, not by suggestion or even persuasion, but by her own failed will.

She knew that he wanted her, but she waited. She had wanted her first time to be with the right man, the way one did in those days, and she knew it was him. It had nothing to do with logic, reason, or common sense; their lives could not have been more separately lived, their backgrounds more dissimilar, their expectations of marriage more different, as her father pointed out when she announced, in June, that she was marrying him. She would not heed the protests of her family—not only her parents, but her aunts and uncles, too, told her not to throw away her life, her brilliant career, on this man, who was clearly unsuitable. He was not stable, they pronounced, making their judgment on the basis of his history, which he presented to them honestly and unalibied or unembellished.

Against the intensity of her passion for Don, their words, their warnings, their imprecations, and even their threats had no power. Since Jeff's breakdown, she had felt the burden of their hopes that she would bring them the happiness and honor, the *nachas* that he obviously never would. Because Jeff was the tragedy of their lives, it fell to her to be the joy, but she would not give up Don because of that obligation.

She wanted him because he saw behind her skin, deep into her heart, past her studied coolness and even, occasionally, through her willingness to let him strut and preen and charm and tease her, dominate her with his superior strength, wisdom, and sophistication. That she was his equal in those ways and perhaps others was a secret they kept from each other.

Effortlessly, it seemed, he cut through all her layers, through to her true core, from which her blood leapt to meet his, through bone, tissue, and nerves, through her skin, which sought his whenever he was in range of her senses. Like a laser, he cut cleanly, leaving no trace of blood except the first time, when, breaching the unexpected barrier, he caused the shedding of the token drops of her virginity. In a moment so brief that later she thought she had imagined it, she felt his cool tears on her breast, and through him a trembling greater than, different from, sexual passion; she had kept the fact of her innocence from him until then, sensing with the same female essence he touched in her the power it gave her over him, for she knew that he was a true romantic.

He overwhelmed her. She would have followed him anywhere; without monogrammed towels and silver teaspoons, without wedding announcements or the blessings of her family and friends, without a single possession or even the promise of eternal love. She knew then, though she never acknowledged it, to herself or to him, that he was not capable of that, but she would be with him as long as he wanted her, and when he did not, when his passion for her cooled, she would understand him so clearly and love him so completely that he could not leave her. Meanwhile, she kept him always a little bit at bay, hiding the intensity of her obsession as well as she could. For if he knew how much she needed him—how essential he was to her happiness, to her very survival—surely he would tire of her. So for a time before they married, and even after, she held herself at a distance she thought a safe remove. And when he stopped wanting her, as she knew from the beginning he would, that fragment of self she had held back saved her.

Until this past week, she had not thought of him in

years, except for occasional flashes of pure anger, close to hatred, when Billy suffered from his indifference, or when she indulged herself in making Don responsible, by his absence, for Billy's problems. She had put the memories of her time with him in a tiny compartment in her head, and she did not take them out very often. Now she tried to call some up, and could not. She wanted to give Billy something to alleviate the fear she knew he must be feeling, some words to reassure him. She wished she had some insight into Don's character or values or habits to indicate to Billy that it would be all right.

They were silent in the car on the way to the airport. Billy fiddled with the radio dial; hearing nothing he liked, he put a tape from his carrying case in the car deck—Pink Floyd's "The Wall," whose nihilist lyrics appalled her. As she drove, she reached for his hand and squeezed it; there was a game they played sometimes when they were in the car. Okay, she'd say, with a little squeeze. Yeah, he'd reply, squeezing back. Sure, she'd venture, squeezing twice, or in a rhythm—shave and a haircut, two bits, say. Absolutely, he'd answer, matching her beat. Even when he wasn't talking much, he'd usually respond to that.

Not now. He took his hand away, not roughly, and hers shook as she replaced it on the wheel. Her son was going to live with his father. She loved him, but she could not help him. She loved him, but he could not live with her. She loved him, had loved and cared for him all his life, and now could not do for him what someone else—someone he did not even know—could do with four simple words: I want you, son.

She did not settle him in his seat with books and magazines and last-minute instructions the way she did when he flew to the East Coast to see his grandparents. They said good-bye at the departure gate. She hugged him tight, trying not to cry. They called his flight and she kissed him; she held him away from her, and said, "He's a good man, Bill. Just different from us." They called his flight again, and he broke away. He turned and walked down the narrow airway corridor to the plane. She looked out through the big windows in front of the boarding gate, where the plane was, trying to catch a glimpse of him in a port-hole, but she did not see him.

She waited in the coffee shop until some time after the plane departed. She ate a rubbery omelet and cold toast and a glass of milk and two cups of coffee and she waited. And then, with a feeling that was part relief and part sadness, she got into her car and drove home.

14 Don woke up from a dream about Anne.

He could not remember any details of the dream except that in it she was pregnant. On the drive to the airport, he thought about her, them, then. About watching her flat, taut stomach round and soften, feeling the baby's first kick. Does it matter if it's a boy or a girl? she asked, and he rested his cheek on the bulge of her abdomen and said of course not, although he was certain she was carrying his son.

He remembered how her rosy aureoles had darkened as her pregnancy progressed, how just before Billy was born her breasts were full of a thin, sweetish moisture he tasted on her nipples in those last weeks when they belonged only to him. He recalled her waiting for him to come home from work, in the wing chair by the fireplace, late into her final month. Her hair was loose, curled around her shoulders; she wore a dressing gown that stretched across her enormous belly. There was a mohair throw tucked around her ankles, a book in her lap. She smiled up at him when he came into the room. He could smell chicken simmering in red wine on the stove and bread baking in the oven.

She woke him just before dawn: Don, it's time. He helped her dress, brought the car around to the front door, and bundled her carefully into it. It was icy on the streets near the hospital; he drove very carefully. And when they wheeled her away to do all the mysterious things they do to women in labor, he went to a florist and filled her room with luxuriant blooms—gladioli and lilies and freesia and roses.

When he held his son in his arms for the first time, he did not think his life was lacking anything. He thought he would be married to Anne for a long time, despite the tensions of the last couple of years, while she was trying to conceive and could not. It's just one of those things, the specialist told them, no telling why some folks don't get pregnant, there's nothing wrong that we can tell, at least not with you, Don. Don already knew that—a woman he'd been running around with for the past few months was pregnant, and it was his. She had an abortion, for which he paid; the irony didn't escape him, but he'd been cheating on Anne enough so that it was probably bound to happen with somebody.

When Anne became pregnant, he vowed to clean up his act, and for a long while he did. For a time it was the way it had been at first, when he'd fallen in love with her. And after Billy was born it was pretty good for a while, too—the baby was new and interesting to him, and so was she. But he could feel the sands of their life together shifting, and he knew he could not keep their marriage from being washed away by the tide—even Billy could not do that.

Their bodies held them together long after they had said all that they had to say to each other. "I can't believe that this was the last time you'll ever make love to me," she said when he took out the suitcases and placed them on the bed whose sheets were still damp from their sex. He had told her that night that he was leaving in the morning; he had spoken the words she knew were coming: divorce, lawyers, papers, and pulled her hands from her ears to make her listen to them. He repeated them until she stopped shaking her head from side to side and twisted away from him to cry, first in a quiet sniffle and then in deep, gut-wrenching sobs. Finally he quieted her in the only way he knew how. She fell asleep right afterward, her dried tears cold and clammy against the curve of his shoulder. In the morning she reached for him, but he packed his clothes and left. Left her and left his son. His son, who was coming back to him today.

At first, at the airport, Don wasn't sure which kid was his. Several teenagers disembarked from the Seattle plane, and it was hard to pick out Bill, who passed him twice before approaching him.

"Dad?" he said. "I'm Bill."

"Sure, of course . . . you've grown so much, I didn't recognize you at first. Still think of you as a kid, I guess," said Don, embarrassed at not having known his own son.

He was a good-looking kid, Don thought—going to get some shoulders on him in a couple of years, maybe not his height, but you never could tell, kids grew in spurts. He was kind of quiet, but that was to be expected, under the circumstances. "Let's go pick up your gear, and get out of here."

They stopped first at the marina, and he introduced the boy to Peggy and Travis—Don was hoping she'd invite them to dinner, but she shooed him off *Pandora* after a few minutes.

"He needs to be alone with you, not us," she said. "Don't be afraid of him—he won't bite you. He looks like a nice kid to me."

On the way to the apartment, Bill said, "You and her have a thing going?" in a flat, neutral voice.

"No, we don't. Why?"

"I didn't mean to be nosey. I mean, I just don't want to be in the way."

"It's nothing like that," Don said. "She just lives at the marina and helps out with the books sometimes. She's a good person."

"Sure," said the kid.

What did he mean by that? Don wondered. Did he think his old man was shitting him? Don sighed—he only wished it were true. He'd gotten a little closer to Peggy McCarthy since that sunset sail. They'd become friends in a casual fashion. He had not made any moves on her—somehow she let him know that they would not be welcomed. Or maybe they would, he wasn't sure. But until he was, he wasn't going to try. Now that he had a kid on his hands, he couldn't be catting around anymore. Since that last night with Barbaralee, he'd led a pretty clean life, except that he wasn't feeling particularly good. In the mornings he coughed a great deal, and he had a few new aches and pains and a funny little bump on his groin he'd noticed a couple of weeks before. Probably something he picked up from Barbaralee, he thought; she got around a lot on her out-of-town layovers. He swallowed some old penicillin pills he had, just in case. It probably wasn't the clap, simply middle age catching up on him.

He pulled the car into the carport and helped the kid get his bags inside. The apartment looked pretty crummy, he supposed; he'd cleaned it the day before, and he'd done the best he could with what he had, which wasn't much. He hadn't had time to paint the second bedroom, but he'd gone to a furniture store in the shopping mall and picked up a bed and a dresser and a desk and chair for the kid. He wasn't much shakes at decorating, but he'd hung a couple of seascapes bought from an artist who hung out at the marina, and Peggy had contributed a striped cotton bedspread and matching curtains. The room didn't actually look as bad as he'd feared, and Billy seemed satisfied.

They cooked hamburgers on the hibachi on the deck adjoining the living room, which faced the ocean. They made small talk during dinner, and did the dishes afterward. The kid said he was beat from the trip and all, and he hit the rack pretty early. Later, Don went in to check on him. He seemed asleep; Don moved closer, watching until he saw the almost imperceptible rise and fall of the boy's chest. He slept curled up in a ball, with his legs folded up close to his chest. In the moonlight that streamed in from the courtyard window, he looked very young and very defenseless.

Don stepped out of the room, into the hall that separated the two bedrooms—one end led to the bathroom and the other to the kitchen, dining alcove, and living room. He took a bottle from a shelf above the refrigerator and poured some Cutty into a shot glass, then sat down in the captain's chair on his half of the deck of the duplex. He stared at the dark ocean for a long time, listening to the waves beat against the sand, and then he went back for some more Scotch. The apartment really was small, he realized. If Billy stayed with him after the summer he'd have to find something else.

After the summer—where had that come from? From the kid, sort of. While they were putting the dishes away they talked about Seattle, and Bill said I can't live there anymore, I can't hack it. He didn't explain any more than that; he didn't need to. Don knew how suffocating living with Anne could be. Maybe Bill was like him, Don thought, feeling so hemmed in, so beached, that he had to get out.

"What are you going to do?" Don asked him, finally.

His son shrugged. "I don't know. Stay here for the summer. Go back to my mom's house in the fall, or maybe go away to school somewhere."

He didn't sound too thrilled with any of the options. Maybe if it worked out between them, Don thought . . . maybe if they got along . . . He stopped himself. Hell, it was too soon to think about that now. It was only the kid's first night, and here he was planning the rest of his life. Feeling somehow guilty, he remembered Anne, and dialed her number in Seattle.

"He got here okay," he said when she answered the phone on the first ring.

"I figured," she said dryly. "I called the airline to make sure the plane landed okay."

He felt defensive—had the kid promised to call her when he arrived? Was he supposed to have reminded him? "He's a nice kid," he said, to cover the awkwardness. "Kind of quiet, but that's fine. I think it'll be okay, after we get used to each other. I've been alone a long time."

"So has he," she said, and he could hear the quiver in her voice. Don't, lady, he prayed silently—don't turn on the waterworks, it's been one hell of a long, hard day.

"Don?"

"What?"

"Thank you for doing this. I wouldn't have called you, asked you for help, if there had been any other choice."

"What do you mean? He's my son, too, isn't he?"

"Yes, he's your son. But he's mine too, and I love him. I worry about him."

"I know you do, but you don't have to. I'll do the worrying for a while. He's my responsibility now."

"It sounds like you really mean that."

"I do. I know you may not believe me, but I do."

"Don, promise me you'll keep me informed about what's happening down there."

"Nothing's going to happen. If he breaks a leg I'll tell you. If there's any shit, I don't need to pass it along to you. You've done your time, Anne. Let me worry about it now."

Finally they finished their conversation, and he turned off the lights. He checked on the kid one more time before he turned in. Tomorrow was going to be a long, tough day, too, and if he didn't hit the rack now, neither of them would get through it.

15 Every day of the week following Billy's departure Anne wanted to call him; every day she resisted she counted as a victory, like a woman passing up desserts when she is dieting.

But after that first week, entire days went by when she hardly thought about Bill. She had expected to feel so lonely without him, so self-punishing for having sent him away and concerned for his welfare that she would be overwhelmed with guilt. Instead, what she felt was an overpowering sense of relief, which she confessed to no one. Instead, she spent the time she had devoted to assuring Billy's comfort and happiness to making her own.

She cleaned her house thoroughly, and closed the door of his room. She became used to returning home after a day at the office or a weekend in the country and finding things exactly as she had left them. She ate and slept when she pleased, played the music she liked, and had a party. In many ways, she thought, she was reacting the same way she had after her divorce, pampering and indulging herself as she had then. Except that then she had Bill, and his needs came first.

Now hers did, and those of her career and her friends. "I really think they're going to offer you the chief attorney's job," Marty said one day after beating her at tennis, which she had taken up again.

"I think so, too. I talked to Phil about it a few months ago, and when I realized what a commitment it was, I waffled. With Billy, and all the trouble with him, I couldn't see it as a possibility. Now I have the energy to devote to it, and I'd really like a crack at it—I think I'd make a good chief attorney, don't you?"

"Always did. But what if Bill comes back after the summer?"

"I told Phil I'd let him know in August. We'll see what happens then," she said.

The first calls were awkward; she found it hard to think of things to say.

"Billy? This is Mom. How's it going?" she asked the first time she talked to him, a week after his departure.

"Fine."

His voice sounded deeper, she thought. "What have you been doing?"

"Going to school."

"How are your classes?" Oops, that's a touchy one, be careful, she warned herself.

"Really easy."

She could not resist. "Are you doing your homework? Turning it in?"

"Yeah."

"What's it like down there? What do you do after school? Are you helping your dad at the marina?" If she asked him several questions at one time, she might get more than monosyllables; she might even learn something, decipher a clue about his new life, which she could not even imagine; she had never been to that place, could not picture it or her son in it.

"It's hot. The sun shines every day. Not like Seattle. I got a surfboard—it's used, a little dinged up, but it's okay. I traded Dylan my Walkman and tapes for it."

"Who's Dylan?" Trading . . . sometimes that was a code word for stealing. Well, she wasn't going to worry about it. Let his father teach him all the things she hadn't been able to—Honesty, Integrity, Honor, all the capital-letter virtues, which is how she thought of them.

"A kid at school."

"Does he live at the marina?"

"Nobody lives at the marina, it's not a yacht club. Except for this one kid, but he's younger than me. He lives on a sailboat with his mother."

She wondered if that was Don's girlfriend, but she wasn't going to ask about that.

Later she did, though. She hadn't been able to sleep one night, worrying about Billy, so she called Don, at home, after she thought Bill would be asleep.

"The kid's doing fine," Don said. "He's a little lazy, but he's coming around. Once school gets out next week, I'm putting him to work in the yard."

"Every day? Give him a break, Don, it's his only vacation since he's not going to camp."

"Vacation from what? He wants money in his jeans, he works for it."

"Aren't you giving him an allowance?"

"Nope. I'm giving him a paycheck, when he earns it."

"How is he doing in school? Is he passing all his classes?"

"Far as I know. I told him I couldn't be bothered going to jaw with his teachers about his not pulling his weight, and that if I had to, I was likely to get cranky. And that I didn't think he'd like to see me cranky, at least not till he could run faster than I can."

She laughed. "It sounds like you've got fatherhood down."

"We're making out." He sounded pleased. "He's turning into a pretty good yard rat. Good with his hands when he's interested. He's rebuilding an old dinghy that washed up after the storm last month."

"He was always building things around here," she said. "Tree houses, stuff like that." He had wanted a jigsaw for the past year but she wouldn't buy it for him—she was afraid of the jagged edges and the power. "What does he do when you're not around?"

"Most of the time I'm around."

"That's a switch." She didn't mean it sarcastically, and she hoped he knew that. She wasn't picking at old wounds. As long as Don was taking care of Billy he could sleep with anyone he wanted to as far as she was concerned.

"Yeah, well we're none of us as young and horny as we used to be, right?" Don said. "To tell you the truth, I haven't seen a woman since Bill got here. Except for Peggy. And Bill's taken quite a shine to her and Travis."

"Who are they?" As long as Don brought it up, she wouldn't resist asking.

"A gal who lives at the marina. Travis is her kid, he's around eight, tags after Bill all the time—thinks he's the cat's meow. Sometimes Bill baby-sits him, when Peggy's going out. She's a good woman, but there's nothing going on between us."

"You don't have to tell me if there is," she said softly.

"I know that," he replied.

Sometimes when she talked to Don it was like talking to a stranger. At other times she remembered details about him she thought she had forgotten, like how straitlaced he could be about some things.

"Dad threw some guy out of here a few days ago for snorting coke in the yard," Bill informed her in another conversation. "He was practically signing the papers on this boat Dad's been trying to unload for a while, and then he pulled out his spoon and stuff and Dad told him to take his business somewhere else."

She wanted to know if Bill was still involved with drugs, but she didn't ask. Maybe she didn't really want to know, she considered later, and probably there was no way to find out. Bill wouldn't tell her, and she was certain Don wouldn't—that was his problem now, and she thought that if it came up, Don would handle it his way and never tell her about it unless he had to.

Bill phoned her the day school let out for the summer. "I got an A, two B's, and a C," he reported, even though she hadn't asked. "I think I might go to school here in the fall. There's a neat high school I'd be going to."

She was pleased for Bill, but she resented the fact that it sounded so easy for Don. Was it as simple as enforcing regular discipline, never bending the rules, not putting Bill's happiness, or un-, ahead of his responsibilities? Maybe she should have scared him into behaving decently; maybe she should have busted his tail, as Don put it, a long time ago. Well, it was too late to change now. She had believed a certain amount of permissiveness encouraged a child to take responsibility for himself—with Billy, the opposite had been true. "How come it seems so easy for you?" she asked Don. "Is it just in the male chromosomes?"

"Hell, Anne, I know because I've been through it. I've been a teenage boy, you haven't. That's all. I had a father who was so strict I didn't have any choice except to rebel totally—there was no middle ground. And Bill had . . . you didn't give him any limits at all to rebel against, let off a little wind. Don't get all huffy now, I'm not criticizing, I'm just telling it like it is. Besides, he doesn't know what my limits are yet—and he's still not sure enough of himself to try and find out."

She didn't argue. It was like a Hollywood cliché, she thought; boy loves father, boy loses father, boy finds father, and they all live happily ever after. And so might she, she realized, as the summer went on, and the new possibilities of a daily life without Bill surprised her; as she woke most mornings with a sense that something wonderful could happen to her that day, and as, on some days, something did.

16 "Hey, man, whatcha doin'?"

"Just looking, that's all." Billy was fingering the new boards at the surf shop in town. There was nothing wrong with his own board—it was old and kind of beat up, but it was fine. Had been, while he was learning how to use it. He had become a very proficient surfer in a couple of months. He found that height and even weight didn't matter that much on a board; balance was more important, and the ability to really feel the waves under his feet, the way he could feel the snow under his skis and skim over moguls that tripped other skiers.

"You gonna get a new board?" Danny Sanchez wasn't really a friend; Bill had met him at school, seen him around a few times, and once he'd come by the marina in a little speedboat that was practically sinking, the keel was in such bad shape. It was his older brother's, he said, the one who had gone to the joint for stabbing some guy in a fight.

"Nah," Bill replied, "I can't afford it."

"I might be able to put my hands on a board," Danny said. "Not one of these new jobbies, but better 'n your junker."

"So?" Billy said. He didn't really like Sanchez all

that much, but he hadn't met a lot of kids, coming to school as late in the year as he had, and sometimes it got lonesome around the yard. Travis was always ready to hang out with him, but he was only a little kid, and Dylan, his only real buddy, was camping in the Grand Canyon with his folks for two weeks.

"So we might be able to come to some kind of arrangement."

"Like what kind?"

"Say, I trade you my board for yours, with a little sweetener thrown in."

"What kind of sweetener? And where did you get a decent board from, anyway? If it's anything like your boat, I'll stick with what I got."

"It's my brother's—you know, the one up at Chino. He ain't gonna be usin' it for a long time, seven years at least. By the time they let him outa there, he ain't gonna be interested in no surfboards. It's just sittin' there, goin' to waste. He said I could have it if I wanted, do whatever I like with it. So I'm offerin' to give it to you, bein' as how you're such an asshole buddy of mine."

"Since when?"

"Since now."

"I told you, I don't have any bread. Maybe a couple bucks, but not enough for a new board."

"Yeah, but you got a couple gallons of bottom paint, up there at the yard where you live. That your old man's yard?"

"Yeah. What do you need bottom paint for?"

"I got my boat hauled up, out in my backyard, I'm fixin' it up. Got the rot out, just cut it away, and got a guy knows how to fix it helping me. I got to paint the keel, though, with some red lead, keep it from gettin' all fouled again soon's I get it back in the water."

"So go buy some. Ricco'll sell you what you need. He's the yard manager for my dad, handles that shit."

"Yeah, at sixty, seventy skins a gallon. I ain't got that kind of dough. All I got's a surfboard that's too fast for an average type surfer like me, who'd be just as good off with a beat-up board like yours."

"You want me to give you two gallons of bottom paint for your board, is that it?"

"And your old board, too. It's a trade."

"Lemme think about it."

"Yeah. But don't take too long, though—I might just bring my board down here and let 'em sell it on consignment. Might get one gallon of bottom paint out of it."

"You need two, though."

"Yeah. Life's a bitch, ain't it?"

"Where'd you get the new board?" Don asked.

"Swapped it with this guy I know. Danny Sanchez. From my school."

"He gave you that for your old one?"

Bill nodded.

"Helluva deal," his father said. "How much extra did you have to give him?"

"I didn't. We just swapped. See, he had this board, it used to be his brother's, but he left town and gave it to him. And he's not a very good surfer—fact is, he can hardly stand up on it. He wanted an old board he could practice on."

"And when he gets better, he'll get another board, huh?"

"I guess."

"Must be pretty well fixed, your pal."

"Yeah, I think his old man's loaded."

"Nice."

"Yeah. Well, I finished the brightwork on the

Windsong, like you told me, and Ricco said there wasn't anything else needed doing. I think I'll go to the beach for a while."

"Suit yourself."

Bill carried his new board to the beach. He surfed until dark, enjoying the way it handled, skimming the waves like they were glass. He caught a big one and rode it all the way in, then slung the board over his shoulder and headed home. He wanted a hot shower and something to eat; his father had talked about going to a movie later on, a new Clint Eastwood they both wanted to see.

"How's the new board?" his father asked when he came in.

"Neat," Bill said. He sniffed the air in the kitchen expectantly. "Wasn't it your turn to cook tonight?"

"I already ate."

"I guess I'll fix myself a sandwich then."

"Pretty hungry, huh?"

"Yeah."

"Too bad you're not going to eat till you've scraped the keel of that thirty-foot Blanchard we got in last week. Enough barnacles on that sucker to keep you going for a couple of days."

"What are you talking about?"

"I'm talking about two cans of bottom paint you took from the shop. You owe me, kid."

Suddenly Bill wasn't hungry anymore; in fact, his stomach rebelled at the very thought of food. "Who says I took it?"

"I do. Ricco does. Well, that's not true, exactly. He says we're two gallons short, that's about a hundred, hundred and twenty bucks' worth of inventory missing. The yard crew doesn't know anything about it, Ricco doesn't have a clue, and you turn up with a new board you got from some guy whose old man is loaded. Seems to me that's a whole bunch of coincidences."

"So?" He's bluffing, Bill thought, he doesn't know I took the paint.

"So I cruise down to the surf shop, look around for a guy named Danny Sanchez. Yeah, says the fellow that owns it, I know Danny. He's trying to unload his brother's surfboard. Seems the brother got himself sent to prison and left Danny his board and his boat. That crappy little stinkpot I remember seeing around here a few weeks ago. That needed its bottom hauled and scraped, and a couple of gallons of red lead, too. Ricco says the kid asked him about buying some but said he didn't have the money."

Billy didn't say anything. If he didn't admit it, there was nothing the old man could do. There'd been nothing his mother could do when she didn't have any proof of his thefts, either. Even when she did, he thought idly.

"You got anything you want to tell me before you get your ass down to the yard and start scraping?"

"No."

"Suppose you just mosey on down there, then. The Blanchard's out in the yard, on the cradle. You put on the yard lights, you'll be able to see what you're doing. Except when the crap falls in your eyes, then it's kind of hard. But at least it's a cool night. Scraping paint is a real bitch in the sun."

"I just have to scrape tonight?"

"I didn't say that. I said you have to scrape till it's done."

"You mean if I don't finish it tonight, I got to do it tomorrow?"

"That's what I mean. Weatherman says it's likely to hit a hundred tomorrow. By ten in the morning."

"What about supper?"

"We'll talk about it at breakfast. I'm leaving now—I want to catch the nine o'clock show. See you tomorrow."

The yard lights brought out the mosquitoes, and Bill was bitten so many times he was one big itch. Except where he was sore, from hanging upside down under the Blanchard's keel, scraping the paint inch by inch, or raw, from where the paint-dissolving chemical dripped on his skin. He was hungry, too—the worst had happened, his father had spoken, and the nausea he'd felt when he knew he was found out had gone, leaving an empty, rumbling stomach. He thought about sneaking home to grab something from the kitchen, then thought what a candyass he'd feel like if his father caught him, not to mention whatever else might happen. He eyed the *Pandora* longingly; Don had taken Peggy and Travis to the movies and they wouldn't be back till late. He could probably score a couple of slices of bread from *Pandora*'s galley, maybe a hunk of cheese or something, without anyone finding out. Maybe later, when I get really hungry, he told himself; it's a fact that nobody ever starved to death overnight. I can be as tough as that old bastard thinks he is, he thought.

At midnight, when his father dropped the McCarthys off at the marina, he wasn't so sure. "Hard to do this job right without daylight," Don commented. "When the sun comes up you see all the places you missed."

Rub it in, asshole, Bill thought, by the time it does I'm going to be finished. His father left, and he went back to the job with renewed energy, fueled by his anger—whether at Don, or at his own stupidity, he wasn't quite sure, but it was anger, pure and red hot, and the madder he got, the faster he scraped.

Around two o'clock in the morning he heard footsteps, and he crawled out from under the cradle to see who it was.

"I brung you something to eat, Bill," said Travis, holding out a peanut butter and jelly sandwich and an apple. "I heard your dad say you weren't getting a mealticket off of him until you paid for it. He told my mom that when we were at the movies. I waited until she went to sleep, it was really hard." He rubbed his eyes sleepily, and Billy wanted to laugh but didn't.

"Thanks a whole bunch, Trav," he said, wolfing down the food. "If I wasn't so hungry I coulda had this finished by morning."

"We're supposed to go fishing tomorrow. You said you'd take me," said Travis.

"Yeah, and I'm going to, I promise. Now you get outa here and get back in your bunk before your ma wakes up, okay?"

"Okay," said the little boy happily. "See you tomorrow, Bill."

"Yeah, see you tomorrow."

He whistled when he went back to scraping, and when his eyes wanted to close and the scraper wanted to drop out of his hands from exhaustion, he thought about what a neat kid old Trav was, and he kept working. When Don came into the yard early the next morning, soon after the sun was up, Bill was just finishing the places he'd missed in the darkness.

"Got it all done, I see," the old man said.

"Near about."

"Going to be a corker today, looks like. Guess you'll be heading home to hit the rack."

"I promised Trav I'd take him fishing."

"You made a promise, you got to keep it."

"Yeah, that's what they say."

"Must be pretty hungry by now."

"Nah, not really. Besides, Peggy's fixing us a lunch."

"You catch anything, we'll have it for supper."

"Yeah. See you."

"See you."

He put the chemicals and the scraper in their place in the supply room and went to pick up Travis, whistling. It was going to be a good day for fishing, he decided.

17 Anne was excited and more than a little nervous; Billy was coming home for a visit. Don had some business north of Seattle, at a yard in Bellingham; he and Bill would fly up together, and he'd leave the boy with her for a few days while he took care of it, he said, if that was convenient for her.

She would have made it convenient in any case; she had not seen her son for nearly three months, the longest they'd ever been separated. When she watched him get out of Don's rented car, from the second-floor landing of her house, she saw that he had grown taller and heavier. He was wearing an unfamiliar blazer, neatly pressed khakis, and a tie was loosely knotted around the collar of his oxford cloth shirt. She smiled; he looked like a copy of Don, right down to the short, neatly trimmed hair. Which was more than her ex-husband had, she thought, looking down from her higher vantage point on the round balding spot on top of his head.

She ran downstairs and threw open the front door.

"Billy! I can't believe it, you've gotten so big . . . and so handsome! I'm so glad to see you!" She hugged him tight, then held him away from her. He was tanned and healthy-looking, smiling and comfortable. He had the faint beginnings of a mustache, and it looked as though he had started to shave.

"Yeah, that's me, a regular gorgeous hunk," he grinned. "You look pretty good yourself."

"Not so bad for a forty-one-year-old broad," said Don, who was standing behind Bill.

"Not for seven more months and you know it," she said. "Come in, come in. I made dinner, it'll be ready in a few minutes."

"I'm not hungry, Ma, we ate on the plane. I gotta call Chris." He disappeared up the stairs, and she turned to her ex-husband.

"Hi," she said, feeling oddly shy. It was the first time in over three years that she had seen him; it was the first time since the divorce that she had wanted to.

"You got a kiss for an old buddy?" he asked, holding his arms out. She went into them and breathed in his remembered smell, felt his body as if hers had never forgotten it. It was as if the lives they had lived separately for so long had not happened, like welcoming him home after a long cruise. She was genuinely glad that he had come. While she was putting dinner on the table and he stood in the dining room with a drink in his hands she studied him covertly. He looked old, a lot older, she thought, and smaller than he had seemed to her so long ago. But time distorted memory; probably she looked different to him, too.

Billy ate with them; he wanted to go right down to Chris's house, as Anne thought he would, but Don said no, not yet.

"Your mother went to the trouble of fixing you dinner, you eat it," he insisted.

"But I'm not hungry, I told her," Bill protested.

"It's okay, he doesn't have to if he doesn't want to," Anne began, but Don was firm.

"When you're a guest in someone's home, you accommodate them," he said.

"I'm not a guest, for Christ sake, I live here!" Bill replied.

"Not at the moment," Don said.

"Yes, sir," Bill muttered, and held Anne's chair out to seat her at the table before taking his own. Bill managed to put away two helpings of everything, and talked freely, easily of his life in California, his friend Dylan, the boat he had rebuilt, surfing, and his special taco recipe.

"You're cooking these days?" Anne asked.

"Every other night," Bill said. "At first we switched around every week, but Dad only knows how to burn a couple of things so I try to space the charcoal out between real food."

"Like tacos?"

"Yeah, and spaghetti and meat loaf and barbecued chicken and stuff. Anyone who can read can cook. Burning food just right, so you can't taste enough of it to know what it is, though, that's a talent, they say it skips every other generation. I guess I missed it."

"Right, along with the one for good looks and common sense, too," said Don. They bantered good-naturedly, and she marveled at how relaxed and open Bill was. For all the flip talk, there was a tone of respect in his voice when he addressed his father, even without the yes, sirs.

After dinner, Bill cleared the table without being asked. "Can I go to Chris's now?" he said, addressing Don.

"If it's all right with your mother."

"It's fine," Anne said. "Don't stay too late, though."

"I won't." He bent over to kiss her on the cheek, unbidden, and Anne watched him leave. She made coffee and took it into the living room. She sat in the wing chair near the fireplace where Don stood, leaning against the mantel in a familiar way.

"Billy looks wonderful," she said. "He's so . . . open, I guess is the word. He laughed tonight when you were telling that story about how I used to sterilize the kitchen sink with hot water from the stove before I bathed him. I haven't heard him laugh like that for a long time. And his manners . . . when he said yes, ma'am, when I asked him a question, I was floored. His clothes . . . you always were neat, paid attention to things, but I could never get him to wear anything but those filthy old jeans."

"Tell a kid he can't go out to dinner with you unless he puts on a clean shirt and a jacket, and there's nothing to eat at home and he's hungry enough, he'll dress right," said Don. "He's got decent manners, you taught him those. You just have to lean on him sometimes to make sure he remembers them."

"He seems to have made some friends there."

"There was one kid I didn't particularly appreciate, but he doesn't come around much these days; I let Bill know how I felt about it. This kid Dylan's okay."

"I never tried to censor his friends. He didn't have so many I thought I should. And besides, kids always glom onto the friends their parents don't like. Sometimes I think that's part of the reason I married you—because my folks were so against it."

"That was different, we were older. Maybe not wiser, but older. Besides, until you sprung me on them, you'd never wanted anything that wasn't good for you. This kid wasn't good for Bill."

"And you were good for me?"

He sighed. "I tried, Anne. I just wasn't good enough."

She felt contrite; she hadn't meant to wound him. "I don't hate you anymore," she said. "My mother asks me how I can just forget everything that happened between us. The times Billy and I needed you and you weren't there."

"What do you tell her?"

"I tell her I don't care about that anymore. What matters is that when he really needed you, you came through."

"I don't know about that, but I'm glad you don't hate me anymore."

"I never did, actually. It might have been easier if I could have." She had not stopped loving him for a long time after the divorce; it was like trying to break a habit, she had loved him so long. Until she was too exhausted to continue. Then she had put him out of her mind, out of her life, banished him from her daily awareness until enough time passed for her to think of him, when she did, as someone she had known long ago. Just like she had with Billy, she thought.

"Anne, that was a long time ago. That's over. We don't need to rake that over the coals again."

He had never been easy talking about feelings, his or hers. In that way, too, Billy was like him; seeing the two together, father and son, she marveled at their similarities. And felt alien, different from them, in a way she never had; not, at least, with Billy. She was used to thinking of him as her flesh, her blood; with a startling immediacy, she remembered that he was Don's, too.

She found her former husband less changed by the intervening years than she felt she was. It was hard for her to remember the woman who had thought him larger than life—larger, at least, than her own. Who had lived only to please him, to hold him. Who would that woman be today if she had stayed married to him? Not who she was now, she thought. If they had never divorced, she would not have needed to invent a new person to cope with a life that didn't work for the old one.

"You're right," she said brightly. "How do you really like it, Don? How is it, living with your son?"

"Well, I'll tell you—say, you have a touch of brandy for this coffee, lady?—thanks. It's like having myself around, me at his age I mean. Christ, he's stubborn sometimes, just like I was. Gets in a snit and gets all quiet. Won't give you the satisfaction of knowing you got to him."

She nodded—she knew what Don meant. She'd wondered, before, at how much like Don Billy was, even though they had not lived together since he was six. It came out in habits that surprised her—the way Billy tugged on his earlobe when he was thinking, as Don was doing now—and in other acts that were painfully familiar, like his ability to reach her with his silences, to wound her with them as deeply as his father had.

"It's not always fun stepping on him when he gets out of line," Don continued. "But you have to do it. I try . . . I don't want the kid making the same dumb mistakes I did, always making things harder than they have to be. I tell him listen, kid, there's an easier way, and the pay is better. It's too soon to tell if he's getting the message." Don sat down on the couch facing her and lit a cigarette. "He wants to stay down there. He'll be going to high school in the fall. That's where he has to turn it around, start shaping up. Without an education—without seeing the thing through—he'll end up like me."

It's not that Don looks old, Anne thought. It's that he looks defeated. "What do you mean?" she asked.

"Oh, hell, Anne, I'm forty-six years old. Owner of a practically worthless lease on a broken-down boat yard in a little beach town. Some months I barely make the rent. I live in a crummy rented apartment. I drive a nine-year-old car. I drink too much, I'm a boat bum . . . I want more than that for him."

"It didn't turn out the way it was supposed to, did it?" She felt sad for him, after all these years; it was hard to imagine him the way he described himself, living the way he said he did.

He smiled gently. "No, I guess not. It didn't for you either, did it?"

"No. It's very different. But it's okay." Better than it was—now.

"Anne, I want him to stay. I . . . we need each other, me and Bill."

"I don't want to lose him."

"You won't. He'll be up here on school vacations, during the summers, whenever. You won't lose touch. I'll see that he writes and calls. I'll take good care of him."

"You have. You will." She felt released, as though an enormous weight had been lifted from her shoulders. "You know, that time before he went to you— that bad time—I thought I was the only one who could help him. Save him. But I couldn't. And I know . . . if I don't want to lose him, I have to let him go. So I'm grateful that there's somewhere for him to go to, with someone who loves him as much as I do." She brushed a tear from her cheek; he knelt next to her chair, and took her hand in his.

"Don't cry," he said. "Please don't cry."

"I'm sorry."

"And don't say you're sorry, either. You did a good job with him. Underneath all that Mickey Mouse stuff, he's a fine, decent kid. You made him that way."

She didn't know why his words had the power to comfort her, only that they did. When he left she said, "I think when two people have a child together, they never really get divorced. Do they?"

"Not that part of them," he replied. "I'll see you in a week. Take care."

"Of him, or me?"

"Both," he said. "Of both of you."

18 When Don and Bill got back to California, the apartment looked smaller and shabbier to both of them. The kid had never complained, but Don wanted something better. Now that he was in high school, he'd want to bring his buddies around, have some room to get away from the old man, some privacy. And Don could use it too, he thought—the one habit of Bill's he hadn't made any headway with was getting him to turn that damn music down. If you could call it that—he'd take Sinatra or the Mantovani Strings, or even the Beatles, any time, especially when the choice was that or Iron Maiden.

It took him until October to find a place he could afford. It was a small house, midway between the marina and the high school, a block in from the beach but close enough to hear the ocean if you left the windows open. There was some furniture in it, and they added more. Don and Bill painted the interior a fresh, clean white and refinished the floors. There was a small yard, and an avocado tree outside the front door. A few days after they moved in, Bill suggested asking Peggy and Travis for dinner.

Don didn't know how he would have managed the

past few months without Peggy—when he wasn't sure if he was doing the right thing with the kid or not, he checked with her. She gave him sensible suggestions. Mostly she made him feel like he was doing an okay job. It was hard to tell from the kid—he didn't talk much. But he seemed content. After the week in Seattle, Anne said he was a changed boy. He couldn't see it, himself. But then, he hadn't seen him any other way, except for that business with the Sanchez kid. If Bill was doing something he shouldn't, Don didn't know about it. And if he was, he figured, he'd hear about it soon enough.

They passed much of their time in a companionable silence, which was okay with Don. At first, Bill had treated him with wariness—not fear, exactly, but his guard was up. He was a lot more relaxed these days. He didn't lip off much, but sometimes he zinged Don with an ironic little crack he hardly felt going in. Then Don would catch that kind of half-grin on the kid's face and know he had to give it to him, he'd gotten the old man again. Of course, he still had to be dragged out of the rack in the morning, reminded about chores, taunted to the barbershop. He spent a fair amount of time at the marina, when he wasn't hanging out with his buddies from his new school, who seemed like a decent bunch of kids—no troublemakers that Don could tell, when he could usually spot them a mile off. And the kid had found himself a girlfriend, too, a cute little redhead who hung on his every word. Don figured he'd better have a talk with Bill about that soon—he didn't want him knocking her up.

His life with Bill had settled into a routine. He got him off to school every day, insisted that he check in at the marina after classes. The kid hadn't wanted to go out for sports, and that was okay with Don, no sense getting the crap beat out of you at football. Between surfing and sailing, he was getting plenty of exercise. And he ate—God, how he ate. He'd put on fifteen pounds since the summer, most of it muscle.

He was in better shape than his old man, Don thought. Between the groceries, the rent on the new place, and buying the minimum the kid needed to dress decently, he was strapped. The marina's cash position was lousy, and Don was hurting for money. He thought for a time that he had a backer lined up, someone to finance the expansion planned for the yard, but the money man backed out. That was the story of his life, Don mused—a day late and a dollar short. Oh well, he had more than he'd had six months ago. He had a reason to get up in the morning, and one to come home at night. He had his son.

"You got the table set yet?"

"I'm working on it, don't blow your cool," Bill said. "It'll all be copacetic when they get here. Ma says the most important thing about having a party is being relaxed yourself."

"She does, does she?" He inspected his son's handiwork and pronounced it acceptable. Bill had stuck some flowers in an old wine decanter and set it in the middle of the table. From somewhere he had unearthed four matching plates and sets of silverware. "First guests in our new place . . . it looks pretty spiffy."

There was a knock on the door, and Peggy came in with an enormous hanging plant of some kind, a bottle of champagne, and two tissue-wrapped packages. "Is this Manning and Son?" she asked gaily. She opened the champagne and Don and Bill unwrapped their gifts, two small nameboards that said "Captain" and "First Mate." Bill got a screwdriver and had them up on their bedroom doors before the coals in the hibachi were ready for the steaks.

After dinner the boys went outside. "Come on, Trav, I'll show you where there's a basketball hoop, out behind the house," Bill told the younger boy. Don and Peggy took the brandy and a couple of glasses to the beach, where they leaned against a washed-up log and waited for the sun to set.

"What happened with the people from First Financial?" Peggy asked.

"No dice," said Don. "Hell, it's a good investment. They can't lose. I used to be a pretty good salesman, but maybe I've lost my touch."

"It probably has more to do with the state of the economy than the project. From a financial perspective it's very solid—the figures don't lie."

"Yes, but nobody wants the truth. They want to have bought Xerox at twenty, like this one man said. Failing that, they want an immediate return, at least what they could get in a money market. And no risk at all, of course. Well, there's a downside risk in this, all right—and an outside chance that even if I got what I needed to do it right, it might not pan out."

"A very small risk," said Peggy. "How would you like me for a partner?"

"I'd like it fine, if I could afford you." He rumpled her hair.

Peggy was as much a part of the new contentment he felt as Billy was. He'd never had this equal kind of friendship with a woman before. It was not as casual as it had been in the beginning. Now there was a different kind of intimacy between them. He could tell her things about himself and she didn't judge him. And he could hear about her vulnerabilities and weaknesses without needing to protect himself, or her, from them. He still had not touched her, beyond an occasional hug or a peck on her cheek. But sometimes he watched her moving around *Pandora*, and desire rose in him unbidden. He didn't act on it; he would go to greater lengths to avoid messing up their relationship. A man could always get laid, but a friend like Peggy was hard to find.

"You can't afford me," she replied matter-of-factly. "But I can. When Nat and I split, I received a substantial settlement. He made a great deal of money when he was playing with the pros and I handled all our investments. I think the marina is a good one."

"I can't take your money."

"I'm not asking you to take it all. I can't put in everything you need, either. Half, maybe, and I'll take stock in exchange for it. You run the yard and ratchet Ricco and the yardbirds, and I'll do the office and the books and manage the business end of it. I'm good at that. I've already cut the overhead by eighteen percent over last year, and prices are higher than they were then."

She talked for a time about margins of profit and investment credits and tax shelters and he listened. She was a smart woman, smarter than he was in many ways, but something didn't sit right with him.

"If you're worried about strings, don't be," she said. "This is a business deal."

In fact, that was what he had been thinking—worrying—about. But not quite the way she thought. He wanted strings . . . as a matter of fact, he wanted the whole ball of yarn. He had never felt that way before, except in the beginning, with Anne. He told her that, and she smiled.

"Billy and me, and Peggy makes three, huh?" she said. "Four, actually, counting Travis."

"I counted him," he said laconically. "It's got nothing to do with the marina, you know."

"I didn't think for a minute it did," she replied. "I care for you a lot, Don. But I'm not ready for anything like that yet. I don't know if I ever will be again."

He wasn't really sad when Peggy turned him down. Maybe he was too set in his ways, too old to try again. He'd dropped anchor once, after all, and itched to cast the lines off most of that time. He was actually somewhat relieved when Peggy made the decision for him, for them. Now he could consider her other offer without feeling pressured.

They signed the partnership papers a couple of weeks later, and dropped Bill and Travis off at a movie while they went to dinner together at the Mission, an elegant Portuguese restaurant on a high hill outside of town. The lights of fishing boats in the harbor twinkled below them, and a sad-faced young man sang fados while they sipped their cocktails.

"To our new venture," Peggy said, clinking her glass against his. She looked especially good that night, with her golden tan set off by a clinging white knit dress, her legs made even longer by the high, fragile heels of her sandals.

"Should we call it Manning, McCarthy, and Sons?" Don asked.

"You have his future all laid out for him, don't you?"

"Not really. Oh sure, it would be nice. A man wants to leave something to his kids, make a place for them, you know. But you can't force them into it. They have to want it for themselves."

"Bill wants whatever you want. He's trying to be just like you. He even walks the way you do, with that kind of rolling gait."

"He's a pretty good kid, isn't he?"

"Yes. At first I didn't know what to make of him.

He was so quiet and serious, and sort of detached, until he loosened up. Travis imitates him the way Bill imitates you—a clear case of hero worship, I'd say. Bill is always so nice to Travis, and so are you. I really appreciate that."

"We Manning men are always glad to oblige, ma'am."

She giggled. "I'll just bet you are. In fact, I intend to discover for myself just how obliging you are, so to speak, later tonight. After we've bedded the boys down in your handsome new digs and I lure you over to the *Pandora* for a little adult entertainment."

"Are you making a pass at me, lady?" Peggy beamed at him, and he grinned. "And here I thought we were just good friends and partners."

"I sure am, mister, and we sure are. I think you ought to seal a partnership with something more intimate than a handshake. Does that shock you?"

"No, it just makes me want to drag the kids out of that movie, that's all. Let's go."

In mid-November, on his birthday, they surprised him with a party. Peggy and Bill had invited the guests. Ricco, his yard manager, came with his wife; in a coat and tie, instead of the coveralls Don was used to seeing him in, Ricco looked nervous and uncomfortable. His wife was a pretty, fat woman who took an instant shine to Peggy.

Karl, the naval architect who signed off on Don's boat surveys, came with his fiancée, a woman Don had once dated and introduced to his longtime pal. "Couldn't have happened to a nicer guy, except me," he told Karl.

"You had your chance and you blew it," Karl said jovially. "The better man won, that's all. Haven't seen much of you lately—guess you're busy with Bill and all."

"Not all the time," Don said. "We'll go out one night soon and hoist a few, before Katy puts you out of commission for hard drinking."

"That'll be the day, I can drink you under the table anytime."

"You're on—I'll collect once I get over the hangover I'm sure as hell gonna have tomorrow," said Don.

Even Barbaralee was there, with a pilot who hardly left her side. "How did she get here?" he asked Bill.

"She called one night, said she was a very close friend of yours, only in town for a few days, so I invited her."

"I'm still waiting to find Mr. First Class," Barbaralee told Don. "Since my favorite layover took the veil of fatherhood, that is. Or is it something else you've taken?" She looked at Peggy with a meaningful stare, but there was no anger in her voice. "He's a nice kid, Don, and she's a nice woman, too."

"She is that. And you're no mean slouch yourself," he said, and meant it. He was glad she had come, glad there were no hard feelings between them.

The party was terrific, and he thanked Peggy several times during the evening. At one point she said, "It was all Bill's idea, Don, I just helped him with the details."

"Yeah?"

"Yes. Don't be angry with him. He meant well."

"I'm not angry, don't be silly. I'm just surprised."

"That's why they call it a surprise party, dummy."

"You don't say?" He was kidding, and she knew it; he was having a wonderful time. Bill had baked Don's birthday cake himself, and Don was proud of him. He was, he realized, happier than he had ever thought he could be again. God must be in His heaven, he thought—somebody sure as hell was.

"Nice party you throw, sport," he said as Bill passed around the chips and dip.

"Glad you liked it, old man," replied his son.

"Old, huh? Well, show a little respect for your elders and get me another beer, will you?"

"Sure thing, Cap'n Manning, sir."

"And by the way, mate—"

"Yeah?"

"You can tell that little redhead who's been waiting outside for you to come in and have some birthday cake, and that all liberty parties are due back aboard at midnight."

"Yes, sir!"

"Don?"

"Mmm hmm?"

Peggy was curled up in his arms, tracing her fingertips over his body. "What's this funny bump here?"

"I don't know. It's been there for a while. I thought it was the clap, but it's not, don't worry . . . hey, don't press, that hurts."

"You should have it looked at."

"You're looking at it."

"I mean by a doctor."

"One of these days. Hey lady, watch your hand there. This is an old man you're playing around with."

"Not that old," she said, and did something tricky with a swivel of her hip, and then with her mouth, and whaddya know, maybe he wasn't so old, maybe there's life in the old goat yet, he thought, as he gave himself up to the sweetness of Peggy McCarthy.

19 "Take a deep breath . . . another one . . . hold it now . . . all right, exhale."

The doctor put away his stethoscope. "That bump isn't anything, just a little oil deposit that got clogged up somehow, a small gland. This is going to sting for a minute . . . there, it's all done. It'll drain nicely, I think. Hold this gauze pad over it for a few minutes, I want to check something else."

Don hadn't thought it was anything, but Peggy had nagged him into making an appointment with a doctor. You're just like my ex-wife, he told her. Every time Billy had the sniffles, she took him to the pediatrician. He's not a baby now, he's almost a man, Peggy said with annoyance. Don't you want to stick around and watch him grow up? Or are you afraid of doctors?

Don't be a nag, Peg, come on over here, ah, that's right, like that. I'm not afraid of doctors, just hate sitting around the V.A. clinic waiting to see them, that's all. She was so soft and sweet; mister, this time you lucked out, he thought. A girl and a son, a business—a second chance at something decent, honorable, and satisfying. He'd wasted the first one, and all

those years in between, but not now—now he was
going to suck the good, sweet, life-giving juice out of
every one of them.

"You had this long?"

"What?"

The doctor at the V.A. clinic was poking around
that fatty place down the side of Don's neck—you're
getting jowls, he told himself when he first noticed, a
couple of weeks back, the softening of his jaw line. So
this was middle age, he thought.

"I don't like the looks of that," said the doctor.

Yeah, well he didn't either, but that was life, what
could you do? He'd put on a few pounds over the
years, although lately his clothes were beginning to
bag a bit on him. He couldn't understand why—since
Billy came, he was eating regularly. He wasn't drinking as much, though . . . he figured that evened it out.

"I want to get a biopsy of that lump," the doctor
went on. "It's a simple procedure, we can do it in the
short-stay unit at the hospital. It may not be anything,
but I'd like to be sure. We'll do a biopsy and then you
won't have to worry about it."

He wasn't worried. Or was he? The little bump on
his groin was nothing, the doctor had said. Most likely
the one on his neck wasn't anything to be concerned
about either.

"I can schedule you on Friday," the doctor said.

"I can't Friday, got to see some people, getting
construction bids. Next week maybe."

The doctor shrugged. "It's your life, pal." He was
a young man, not more than thirty, Don guessed, although the white coat made him look younger. "It
doesn't work that way around here. At the V.A. Hospital it will be at least another month before they can

fit you in. I wouldn't wait that long if I were you. That could turn out to be nasty."

"What do you mean, nasty?"

"Anybody in your immediate family have cancer?"

"My old man died of it, why?"

"We don't know, sometimes there are hereditary links."

"You think I have cancer?"

"I think we ought to take a look at that lump. It's probably benign, but we won't know for certain until we get a look at it under a microscope. You smoke?"

"About a pack a day."

"Any pain anywhere? Headaches, dizziness, nausea, night sweats, weakness in the limbs, coughing?"

"I cough a little in the mornings sometimes, everyone does that." Headaches—sure he had those, hangovers usually. Matter of fact, he had a bitch of one right now. He and Karl had put away a fifth of Cutty last night, going over the plans for the marina, making changes, making choices.

The doctor made some notes on a pad of paper. "I want some blood tests, a chest X ray—when's the last time you had one?"

"I don't know, fifteen, sixteen years ago, maybe. When my kid was born I had to have one for the insurance." He'd canceled that, cashed it in once when Anne threatened to take him to court for not paying support. He used the money to buy a plane ticket, flown up there to try to talk her out of it, bought some Christmas presents for the kid. It hadn't been much, a few years of premiums, less than a thousand dollars.

"It's time you had another one. Shall I schedule you for Friday?"

"No, I can't do it then, I told you, I have a very important appointment."

"How about . . . let's see, there's a cancellation down here next Wednesday, at three fifteen."

"Nope. Wednesday I have to see the port commission, get them to approve the final drawings. I've been waiting three months for that meeting. No, I can't do it Wednesday either, sorry about that."

"Like I said, it's your life. See the nurse on your way out, she'll give you an appointment for next month."

"Hey, Dad, where you been? What's under the tarp in the pickup, huh?"

"Slow down, son." He got down heavily from the cab. "Got your chores done?"

"Yeah . . . yes, sir."

"How about your schoolwork?"

"Finished. I aced a math test today."

"You did, huh? You must have been doing your work while I wasn't looking. Seems to me I haven't seen a math book around here for a while."

"I guess I'm just naturally brilliant. It's in the genes. Mom's, probably."

"Probably." The kid was cocky sometimes, and that was okay, as long as he kept it together, which he seemed to be doing. As long as he toed the mark. He'd brought home a warning slip in English, more embarrassed than afraid, it seemed to Don. Guess there goes the redhead for a few weeks, Don told him. I got to go down there and rassle with the teachers, you better kiss her ass good-bye for a long time. And your board, too. It seemed to do the trick; the kid had pulled his grade up, anyway. "Glad to hear you're such a whiz with numbers. Come in handy when we go cruising."

"We going cruising?" The kid was excited, but trying not to show it, trying to act cool.

"Yeah, I think we'll take the monk, go down to Baja, maybe to Cabo. You could crack a beer for your old man and then take a look under that tarp, you want to."

"Already cracked you one." The kid came down off the porch and held out a bottle of Bud with the frost making patches of sparkle on it. Probably sneaked one for himself before I drove in, Don thought. What the hell, a beer once in a while couldn't hurt, long as he didn't overdo it.

"A Windsurfer . . . hey, Dad, that's neat! Where'd you get it?"

"Made a deal with a guy down the beach who sells them." And taken it in the shorts, too, but it was only money. Besides, it looked like he had a sale coming up on the Blanchard, the one the kid had scraped that summer. The young couple who wanted it had been to the marina twice, and brought the woman's father to see it the second time.

"Is it for me?" The kid was crazy about it, he knew, but he was keeping it in his pockets.

"Well, I figure I'd want something a little sturdier between me and the water, personally. You'll build up your quads and pecs with that thing, it's not easy to use at first. Now you're growing so much, need to put a little muscle on you. Say, are those the last pair of jeans I bought you, halfway up your legs already?"

"Yeah. Hey, Dad, thanks. Really . . . thanks."

Don didn't hold much with overpraising a kid for the things he was supposed to do in the first place. Not like Anne did. She made such a big deal of it whenever the kid did anything right you'd think he'd performed a miracle. Like finding a cure for cancer.

He put that thought out of his mind—the doc had said it was probably nothing, hadn't he? "The Windsurfer's an early Christmas present," he told the kid.

"Since you're going to be at your mother's house then."

"Sure . . . hey, Dad? Do you think I could just go up there for part of the time and come back early, and maybe we could go to Cabo then? I have three weeks' vacation."

"Maybe. I'll talk to your mother, see what she thinks."

20 Anne was packing for a trip to Hawaii. How lucky that Bill was going back to Don early, and that David's trial schedule had a hole in it that one week between Christmas and New Year's, and that she could get away, too.

A smile curved around her lips as she folded a filmy nightgown and thought about David. She had met him at a Fourth of July picnic at Carol's, and now they were engaged in a lively courtship, marked by boisterous, highly partisan disagreements about everything that didn't matter at all—such as whether there could be too much garlic in a pesto sauce, a possibility David considered highly unlikely—and a surprising unanimity about everything that did.

"Do you think we should move in together?" David asked one morning, dressing in the same clothes he had worn the previous day. "Two large houses for two single people seems ridiculous."

"Not especially," said Anne. "For one thing, I'm not one single person. Billy might not stay with Don. And for another . . ." her voice trailed off.

"For another, you don't believe in living together without being married," said David. "Right?"

Anne colored. "Embarrassingly enough, in this liberated era, that's right. I don't think it's wrong, exactly. It's just . . . not for me."

"Or me," David said. "If two people love each other enough to put their toothbrushes in the same glass, they ought to get married."

"I'm glad you feel that way, too," said Anne. "But you can still leave an extra shirt here once in a while. Without compromising your position, I mean."

And there they left the subject of marriage, for the time being. Anne wasn't ready to think about it. She didn't love David with the same passionate intensity with which she had loved Don, and she was glad of it. She was afraid of being consumed by that intensity of emotion again. Meanwhile, it was enough that as the weeks and months went by he became increasingly important to her; she found more qualities in him to admire and cherish and, more important, none that she could not accept.

"You knew David Michaelson for three years before you introduced us," she said to Ted Cain. "How come you held out on me for so long?"

Carol answered the question Anne had put to her husband. "Because you weren't available before now," she said.

"I've been available for almost ten years," Anne argued.

"Not really. You couldn't share your responsibility for Billy with any man. You wouldn't let anyone else help, except psychiatrists. Look what you did to Patrick. When Billy was really jerking you around, he tried to be there, but you threw him out."

"Not exactly," Anne protested.

"Close enough," Carol insisted. "You had it set in your mind that Bill was completely your own burden, and you wouldn't inflict him on any man."

"No one else had the same emotional investment in Bill that I did . . . do," said Anne. "Except Don, now. I'll tell you, I certainly feel available in some different way now. I think I'm open to falling in love again."

"I'd say David is a pretty likely candidate," offered Ted Cain, and Anne was beginning to agree. David was a kind man. He was much more, certainly— bright and funny, ambitious for what she thought were the right things, and for the right reasons. He was also direct and outspoken, in ways she sometimes found uncomfortable; he criticized her for rationalizing and making excuses, for her own behavior or anyone else's, including Bill's. David was not a man of big, romantic gestures, he didn't have Don's easy charm and confidence with women. But he had other qualities that mattered to her now. He could be relied upon. She could count on him to be there when she needed him, to be rational without being cold, to be wise without being patronizing. And for now, she thought, that was enough.

She had been nervous about Bill's first meeting with David, but it had gone smoothly enough, and her son seemed comfortable in her lover's presence. "You going to marry him?" he asked after David left one night. The three of them had gone to a Sonics game, and David dropped them off; she wanted him to spend the night, but he refused, saying that there wasn't any good reason to stir Bill up, just in case his presence in her bed might bother him. They were going away in a few days, he said, he could take a cold shower if necessary.

"I don't know," Anne answered Bill. "Maybe. How would you feel about that?"

"It's your life," he said. "Do what you want. He seems like an okay guy to me."

It was almost irrelevant to Bill, Anne thought, whether she married David or not. He might be a friend to her son, and she hoped he would, but he would never be a father. That position was taken, and she was grateful that it was. It made her own choices a lot easier, her own options wider.

Billy had changed. She was startled by how much he had grown in a few short months. It was as if some spring had been uncoiled in his DNA, some message transmitted to his cells to resume or continue a process. His whole body is different, she thought, watching him as he sat at the kitchen table, doodling on a pad of graph paper. His chest had broadened, his arms lengthened; his entire presence seemed to fill the space where less than a year before a thin, slightly undersized fourteen-year-old had sat and picked desultorily at his food. Now he was ravenous all the time—she never had to call him for meals, and the food vanished from the refrigerator like cards disappearing up a magician's sleeve.

"What's that you're drawing?" she asked.

"Just some boats. See this hull design? It's just a Boston whaler, but if you rigged it like this, see—"

"Your father used to do that, too. Sit at the table every night and design sailboats."

"He still does. See, if you put a cutter rig on it, it would . . ."

How uncannily like Don her son had become. More messages locked in the cells, she thought, the mysteries of the genetic code. Perhaps living with Don had been the catalyst; whatever the explanation, she was satisfied with the changes she saw and the others, less visible, that she sensed and experienced.

Bill was comfortable in his own skin in a way he'd

never been. When he teased her, there was no sarcastic edge in his voice, no bitter underlay. He was affectionate with her, in an easy, unstrained way, and talked freely and happily about his life with Don. She heard about his Windsurfer, and the dinghy he'd rebuilt, and Ricco, the yard manager, who'd had a son killed in Vietnam and sometimes absentmindedly called Bill by his son's name. "But he's real sharp, otherwise. Dad says he can smell a diesel and know what's wrong with it, and he's great at handicapping horses," Bill said. "We go to the track sometimes, me and Dad and Ricco. He has this scar down his face, he says a shark got him, but I heard from Karl he got it in a fight the night he heard about his son."

"Who's Karl?"

"He's a naval architect, he and Dad are pretty good friends. He's got a dinky little practice, because he only likes to design wooden sailboats, and most people want fiberglass stinkpots, they don't want to be scraping paint all the time." He grimaced, as if remembering something unpleasant. "He helped Dad with the plans for the marina—we're going to rebuild some of the piers and add more haul-out space and stuff, maybe put in a restaurant for the fishermen, a short-order place," Bill said. "He's an okay guy, Karl. Before he got married, he and Dad used to cat around all the time."

Bill told her about taking the rebuilt boat over to an island a few miles from the marina and spending the weekend there with his friend Dylan.

"Alone?" Anne asked. "Just you and Dylan? Don let you do that?"

"Sure. He leaves me alone plenty. Well, actually, only once in a while. Like if he spends the night on Peggy's boat. He's just down the road aways, Mom, I could holler if I needed him. He doesn't do it very often. Don't worry, he's not neglecting me."

"I didn't think he was." She hesitated. "Does he come home late a lot?"

"Not as much as he used to. He says he's slowing down some. Once in a while he and Karl and Ricco tie on one. He's sure a bear in the morning after a night like that."

Don didn't seem to have adjusted his life-style to the demands of a child, Anne thought. But then, Billy wasn't a child anymore. He had his father now, and he did not need her, nor she him, in the old desperate way.

She liked being a vacation mother, she decided, putting her new bikini into the suitcase. She enjoyed having Billy home every few months, buying him treats, having a good time with him, not having to cope with his problems on a daily basis. He still had problems, she knew—she didn't think the months with Don had solved all of them. There would be rocky times ahead for her son, and bigger challenges to grapple with than sailing a small boat to a nearby island or passing a math test. She thought of all the dangers growing up entailed, and shuddered. Driving . . . soon he would have his license. At least she would not be the one who stayed awake at night worrying about that. Or sex, either. Don could worry about him getting some girl in trouble, too.

Don had always said that he didn't have much use for babies. Give me a kid when it's able to change its own pants and old enough to reason with, and I can handle it—that was his attitude before Bill was born. But by the time Bill was five, he was gone, and she'd had to negotiate all Bill's in-between years, from toddler to teenager, alone. And now, a few years short of the end of endless mothering—if there was an end, which she doubted—she'd been given an unexpected parole. Don had done that. He had appeared as if on cue, the hero who rescues the girl. Although this time he had rescued the boy as well.

She packed a long eyelet skirt, and a gauzy scarf Bill had given her for Christmas. She knew Don had helped him choose it—it was a shade of blue he had always liked her in. Tomorrow she would wear it for David.

21 It was weird being in Seattle again, Bill thought. His mother had repainted his room, and she had a new boyfriend, who seemed like a pretty decent guy, but you never could tell—she'd collected her share of losers, and maybe this guy would turn out to be one, too. She didn't seem as uptight as she had been in the past—at least, she didn't bug him the way she used to. She was familiar, but different, too. Like Chris.

Chris was all hot to go skiing, but they only got to go that one night at Alpental right after he got home—there hadn't been much snow in the mountains that winter, and the lift lines were so long he only got in a few runs. His ski boots were too small for him; his mother wanted to get him new ones for Christmas, but he said no thanks, he probably wouldn't be doing much skiing, so she bought him a stereo instead.

Skiing was kind of a washout, and so, in a way, was Chris. One afternoon they went down to the tree house and found it all busted up.

"Some little kids must have raped it for the lumber," Chris said. "I haven't been around here much lately."

"Yeah? What have you been doing instead?" Bill asked.

"There's the girl, Debby. She's in my class at Ingraham. I hang out with her sometimes. You got a girlfriend in California?"

"Sort of." In fact, Melissa, the redhead he'd been hanging out with, as Chris put it, had dumped him rather unceremoniously a few weeks before for a senior. But he didn't tell Chris that.

"Yeah, well, you know how it is, girls take up a lot of time."

"I know."

"And Kevin and me've been going jeeping up on Tiger Mountain. We go four-wheeling all over the trails—it's really neat. When I get my license I'm going to buy a jeep—a Cherokee like his. I know this place down Renton, you can get a good used one cheap."

"Where you getting the bread?"

"I'm thinking of dropping out of school, maybe getting a job. They're hiring down at the Burgerchef on Rainier."

"You gonna fry burgers for bozos the rest of your life?"

"I dunno. College sounds like a drag, tell you the truth. Besides, I want to get out of the house. My old man's driving me nuts—Chris, do that, Chris, do this. Shit."

"Yeah."

"Yours too?"

"Not so much."

"You're lucky. Hey, you want to smoke some dope?"

"Sure, why not?"

Chris offered to have his girlfriend find somebody for Bill, but he said no, that was okay, he didn't want to. "I see your old girlfriend Clary at school," Chris said. "She's going with Todd Lewis now."

"The world's champion asshole, huh?"

"Ah, he's not so bad, once you get to know him." Hah, that was a laugh. Chris had known Todd Lewis as long as he had, and the one thing they had agreed for sure was, the guy was an asshole.

"You getting much down there in sunny California, man?" asked Chris.

"Enough," Billy said cryptically. You could call it that, he supposed. Lately he was whacking off three or four times a day. He'd be sitting in class or working around the yard or out in the dinghy and have to sit on his hands to keep from flogging it. It nearly drove him nuts thinking that at that very second people were doing it by the zillions, in Shanghai and Sioux Falls, in Portland and Pago Pago. Fucking in Frankfort, getting blown in Bombay, screwing around in Seattle. He was horny all the time, and it only made him feel a little better to hear from Don that he had been the same way when he was Bill's age.

"Must be great-looking chicks down there," said Chris.

"You can say that again," Bill replied. "Jesus, I'm stoned. I haven't been this stoned for ages."

"You're not getting any of that Mexican weed, huh?"

"Not really."

"How come?"

"Just haven't."

"Too bad."

"Yeah."

It wasn't that he didn't like getting stoned, Bill considered. He liked the dreamy, hazy way nothing seemed to matter very much when he did. His favorite thing to do was zonk out on the end of a dock and stare at the water, watch the light make patterns on the waves, think about sailing around the world or going to war or getting laid, or being an adult and doing whatever he wanted to do, on his own time, in his own way. His father found him there one afternoon when he was supposed to be fixing the flat on the pickup.

"I told you to get that tire changed, Ricco needs the truck," Don said.

"I couldn't find the jack."

"You try looking under the floorboard in the bed?"

"No."

"Well, where did the hell you think it was, in the head?" His father was pretty pissed.

"I'll get to it," Bill said, and his father picked him up off the dock by the scruff of his neck and spun him around. He looked at Bill's eyes, which were dilated from the grass, and snorted in disgust.

"Been smoking a little something, huh?" he said.

Bill didn't reply. He knew his father's views on drugs, and he knew he was in for it.

"Well, you'd better wake up pretty damn fast and fix that tire," the old man said. "And then you can clean the bilge in the monk—it's about as filthy a bilge as I've ever seen, and I better be able to eat off the engines when I come down there later."

"I was going to the movies with Dylan later."

"Forget it. You're not going anywhere till the work is done. Except overboard." And with that, his father threw him in the bay, which was fucking freezing in the middle of November—nobody even surfed then without a wetsuit. He came up gasping and choking, taken by surprise, his balls damn near frozen off, and the old man was laughing. "Dirtiest bilge I ever saw, bar none," he said. "That ought to keep you busy most of the night, and pretty much all weekend, too. You want to get stoned when you're done with that, be my guest—I got a lot of stinking jobs need doing around here, and for every time I catch you stoned, there's one with your name on it."

Bill sighed. Sometimes his father was a tough old bastard, but at least you knew where you were with him. You might not know exactly what he was going to do when he caught you fucking up, but two things you knew for sure: he was going to catch you, and you weren't going to like it.

Bill was glad to be back in California. His father had met his plane, and now they were driving home from the airport. In the back of the pickup were his new stereo and his other Christmas gifts; he'd had to bring back an extra duffel to hold the stuff he'd taken from his old room. It looked pretty empty when he took the posters off the walls and the books from the shelves. His mother looked sort of funny when he did that, so he tacked a couple of the posters back up and left a few of the books he had planned to take back to California.

"What's that bandage on your neck for?" he asked as Don swung the pickup onto the freeway.

"Cut myself shaving."

That was a weird place to cut yourself, Bill thought, and besides, he uses an electric razor. But something in Don's tone warned him off. "We going to Cabo?"

"Looks like it."

"Taking the monk?"

"Nope. Sold it to a fellow from Santa Barbara. Taking the *Pandora* instead."

"Peggy and Travis coming too?"

"Yep. That okay with you?"

"Yeah, sure." Boy, that ought to be something. He and the old man had been sailing with Peggy before. Heavy weather came up one time and his father took over, barking out orders—"Ease up on that tiller, it'll tack by itself!" "Reef that sail—let go of that halyard, no, not that far, just a few feet . . . hook the tack, Peggy, for crying out loud, take up on the clew . . . no, not that way, here, I'll do it." It looked to Bill like she was doing fine but the old man was all over her. Until finally she stood there rubbing her head where the boom had grazed her when Don came about un- expectedly and said, "Why don't you sail it, then?" in a funny, quiet voice. She'd gone below and crashed around in the galley for a few minutes, banging every pot and pan on the boat, and his old man didn't even know she was mad, that's how dumb he could be sometimes.

"Who's going to be the captain on this trip?" Bill asked Don.

"Why? You bucking for the job, sport?"

"No, I just wondered, that's all. Last time Peggy said she wouldn't sail with you again if you were Christopher Columbus and she was Queen Isabella."

"Yeah, well, we settled that."

"Want to fill me in, since I'm going along on this trip? I just want to know what's what, that's all."

"You do, huh? Well, for your information—for this trip only—she's the captain, I'm first mate."

That ought to be worth a few laughs. He could just see his father taking orders on a boat—Peggy's or anyone else's. Sometimes Don and Peggy yelled at each other so loud he thought his ears would burst. Peggy was a peppery gal, as his father said—she didn't take the back of anyone's tongue, not even Don's. The first time Bill had seen them fighting he got scared—they were really mixing it up, and he thought they might never talk to each other again. But then Peggy dumped a bucket of seawater on Don's head, and they ended up laughing and tickling each other. They never stayed mad for long, though. After Peggy doused Don that time, the old man said that gal sure doesn't take any shit from me, does she? but there was a grin on his face when he said it. Still, Bill wished he hadn't traded his Walkman—it was going to be one hell of a noisy trip.

It wasn't, though. Peggy handled the tiller most of the time, and when she gave his father orders, Don carried them out without protesting, even when you could tell they were pretty dumb. Coming out of the harbor at Cabo, crowded with fishing boats and pleasure vessels of all sizes, she practically took the paint off a beautiful old Sparkman and Stephens motor-sailer, and his father winced but didn't say anything.

They fished out of Cabo for two days, and his father hooked a humongous tuna but gave it up after ten minutes of playing it, cut the line and let the sucker go. Let the big fella have another chance, he said, rubbing his shoulder below the bandage he still wore on his neck. He was even quieter and more taciturn than usual. He didn't get mad, though, not even when Bill dropped the marlinespike over the side by mistake, or when Travis messed up the drafting set Peggy had given Don for Christmas.

They slept on the boat and went ashore when they weren't cruising the waters around the quaint fishing village at the tip of Baja. They ate some kind of chicken with, of all things, chocolate sauce, and Bill put away a few Tacitas when the old man wasn't looking. He and Travis went in and out of the *panaderia*, the bakery, at least twice a day, and porked themselves stupid with those little sugared tortilla things the old lady in the heavy black dress gave them in exchange for their pesos. Bill tried his high school Spanish out on a few of the street vendors, and was surprised to learn that they understood him. Or maybe they didn't, but they gave him what he ordered, anyway.

On New Year's Eve they anchored the *Pandora* in a little cove. Peggy brought out her guitar and sang good old tunes like "Margaritaville" and "Blowin' in the Wind" in her deep, warm voice, and his father sang, too, off-key, of course, but okay-sounding. The music echoed out over the water, and a couple of porpoises came up on *Pandora*'s starboard side and leapt and played in the moonlight. Bill sat sort of curled up under his father's arm and watched until they disappeared as silently as they had come. All in all, thought Bill, it was a pretty good trip.

"How do you feel about staying on *Pandora* with Peggy and Travis for a few days?" Don asked, a week after they returned from Cabo.

"Okay, if I have to." Bill looked up from *The Once and Future King*. This guy White could really write. He imagined how it was for Arthur—Wart, they called him—to find out he was really the son of a king. He was almost to the part where Merlin was going to tell him so he wasn't paying much attention to his father.

"I'm going to the hospital," Don said.

"How come?"

"They want to take this thing on my neck off."

"Your head?"

"Very funny, very funny." His father touched the place where the bandage had been. It was like a lump with a hole in it. It didn't look like any razor nick Bill had ever seen. "This bump over here."

"Why?"

"They think I'll look better without it."

His father was a great kidder in a sort of droll way. Ironic, sometimes. But he didn't seem to be kidding around now. He looked pretty serious, come to think of it. Bill suddenly felt cold. He turned down the corner of the page and closed the book on Wart.

"How long are you going to be in the hospital?"

"Couple days, maybe. You mind staying on the *Pandora*?"

"No, that's cool. I can watch Trav for Peggy if she needs me to. Which hospital you going to?"

"The V.A."

"Can I come see you?"

"Nah. I'll be back before you know it. It'll give me a chance to get a little peace and quiet without that rock music blaring all the time. Can't hear myself think since you got that fancy stereo."

Ouch. He tried to keep the volume down, but the speakers were real powerful, and A.C.D.C. and Iron Maiden weren't real good if they weren't loud. "I could get some earphones if I had about fifteen more dollars," he said hopefully.

"Sure, and if a pig had wings it could fly. You fixed the hitch on the boat trailer like I told you?"

"No."

"No what?"

"No, sir."

"Why not?"

"I couldn't find the pliers. I looked in the tool kit."

"So you decided not to do the job."

"Well, not without the pliers."

"Ever occur to you to go find another pair of pliers?"

"I didn't know where else to look."

"How about in the dinghy, where you left them?"

"Oh."

"Listen, kid, you have a tendency to give up too easy, you know that?"

"If you say so."

"I say so. Now, why don't you just walk out that door and get the damn pliers and fix the damn trailer hitch. Yeah. I know, it's a little on the damp side out there, but you're used to that, being from Seattle and all."

A little on the damp side, sure. It was a fucking monsoon out there, and nobody needed the damn boat trailer, anyway. Inside the marina office it was warm and pleasant—the little wood stove kept it cozy on a day like today, the kind of day when he liked nothing better than to be totally into a good book. His mother liked that, too—if this was home, there'd be her in the rocking chair, him on the couch, with the fire in the fireplace and a bowl of popcorn between them, both with their own books. Whatever it was he was supposed to have done, she'd say forget it, you can do it later. If this was home.

"My dad come home yet?"

Peggy was in the office when he came home from school. Her eyes looked funny, like she'd been crying. "No," she said. "They're going to keep him there a few more days."

"How come? He said they were just cutting that thing off his neck, he'd be home this afternoon."

"They want to do some more tests," she replied.

"Why? What are they testing him for?"

"I don't know." That was sure a crock of shit— Peggy knew all right. He could tell, she was a lousy liar.

"We going over to the V.A. to see him tonight?"

"I was there until just a while ago. He's kind of tired. He said he didn't want any company tonight."

"I'm not company."

"No, you're not. But he doesn't feel so hot, he wants to be alone."

"He say anything else?"

"He said to tell you . . . he loves you."

"He said that?" It didn't sound like his old man to him.

"Actually, he said tell the kid I kind of miss his lousy music and his pointy little head."

That sounded more like him. "Peggy?"

"Yes?"

"Is he going to be all right? I mean really?"

She turned her face slightly away from him, but not before he saw the tears well up in the corners of her eyes. "I hope so, Bill. I really hope so."

22 Ricco brought Don a work order to sign, but when Don put the pen to the clipboard the damn thing skittered all over the page. He tried holding the board with his weak left and writing with his other hand but he didn't have the strength or control to steady the board. "I'll just take this into the office and look it over first," he told Ricco. "Make sure we're not going to take a bath on this job."

He put it on the desk and scrawled his name quickly, then took it back to his yard manager.

"Everything okay?" Ricco asked.

"Looks okay to me."

"You still want me to run every one of these by you? I can handle it, it's no trouble."

"My name's on the bid, it's my ass if we underestimate."

"Sure, boss."

The doctor had told Don that his arm would get stronger, and his coordination slowly improve. They'd had to cut some muscles in his neck and just below it to free the tumor and one shoulder was considerably lower than the other. He looked, he thought, like an old man with a lousy tailor.

After the needle biopsy they told him it was malignant. They wanted to schedule him for surgery the next day but he said no, he'd promised his kid a trip to Mexico, that came first. Then he had another meeting with the port commission for one last run-through on the plans; if there was any further delay in construction, they'd have to pay a full point more interest on the loan, or maybe even more, the way the prime was climbing.

"Why are you delaying this?" Peggy asked, exasperated with his explanations. He told her about the biopsy report that New Year's Eve in Cabo, after the boys were asleep. They made love as quietly as possible in the forward cabin, and then he told her. He couldn't bullshit her—in spite of what they both said about no strings, they were there all right. Gossamer thin, but he felt them, and most of the time they were a comfort. He couldn't get away with being anything other than completely honest with her, and he did not want to. She never smothered him. She was strong, so he didn't always have to be. She was vulnerable, too, soft like most women are, and as much as she would allow herself to need a man, she needed him.

"I wanted to make the trip. And the meeting with the port."

"I could have handled the port—maybe not as well as you, but enough to get through," Peggy said.

"Getting through isn't enough. You have to sell them. You're a lousy salesman. You let that guy go out of the marina the other day, the fellow looking at the Concordia 28, and you never asked for the order."

"He came back and bought the boat, didn't he?"

"Not exactly. He came back and then I sold him the boat."

"Don, you're avoiding the issue. The way you're avoiding the surgery."

"I'm not avoiding it, just taking care of business."

"What business is more important than your health? Than your life?"

"Hey, settle down. The doc said one more week probably won't make any difference. They'll go in, they'll get it all, and that'll be that. I don't want to talk about it anymore."

They'd gone in, and they thought they'd gotten it all. They took some tissue from a few places near the site, but those were clean. They wanted him to undergo radiation—a prophylactic measure, they said. The young doctor he'd seen the first time told him what the side effects were, and laid out the odds, and Don placed his bet. He remembered his father after the radiation. He didn't tell Peggy any of that part; just that the prognosis was good, they thought they caught it before it metastasized, and by the way, had the work been started yet on the pilings for the new docks?

He hadn't known what to tell the kid, so in the end he told him the truth.

"I guess you're wondering why I didn't want you coming to the hospital," Don said when he came home six days after the surgery.

"Sort of," the kid said.

"I didn't look so great. Tubes and drains and IVs. That lump was bigger than it looked. They had to cut a few muscles, which is why my arm's not as strong as it was. It'll come back, pretty soon. Long as I can still whip you with one hand tied behind my back, I figure you got nothing to worry about."

"Yeah. Was the tumor malignant?"

Shit. Kids know everything these days. "Yes. But they're pretty certain it hasn't spread anywhere else. They took out a lot of extra tissue and muscle to be absolutely sure."

"That's good. You feel okay?"

"Not yet. But I will. Is there a beer around this place?"

"Yeah, Peggy went to the store before she picked you up, you want one?"

"That'd be nice. Bill . . . there's nothing to worry about, you know. The old man's fine."

"Sure. I know."

He figured he ought to tell Anne. If she found out from Bill, she'd get all bent out of shape. Still, he put the call off as long as he dared. He gave her the same facts he'd given Peggy and Bill, and, predictably, she started to cry.

"For crying out loud, don't bury me yet," he said irritably, and from her sharp intake of breath he knew he had reached her.

"You haven't told Bill, have you?" she asked.

"Of course I have," he snapped. "You think he's a baby, still believes in the Good Fairy? He lives here, he sees me, he knows I was in the hosptial for a week. What am I supposed to tell him, I had my tonsils out?"

"How did he take it?"

"Like a man. Bill's okay."

"He may act that way, but how does he feel?"

"How the hell should I know?"

"By asking him, Don," she said, as if he were a child who could not remember the simplest fact. Bill called it her Long Suffering Voice, which was the way he'd always thought of it, too. "Ask him if he's worried, or afraid."

"I don't hold with that, Anne. Just trust me, okay?"

"Maybe he should see someone . . . just to get it out, talk about it."

When he was discharged from the hospital, the physical therapist had recommended that he squeeze a tennis ball frequently to build up strength in his arm and hand. Now he squeezed the tennis ball as hard as he could, gritting his teeth; he imagined it was her throat. "Bill doesn't need a shrink, Anne. He's fine. If there's something on his mind he'll tell me. If he wants to talk, I'll listen."

"Don, he never wants to talk."

"Like I said, he does if you listen."

"Are you implying that I don't?"

"I'm not implying it, lady, I'm telling it!" He squeezed the yellow ball so hard he could feel it give. "Listen carefully," he said. "I had an operation. I'm going to be fine. I told your son the truth, as far as I know it. He's getting up in the morning and going to school and doing his work and sailing his boat and whacking off about the right amount for a kid his age. He's making out okay. He doesn't need to see a psychiatrist and I don't need to hear any more suggestions like that from you."

"Okay," she said, in a remembered tone that made him feel as if he were bullying her. Maybe he was, he thought. But sometimes that was the only way to shut her up.

23 That April, during his spring vacation from school, Bill and Don flew to the East Coast. The only rental cars available at the airport in Baltimore were stick shifts. Bill sat close to his father all the way down the peninsula, helping him shift; Don still didn't have a lot of strength in his arm, and Bill could tell it bothered him.

They spent the night at the Tidewater Inn in Easton, and in the morning they continued driving south. At a dock in Chincoteague, they rented a small skiff and made the brief crossing to Captain's Island. His father showed him the cabin, and together they unloaded their gear. Don took a nap while Bill explored the island. For supper they heated soup and made sandwiches. "Tomorrow I'm counting on fresh fish," Don told him. "You're chief supply officer."

"What happens if I don't catch anything?"

"Guess you don't eat."

In the morning Bill woke to the sound of wild geese calling, honking like drivers in a traffic jam. His father told him they were returning to Canada and the Arctic for the summer; in the fall, he said, this island is one big duck blind. They went to the small freshwater stream for water, and then walked along the beach. They watched mallards and teal and canvasbacks and mud ducks and a zillion other waterfowl. His father knew them all, their colors and markings and habits.

Bill caught two small fish and brought them back to the cabin. "Dinner," he said offhandedly, and Don nodded.

"What took you so long?" he said.

"I was busy throwing the rest of them back. Thought I'd leave some for tomorrow."

"Tomorrow we'll get ourselves some meat. There's plenty of small game around here. Ever handle a gun?"

"Not really." That time with the revolver didn't count, did it?

"Get my old shotgun out of that duffel there. You get your first lesson after supper."

"I get to shoot it then?"

His father snorted. "You don't get to pick it up until I tell you about how to use a gun. When and why. Then you clean and oil and load it. And then we'll see."

"Can you shoot it? I mean, with your shoulder and all?"

"Guess you won't know till I try it, will you?"

"Guess not."

His father shot a rabbit the next day, and Bill noticed him wince when the recoil slammed the gun back into his shoulder. Don showed him how to skin and cook it. Bill thought it tasted terrible, but there was something kind of neat about his old man nailing it on his first shot.

It was his last one, too, but he made Bill practice with the shotgun until he could blast a tree at twenty yards, get the circle right in the middle of the target his father found in the cabin. It was riddled with holes whose edges were ragged and brown with age.

"This was mine," he said, as they nailed it to a tree. "My father taught me how to shoot here. The captain." Then he added, "He was one tough sonuvabitch."

Bill waited for Don to continue, but he didn't. Later he asked Don if he and his father had gotten along.

"Like oil and water," said Don. "He only knew one way to do things—his way. Sometimes his way didn't sit so well with me."

"Then what happened?"

"I did it his way."

"All the time?"

"Till I got bigger than him."

"Oh."

Don smiled in a sort of gentle way. "Think you'll ever get bigger than me?"

"One of these years, maybe." His father seemed to have shrunk since the operation. He looked, Bill thought, like a snowman that has just begun to melt.

"I want to see that," Don said.

"All you got to do is stick around."

"Nothing to it."

"Nope."

They stayed on Captain's Island for four days, and then they packed their things in the skiff. Bill collected some stuff he wanted to bring home—a goosefeather, some seashells, the starfish and rocks he'd picked up on the beach, a few spent shells from the shotgun.

"What's all that junk?" Don asked.

"Oh, just a few souvenirs."

"We'll come back in the fall when duck hunting starts."

"I know, but I want to take these things anyway."

"Suit yourself," Don said.

They returned the boat and retrieved the car and drove farther south down the Shore. They stopped in the little town of Wachapreague, and Don showed Bill where his grandmother—Billy's great-grandmother—had lived.

"She made the best crab cakes you ever tasted," he said, "and the best peach pie. Once I took a pie when she left it to cool on the back porch there, and she brained me with a rolling pin. Nearly bashed my head in." He chuckled.

"Do you have any relatives around here?" Bill wanted to know. "Do I? You know, like second cousins or uncles or something?" He knew practically every one of his mother's relatives, after spending all those summers in Westport, but he hardly knew anything about his father's family.

"Uncle Jim had a daughter, Martha, who married the Sykes boy. They had a couple of kids, moved down to Newport News."

"Can we go there?"

"It's a long drive, even with the bridge-tunnel across. I don't think your old man's up to it, sport. Maybe when we come back in the fall."

"Yeah."

Peggy met them at the airport, and Bill was glad to see her—relieved, in a way. His father didn't look so hot on the flight home. Not like he was gonna keel over or anything, just sort of pale under his tan, a kind of yellowish color. He'd drunk four or five of those little bottles of Cutty Sark and hadn't said much.

Bill wasn't sure if his father had had a good time on their trip or not. There was something weird about the way he looked at everything, like he was memorizing it. It was like he was trying to tell Bill something, but he didn't do it in words. The only thing he said was they would come back in the fall.

Bill wasn't sure he was ever going to meet those cousins in Newport News, though. And right now, all he wanted to do was get on his board and paddle out beyond the surf and put his face in the salty water, where nobody but the fish would know if there were tears mixed in.

24 The construction was behind schedule; every day of delay, of hassles with the contractor, was wearing Don down. Ricco was fighting with the job super—there was friction between his husky blond crew and the mostly Mexican workers who hauled and caulked and tuned and repaired to Ricco's loose directions.

The headaches were almost constant now; he swallowed the codeine and aspirin tablets the doctor had given him but they made him groggy, and booze seemed to work almost as well. Tasted better, too, although nothing had much of a taste these days.

"The pickup took two quarts of oil today," said Peggy. Since it was still hard for Don to shift gears, he'd switched vehicles with Peggy. He drove her automatic sedan, a big Buick that responded easily to his touch. It also had power brakes, which he disliked ordinarily, but there was a nagging weakness on his right side; sometimes his leg almost buckled under his weight. He was nauseous from the pills they'd given him at the hospital; they recommended chemotherapy in cases like his. They'd even given him cannabis to settle his stomach, increase his appetite. The kid was very interested in that.

"That's the real stuff, huh? Certified by the federal government, a hundred percent sure to get you high?"

"So they say."

"I don't suppose I could try a little, huh? Just to see what kind of stuff the feds smoke?"

"You do and I'll tan your butt. You know how I feel about that."

"Yeah, I know. Sir."

Peggy mumbled something. "You talking to me?" he asked.

"I said I put two quarts of oil in the truck today."

"I heard you the first time."

"Ricco said you fired the crew today."

"I told them if they couldn't keep their damn ethnic shit out of the yard they could get lost."

"Don, we're not in any position to go out now and find another construction crew. We've got to take what we can get and—"

"I don't have to take anything."

"Hell's bells, Don! You're being unreasonable. Stubborn. Stupid."

He swiveled his chair around, deliberately turning his back on her.

"Don?" He didn't hear her; there was a deep, knifing pain in his head that was louder than her voice. He felt her hands on his face; her fingers were cool. She came around to face him, and her eyes were full of concern.

"Don, did you see the doctor today?"

"What doctor?" He didn't know what Peggy was talking about.

"Don, you were supposed to go to the hospital today for your follow-up."

"Oh, yeah. I guess I forgot."

She wrinkled her nose; she was cute when she did that.

"How could you forget it? I circled it right here on the calendar . . . look."

The water looked cool and blue beyond the jetty. He imagined floating on it, his arms and legs weightless, the sun on his face, a gull flying overhead.

"Don, I want you to phone the hospital and make another appointment."

"What? Appointment? What kind of appointment?"

"Don, honey, why don't you go on back to the house and lie down for a while? You look like you could use a nap. I'll see that Bill gets home . . . I'll pick up supper for us and bring it over later."

"That's a good idea. To tell you the truth, I feel a little peaked today. Hey, Peg, have you seen the crew around? Damn guys, they got their union behind them, think they can just walk off a job whenever they feel like it."

"I know, Don," she said soothingly. "I'll talk to the super, see what I can do."

"Bill, where's the Phillips screwdriver?"

"On the tool rack, same place it always is."

"No it's not." He went into the kid's room. "You didn't put it back last time you used it."

"I haven't used it in weeks."

"Then why isn't it on the tool rack?"

"It's there, you just didn't look."

"Don't tell me I didn't look. I looked and it's not there."

"Well, don't look at me, I didn't lose it."

"Don't give me any lip, Bill, just get me the screwdriver."

"I don't have the goddamned screwdriver!"

"And I don't like that tone of voice, either."

"What tone of voice?"

"That one. That sassy voice. Don't you talk back to

me, kid, I'm still big enough to bust you in the chops, you talk to me like that!"

"Dad, I don't have the fucking screwdriver, I'm not—oww! Why'd you hit me like that?"

"I hit you so you'd learn not to talk back to your father without a little respect. You think you learned that yet? Huh?"

Billy wiped his lip with the back of his hand. It might have stung, but it wasn't bleeding. Why was he looking at him like that? There was something familiar in the kid's eyes . . . Anne? Was it Anne's eyes staring through Bill? No, not Anne. It was like him, Don—it was like he used to look when he was scared of his old man. Really scared.

"Dad?"

"Yeah?"

"Here's the Phillips. It was on the tool rack, where I said."

"Oh, that's good. What are you giving it to me for?"

"I thought you wanted it."

"What made you think a thing like that? Hey, Bill, what's the matter with your lip? It's all swollen . . . too much kissing, probably, you and that girl, what's her name, Melissa?"

"It's Jean, Dad, me 'n' Melissa broke up a long time ago."

"Yes, Melissa, that's right. Better watch that kissing, son."

"Sure, Dad."

Peggy was driving him to the hospital. He'd told her he could go alone, but she was insistent. She said he'd missed his last two appointments.

He told the doctor about the headaches. The doctor gave him more pills and suggested radiation again. When he came out of the hospital, Peggy was waiting for him.

"What did he say?"

"He said I'm doing fine. He said the only thing wrong with me was that I wasn't getting enough sex. He gave me a prescription for it. You know where I could get something like that filled, lady?"

Her eyes were merry again, and she kissed him a big, wet one.

"Watch it, lady, this is a public place."

"Let's go to a private one."

They made love slowly; it was early in the afternoon, and the sun made puddles of sunshine on the quilt on *Pandora*'s forward bunk. She made him lie on his back. Let me, she said, let me love you. She clasped him tight inside her velvety walls and rocked her hips back and forth, back and forth, and the boat rode easily in the water with their movement, rising and falling beneath them. Later she lay with her head on his chest, her small body curled up alongside him, her leg between his.

"Pretty quiet down there," he said. "What are you thinking about?"

"Bill," she replied. "You're ragging him pretty hard these days, Don. Are you aware of that?"

"No," he said. He was confused. It seemed to him that he and the kid were getting along pretty well. "He tell you that?"

"No, he'd never complain or say anything against you. I've noticed it, though. So has Travis."

"If you say so. Maybe we ought to take a trip together, me and the kid. I ever tell you about this is-land I own, down on the Eastern Shore? My old man used to take me there when I was a kid. You think Bill would like a trip like that?"

Was it his imagination, or was she crying?

"Sure, Don. I think some day he'd like to go there with you."

No question about it, she was crying. Women. Sometimes you never knew what set them off.

25 When Anne first learned of Don's cancer, she began to imagine symptoms of her own. She constantly felt her breasts for lumps, and she stopped smoking. She woke up in the night sometimes, afraid. Once she called the marina to talk to Don, and Peggy McCarthy answered.

"This is Anne," she said. "Anne Manning. Bill's mother."

"Yes," said the husky, soft voice. "I know. Bill talks about you often."

"How is he?"

"He seems to be handling a difficult situation with a great deal of maturity. He's a fine boy, Anne."

She liked the way Peggy McCarthy sounded. And because she knew she had a son, too, Anne trusted her. "He likes you a lot, too," she told Peggy. "I've wanted to thank you for a long time for being so good to him."

"It's no problem. He's an easy kid to be good to."

"How is Don?"

Peggy's voice was even. "He has his good days and his bad days. Right now he's very involved with the work on the new addition—I guess he's told you about that."

"He mentioned it. Is that wise? Right now, I mean?"

"Don wouldn't consider putting it off. It's very important to him. He plans to be around to see it pay off."

"I'm very glad you're there to keep an eye on things. Not just the business. You must—it sounds like you care a great deal about them—Don and Bill."

"I do."

"Look, if there's anything you think I should know about . . . sometimes Don doesn't say a lot. Or Bill, either," she finished awkwardly.

"I'll keep in touch," Peggy McCarthy said. "Don't worry, Anne. He's going to be all right."

Did she mean Don—or Billy? Anne wasn't sure, but she slept soundly that night, and she began to believe that maybe, just maybe, Peggy was right.

Anne's first warning came not from Peggy McCarthy but from Bill. He came home for a two-week visit right after school recessed for the summer. Driving in from the airport he said, "Dad's acting pretty weird these days."

"Oh?" It was five thirty; the freeway was crowded with commuter traffic from the Boeing plants south of the city.

"He jumps all over me for no reason. He's on my back all the time. Everything I do is wrong."

So the honeymoon is over, she thought. Bill must be testing the limits, pushing Don. She knew how infuriating that could be, how frustrating, and Don had never been a patient man. "Maybe you're not behaving the way he thinks you should," she said carefully.

"No, Ma, it's not that. I'm not doing stuff like that anymore. I'm not . . . it's not the way it used to be. Here, I mean."

"How did you do in school this term?"

"Three B's and two A's."

"That must have pleased your father."

"He said it should have been all A's. He yelled at me about it. I told him those were the best grades I ever got and he called me a lazy bastard."

"He did?"

"Yeah. He's always hitting on me for stuff I didn't do. Loses his temper all the time—snap, like that. Over the least little thing."

"Have you tried talking to him about it? Directly, I mean? Telling him how you feel. You know, like, Dad, I feel like you're angry with me and I don't know why?"

"That's that psychobabble of yours, Ma, it doesn't work with him. And besides, it's not just me, he gets mad at Peggy a lot, too."

"Maybe he's . . . tired of her." That wasn't the way it had been when he tired of her. He wasn't angry then, just withdrawn and distant. And when he looked at her, she saw guilt in his eyes, and maybe pity.

"I don't think so," said Bill. "They like each other a lot. He'll get real mad and blow up at her and she'll yell back at him and a few minutes later it's over."

"How is it different now?"

"I think because she doesn't yell back at him. She just looks sort of sad and goes away for a while. I don't think he remembers it after he gets pissed off at her. He forgets a lot of things, too. You tell him something, an hour later he asks you a question like he never heard you."

"Well, he has a lot on his mind these days. The marina, and you, and Peggy, and . . . his illness."

"I guess. But he sure is acting weird. I didn't think a tumor on your neck could make you act weird."

"Usually it doesn't. It may have nothing to do with that at all. Sometimes adults worry about things that don't occur to children. Things you never think of."

"Ma, I'm not a child anymore, and I hate it when you say that."

"That's right, you're not." And if you were, Anne added silently, you won't be much longer. Watching a parent sicken, and maybe die . . . it was a hard way to grow up, and she knew that her son would have to do it without her.

"Don't you think you should call your father and see how he is? You've been here for an entire week, and you haven't spoken to him once."

"If he wants to talk to me, he knows where I am," said Bill. She wondered how they would make it up if neither said I'm sorry first.

She watched for signs from Bill, indications that he was depressed, worried or unhappy. There were none. The house was full of kids; she knew Chris, of course, and a few of the others, but most of them were strangers to her. They came to the house at all hours—early in the morning, before she went to work, when she was drinking tea in the kitchen, and late at night, when she yearned for the peace of a silent house to envelop her. In Bill's room the music was very loud. She came home one day and thought she smelled the odor of marijuana, but she said nothing to Bill about it. Not because I'm afraid of him, she told Carol. That's between him and Don now. He's sixteen now—all the kids his age use it. If he does it down there, he knows his father will kill him.

Except for that incident, which she did not allow to become one, having Bill home was enjoyable. He told her ridiculous jokes and he carried in the groceries from the car and put them away without being asked. He showered and changed his clothes every day. He was much more gregarious than he had been—the telephone rang often for him, and he always seemed to have other kids around. He was unusually solicitous of her well-being—you look beat, he'd say when she returned from the office, did you have a hard day? He was gentle and loving and easygoing, and she did not wonder if he was concealing something else. Sometimes when she was washing the dinner dishes at the sink he put his arms around her and buried his face in her neck.

She found him in his room alone one afternoon, moving the furniture around. There were new posters on the wall, she noticed, and a picture of Don, Bill, and a woman and child she assumed were Peggy and Travis McCarthy on Bill's bureau.

"You like the room better this way?" Bill asked her. "There's a lot more space when you take that old kiddy desk of mine out."

"You're right, it does look bigger," Anne said. "Bill, do you still want to stay in California and go back to school there in the fall?"

"Kind of."

"What does that mean?"

"It means I do," but he didn't meet Anne's eyes, and she pressed him.

"Bill, are you worried about your dad? I mean, about his health."

"Not really."

"Are you scared?"

"About what?"

"About Don getting sicker."

"Sometimes."

She sat down on the bed and gestured for him to sit by her, but he kept a distance between them. "Me too," she said. "I'm scared, I'm worried, and sometimes I'm really mad."

"It's not his fault he's sick," Bill said defensively.

"Oh, sweetie, I know that. I didn't say my feelings were rational—they're just there."

"Yeah. Look, Ma, let's not talk about it, okay? Let's just not talk about it."

"Sure, son. You want tacos or burgers for supper?"

"Whatever."

"Okay. I'll call you when it's time to eat."

Some kids came over to say good-bye the night before he left for California. It was a warm night; she sat in the window seat on the landing and listened to the babble of youthful voices. She was not eavesdropping—the window seat was her favorite place to read.

"You must be glad you're going back, I might go to California sometime. My old lady keeps promising. She says we're going to Disneyland. Can you believe it—Disneyland? She thinks I'm still a little kid." That was Chris—she knew his voice. She had heard it change the first time, deepen, a few months before Bill's did, and she had thought, so that's what it will be like.

"Disneyland's boring." It was Bill, responding to Chris.

"Maybe if I come she'll let me stay with you and your father and she and my little sister can go to Disneyland. My sister's dying to see the Magic Kingdom, she's such a weird creep."

"Yeah, that'd be neat."

"Will your dad let us take one of his boats and go sailing?"

"Maybe."

"Could we go to that place he caught the big fish—that Cabo place?"

"Cabo San Lucas. Maybe."

"Hey, Bill, you think you'll ever live here again?"

"I dunno. Maybe."

"I hope you do. If you were going to Ingraham, too, I wouldn't drop out."

"That's good."

"If you came back here to live would you bring your Windsurfer?"

"Maybe. Or maybe I'd leave it there for when I went back on vacation."

"That makes sense. I sure hope you move back."

"Me too. But I can't. Yet."

The next day, while he was packing, she asked him again if he wanted to live at home.

"In a way I do and in a way I don't," he replied. "I like it down there a lot. But I miss being here, too, if you know what I mean. Everything's different. A lot of the kids are changing."

"So are you."

"How so?"

"You've matured a lot—it's a good change. I really have enjoyed having you home with me this vacation. It's not very lively around here without you."

"There were times it was pretty lively, all right," he said with a trace of irony. "I don't think David would dig it."

"David doesn't matter. You matter." That was not entirely true. David did matter—she loved him, and she was probably going to marry him. But Billy was more important than that. "If you want to come home, you can," she told him. "I think perhaps we could manage it better this time."

"Maybe next year," he said. "I think it's time to leave for the airport now."

A week after Bill returned to California, Peggy McCarthy called Anne at the office. Her voice was exceedingly controlled and very calm. "Anne, Don is in the hospital again. I thought you should know."

"What is it? What happened? How's Bill?"

"Bill's doing okay. Don was having a lot of pain. He was acting odd—forgetting things, losing his temper over nothing important, acting irrationally."

"Bill mentioned that. I thought they were having your basic father-and-son conflict."

"No, it wasn't that," said Peggy. "I took Don to the hospital yesterday. He . . . this is hard to explain, you'll have to bear with me . . . he opened his mouth to talk and the words wouldn't come out. You could tell he knew them, they were in his head, but he couldn't get them out. Then he . . . then . . ." She broke down for a moment, and Anne wanted to weep for her, for how much she loved Don. "He went to sleep for a while, and when he woke up he was confused. He thought it was three months ago. He kept telling Bill to put more wood on the fire . . . he was drifting. I think he was remembering the trip they took to the Shore. Anyway, Bill called the doctor, who said to bring him right in. They did a bunch of tests today. A brain scan. They think it broke off and . . . they think the cancer is in his brain. That his brain was the original site, and the cancer metastasized to his neck first, where the tumor was. They won't know anything definite for a day or two."

"I see. Do you think I should come down there?"

"Not yet. Bill seems to be handling things well. He didn't want to go back to the hospital this afternoon for visiting hours, so I didn't push him. When I got back there, Don seemed much better, more in touch. I think right now might not be the best time to come. It would probably upset him . . . Don, I mean."

"But what about Bill? His father is dying, he must be scared. He needs me."

"I know how you must feel. If it were my son I'd feel that way. But I don't think there's anything you can do for him. I think Bill needs to hang in there himself through this one."

"He must have known . . ." Anne began. "When Bill was here, he wasn't all that enthusiastic about going back. There was something in the way he talked about it . . . I don't know. Damn it, Peggy, he should not have to face this alone!"

"He's not alone. There are people down here who love him."

"Yes, I know. But still, he shouldn't have to watch his father die . . . I'm sorry, I know how hard it is on you, too. Except you're older. It's different."

"Yes, it is. Except I've never had to do this before, and neither has Billy. We're sort of showing each other how." .

"Have you told him what the doctor said?"

"No. They don't know anything for sure yet. There's time enough for that. And I don't know how Don plans to handle it . . . I'd feel as if I were intruding on the two of them if I told Bill. Anne, believe me, I'm here for Bill, I won't abandon your son, no matter what. If he needs you, I'll tell you."

How would she know? Anne wondered. Bill wouldn't tell her . . . he wouldn't tell anyone. "But you'll call me as soon as you know anything, right?"

"Right. I'll call you."

That day Anne made reckless bargains with God. Don't let it happen, she beseeched Him, not now . . .

not yet. They've only had this short time together, less than two years. Lord, give them more time. Give me more time. I'll be a perfect mother, I won't ever lose my temper with him again. I won't apologize when I haven't done anything wrong, I'll be more understanding. If You want, I won't marry David, I won't even see him again . . . please God, don't let it happen.

Don't let what happen? she wondered. Don't let Don die . . . or don't leave me alone again with Billy? She didn't know, then or later, what she was praying for.

At the end of August Anne went to California. She arrived in midafternoon on the last day of Don's radiation treatments.

She was not sure what she expected. She had talked to Don and Bill on the phone a few days before. Come on down if you feel like it, Don said, as long as you're in the neighborhood. He was breezy and casual, as if it didn't matter one way or another. And perhaps to him it did not.

It mattered terribly to Anne, though she could not understand why. Bill, of course—she wanted to see him, assure herself that he was, indeed, coping with the ordeal of Don's illness. "What does coping mean to you?" David asked her. "That he's able to express his feelings verbally to you, that he hasn't run away, that he's not acting out destructively?"

"I'd settle for that," Anne replied. "That would be quite a lot, under the circumstances. But I guess what I really want is just to hug him. I know, I know . . . I'm acting like a Jewish mother. Well, damn it, I am a Jewish mother, and I want to make sure my baby's all right. Yes, he's not a baby, but even teenage kids need their parents to hug them once in a while. And whatever Don's doing, he's probably not doing that."

"Then go," said David, and she did. It had been Peggy's suggestion that she tell Don she had business in Los Angeles and thought she'd rent a car, drive down and say hello. "He'd get worried if he thought you were coming to see him on his deathbed, Anne. He's saying he's really fine, it was just a temporary setback, and he's planning to go back to work in a few days."

"Did the doctors tell him?" Anne asked. They had told Peggy—she had no status, she wasn't a relative, but she bullied them into telling her, she told Anne.

"They said they told him what they told me: Two large tumors, not operable, according to the brain scan. But I don't know if he remembers. He's still pretty foggy from the radiation and the medication. They have him on steroids to reduce the swelling in the brain. That causes his mood swings and some disorientation. Tonight he was in a good mood, very excited. He was more interested in what's going on at the marina than anything else. It's become very, very important to him to get the project completed before . . . well, to get it done," Peggy reported.

"How long? How long will he . . . does he have?"

"They don't know. A few weeks, maybe. Possibly longer. It's inoperable, but it's not untreatable. Occasionally the radiation shrinks the tumors enough for a remission for several months . . . in some cases, years." She hesitated. "Anne, if it were me, I'd come now."

She was shocked when she saw him. He moved with a shuffling gait, like an old man; he dragged his right foot slightly behind him, and he sagged on one side like a doll with its stuffing gone. His skin was reddened, as if he'd fallen asleep in the sun with one side of his face and neck exposed for too long. He looked completely exhausted; he explained that the radiation did that, he'd be fine after a few hours of sleep.

"You look like you went a few rounds with Joe Frazier," she told him, and when he grinned she saw the man she had loved for so long. An awful, suffocating, deep burning pain seized her, took her by such surprise that she could do nothing except put her arms around him—gently, carefully—and lay her head on his chest, underneath his chin, and squeeze the tears in her eyes to keep them from overflowing.

"The worst part of it is losing my hair," he said. "You know how particular I am about my hair."

"I remember." His father had gone bald early; Don's own thick, wavy hair, he said, had been a personal affront to his old man.

"Bill ought to be home any minute," Don said. "He had an errand to do. Meanwhile, how about a drink?" He led her on a tour of the house, which was, she noted, much cleaner and neater than her own; in the early years of their marriage, she had attempted to satisfy his standards, the result of his own father's constant white-glove inspections. After he left, she lived in almost compulsive disorder, a tendency she controlled but had not conquered.

At the door of Bill's room, Don hesitated. "The kid is pretty set on his own privacy—why don't you let him show you around?"

"Don't you ever go in there?" she asked.

"Only for weekly inspection, only when he's there."

"But how do you know if . . . what kind of assurance do you have that he's not—," she began, and Don stopped her.

"I know," he said firmly. "And if he does, or if he is, whatever it is you're worried about, I know about it. I'm smarter than he is, and besides, I've done it all.

I've been there. So maybe it won't take him as long as it took me to wise up."

Bill came in then, and looked relieved to see her—or was that only her imagination? She was so acutely conscious of Don's physical deterioration and so upset by it that she was certain Bill must be, too; only with great effort was she able to maintain a cheerful casualness during dinner, and avoid mentioning or even alluding to Don's condition. Bill barbecued steaks and baked potatoes in the coals; before he brought his father's plate to the table, she noticed, he cut the meat into small pieces and split and garnished the potato. When she watched Don struggle with a roll and butter knife, she understood, and a wave of sympathy for her son washed over her.

Without comment or request, Bill did the dinner dishes. He and Don spoke softly to each other; they talked their own language, and discussed people, places, and events shared or planned, stopping occasionally to explain to her, to translate. She was glad that she did not have to carry the conversation; instead, she sat and watched the two of them together, and felt the bond between them with pleasure tinged by resentment. She was the outsider here.

Peggy McCarthy and her son Travis arrived, and Don played the genial host. He had only picked at his dinner, but he seemed stronger, more his old self. "Why don't you make us some coffee," he said to Anne, "and I'll get these folks a drink. Travis might like some of that pie we had for dessert." In a quite natural way, Anne took over as hostess, and Don did what he had always done at parties they'd given when they were married, cueing her with a look or a gesture to refill glasses, find an ashtray, keep the conversation going. Anne had a feeling of déjà vu; they had done this so many times, in another life, and now it seemed like the intervening years had never happened.

Peggy McCarthy was exactly as Anne had pictured her; a little older, maybe, a woman who proved in person to be as direct and unaffected as she had been in her letters and phone calls. When she came in with Travis, her eyes sought Don first, and a funny little nod passed between them, which caused in Anne the same combination of acceptance and resentment Bill's closeness with Don had aroused. It disappeared when Peggy embraced her warmly and sincerely. "I'm really glad to meet you at last," she said. "Bill, your mother is just as beautiful as you told me she was." She turned to Anne. "They may not show it, but these guys have been really excited about seeing you. We've all been." She made Anne feel welcome, as if she sensed her uneasiness.

Anne had not wanted to make this trip; she had come to California because, she explained to David, she thought she ought to. "It may be my last chance to see Don, if the radiation doesn't work," she said. "I don't want to go, but I think I should. After all, he's my son's father. We were married—he was my best friend for a long time. And there are some things we should settle, I guess, about Bill . . . legal things, stuff like that." To Carol she gave a simpler explanation— "I need to finish my business with him before he dies."

When Don left her, she was frustrated for a long time by the things she had meant to say to him but never had. Now there were other words that needed saying, and this might be her only chance, ever, to voice them.

It was still early, not yet nine o'clock, when Peggy and Travis went home, and the three of them were alone again. And then Don and Bill had the argument.

It wasn't a big argument—at least, it didn't start that way. It had something to do with a dripping toilet Don told Bill to repair—had told him two days before to fix. "I've been waiting for you to get around to it, but you blew it. Fix it now," he said.

"I was going to take a ride with Mom, show her around," Bill replied.

"First you fix the faucet, then we'll see."

Bill went into the bathroom with a tool kit, and came out ten minutes later, looking embarrassed. "I don't know how to fix it," he told Don.

"Then I guess you'll have to figure it out pretty quick, unless you want to spend the night in there waiting for it to stop leaking on its own."

"But I told you, I don't know how—"

"No buts, sport. Get in there and fix the damn thing. What kind of kid can't replace a bum flush unit?"

"We don't have a replacement. And there's no plumbing store open now."

"You should have thought about that earlier. Now I guess you'll just have to take the old one apart and fix it."

"I never did that before, Dad, if you showed me I could—"

"Show you? If I wanted to show you, I'd do it myself. You're a smart kid. Go figure it out. Stop making excuses and do it!"

Bill went back into the bathroom, scowling darkly.

Anne was disturbed by the exchange. "Don't you think you're a little out of line?" she said to Don. "He doesn't know how to do it, that's all. He never did anything like that at home—when there was a problem, I called a plumber. Why don't you go explain it to him?"

"He's lazy, wants someone else to do it for him,

that's all. He stays in there long enough, he'll figure it out," Don said.

He didn't, though. He stayed in the bathroom for half an hour, and then came back to the living room and dropped a pipe wrench at Don's feet. "I can't fix it," he said. "I don't know how. You want it fixed, fix it yourself." He went to his room; Anne heard the door slam, an unpleasantly familiar sound, and listened while Don raged about dumb, lazy kids until she'd had enough. She went to her son.

He was crying; his face was red with anger and shame. "Son of a bitch," he muttered, "goddamned bullying sonuvabitch, is it my fault if I don't know how to fix a fucking toilet?"

She sat down on his bed and put her arms around him, holding him close to her breast until his body stopped shaking and he was more in control of himself. "He can't help it, honey. It's not him. It's his illness. Don't be angry with him. He wouldn't be like this if he were well."

"Oh, yeah? What do you know? He can be a fucking stone face forever, never let you know if you're doing stuff okay, and if you're not, or he doesn't think you are, he just lands on you, whomp, like that. Never gives you any chance to explain. And when you cross him, even accidentally, he can be a real sonuvabitch, a fucking Hitler. Is that the illness? Is it? Well, you were married to him, you should know! He's always been like that, right?"

"Kind of," she answered. Don had been like that sometimes with her, especially when she didn't know or couldn't do something he thought everybody knew or could do . . . sail a boat, replace a fuse, conceive a child. She hadn't been angry at him, not the way Billy was now; she had apologized for her inadequacies and tried to remedy them.

"What has Dad told you about his illness, Bill?" she asked.

"Not much. He says the doctors wanted him to have the radiation as a prophylactic measure, be sure they'd gotten all of the tumor. But it's spread, hasn't it?"

"Yes. It's in his brain now. Two tumors."

"Can't they operate? Dylan's mother had cancer and she had an operation. She's all right now. She only has one, uh, breast now, but she's okay."

"They can't operate on your dad. They'd have to destroy too much of the brain to remove the tumors."

"They can do a lot of stuff with lasers now. I read an article about them in *Omni*."

"No," she said, "they can't. Not where the tumors are. But sometimes radiation can shrink the tumors. They don't think there's any cancer anywhere else. His chest and lungs are clean, they think."

"He's still smoking those damn Camels. I tell him to stop, but he keeps on smoking."

She sighed. "Maybe it doesn't make any difference, Bill. Let him have what he has left."

"He has me left, damn him! Aren't I just as important as a fucking cigarette?"

"Of course you are," she soothed him. "Of course you are." Her son buried his head in her lap and she stroked it gently. He reached for her hand and they played their old game . . . hi, okay, yeah, sure, all the silly meaningless words.

"Bill, maybe you ought to come home with me," she said after he had let go of her hand and sat up, wiping his eyes as he did so.

"This is my home," he said firmly.

"Still, I think you'd be better off with me."

"No." He was silent for a time. "He's gonna die, isn't he?"

"We're all going to die, sometime."

"Don't give me that crap," he said fiercely, challenging her.

"Oh, Bill, I'm not God, how do I know? Yes, he's going to die. What he has is terminal. When, I don't know. Nobody does. It might be very quick, or it might not. I don't want you to have to go through this. School starts in ten days. Come home with me and start classes. Peggy will call us. You can come back and see him before . . . before . . ."

"What if he gets better? If he has a, whaddyacallit, remission?"

"Then you can come back here and live with him again. After Christmas, maybe."

"No. Not that long."

"You can't just switch schools in the middle of the term like that."

"Then I'll drop out for a semester."

"Your father wouldn't allow that."

"Would you?"

"I don't know, I haven't thought about it." She did, for a few minutes, trying to sort it out somehow. "There's another option. I could take a leave of absence for a while and move down here for a month or two until we see . . . until your father gets better. I could take care of you. And him, too, of course."

She wondered why she was considering it. It would mean leaving her job, the chief attorney position she had held for less than six months. It would mean leaving David, at least for a time. And it would not be easy—Don did not tolerate ill health well, particularly his own. But she was all he had.

There was Peggy, but she had her own life—her child, her boat, and her interest in the marina to protect. Bill said that, in Don's absence, Peggy was having problems getting anything accomplished there. "Guys like Ricco, they don't take orders from women," Bill told her. Anne liked Peggy very much, but she wasn't family. She wasn't Don's wife, Don's family. Bill was, however, and so, in a way, was she. It was true, what she and Don had agreed the previous summer—people who have a child together and then divorce never really stop being a family. Don was alone in the world, except for her and Bill; his parents were dead and he had no siblings or close relations. She thought about his dying alone, and she felt sad.

There was another possibility, and she thought about that. She could move Don back to Seattle, install him in her house—their house. There was a veterans' hospital in Seattle, and a major cancer center. But she didn't think Don would agree. He would not admit that great a dependence on her or anyone. He had left the city he'd brought Anne to many years before, and it was no longer his home. His home was here. He had friends, a business, a lover here. And a son, she realized: I cannot take Bill away from him.

She doubted that Bill would come. She knew that he wanted to leave, and she knew as well that he would be ridden with guilt if he did. And so she did not argue when Bill said, "Ma, I'm staying here. For now, anyway. I don't think you should move down here. I don't think that's a very good idea. I'm staying here."

"Whatever you want to do, Bill."

"It's not what I want to do, it's what I have to do," he said, with a solemnity that touched her heart. "Like Dad always says, some things you can't run away from."

This is the son that Don has made, she thought; they are lucky to have—to have had—each other.

She and Don took a walk on the beach one evening while Bill was out with his friend Dylan. There was fog rising from the surface of the ocean; a mist shrouded the harbor and obscured the jetty against which waves lapped with a steady, reassuring rhythm. They sat on the sand, their backs against the seawall.

"Ocean never stops, does it?" commented Don. "Just keeps on coming." He took a cigarette from a crumpled pack and lit it. "Are you going to marry that man . . . what's his name? Bill told me . . . I forget."

"David. His name is David. I don't know. It . . . depends."

"You ought to get married again. Be good for you. I know you like taking care of yourself and all, being independent, but a woman needs a man."

"Some do," she said. "I did. I don't know if I do, anymore." In a lighter tone, she added, "You're still the complete male chauvinist, aren't you?"

"I guess so. You used to like it, though."

"Want to know something? I still do."

He took her small hand in his big one, and she remembered how special he had made her feel, how cherished and protected. "A secret yen for male chauvinist pigs, huh?"

"No," she said, "not pigs. You were never a pig. A stubborn ox, sure, but not a pig. Billy's a lot like you in that way. Stubborn."

"I'm glad he went out with his pal tonight. He's been hanging around the house too much lately."

"He worries about you."

"No need for that. I'm going to whip this thing, you know. My old man held on for four years. I'm going to beat him with time to spare. A lot more people whip it than you think."

"Yes."

They sat in companionable silence, holding hands,

thinking their own thoughts. She knew there were things she should discuss with him—Bill's education, wills, insurance—but she did not know how to begin without sounding as though she did not believe him, thought there was no hope.

"As soon as I'm rested up a little from the treatments, I'm going back to work," he said. "Got to get the first stage of the construction done so we can raise money for the next. I have to see some people from San Diego who might be interested. Next week, when I'm not so tuckered out. Got to get what hair I have left trimmed first, though. Took a look at myself in the mirror today, thought I look like a junkyard dog with the mange."

She couldn't bring up money now. She couldn't ask him if he had made a will, if he had a lawyer, a safe-deposit box—all the things she should know. Whatever estate he had would go to Bill, and she was Bill's legal guardian. They hadn't bothered with modifying the custody agreement when Bill went to live with him—it was just between them.

A breeze came up from the ocean and she shivered. Don put his good arm around her, and she snuggled close to him. "We go back a long time, you and me," he said. "It wasn't all bad, was it?"

"No," she told him. "It wasn't all bad." Grief cascaded over her like a wave that catches a swimmer unaware, and she bit her lip to keep the anguished wail that choked her from escaping. She got up and went to the water's edge; the noise of the surf muffled her sobs, and the wind dried the tears that spilled from her eyes. Then she went back to where he sat and helped him up and they walked slowly home together.

26 Bill came home from school one afternoon a few weeks after his mother's visit and found his father packing his old Navy duffel, the one with his name stenciled across it in faded block letters. He was stuffing books, clothes, and his foul-weather gear into the bag, and muttering to himself.

"Hey, Dad, what are you doing?"

"What am I doing?" Don said irritably. "I'm packing, what does it look like I'm doing."

"Where you going?"

"Got to be on board the *Glacier* at sixteen hundred hours. Operation Deepfreeze. You know. The Pole. And liberty in Wellington. Great place, Wellington. Be good to see it again. You seen my drafting tools anywhere?"

"Sure, they're on the table in the kitchen. Uh, Dad?"

"Yes, what is it? Speak your mind, boy, no time to dawdle. Can't miss vessel movement, could lose a stripe for that, you know."

"Dad, it's tomorrow the *Glacier*'s sailing, not today. Why don't you take a little rest and I'll get your gear together for you."

Don lifted himself up from the floor of the closet with slow, stiff movements. "That's a good idea, son. You're right, I'm feeling a little peaked, must have really tied on one last night. You be sure and get me up. Got the dogwatch tonight."

"Sure, Dad, sure I will. Come on now, I'll help you."

"'S all right, I can make it, no sweat. Don't forget, now . . . sixteen hundred hours."

"I won't forget."

Sometimes his father was there, and sometimes he wasn't. Some days he was completely himself and impossible to please, like a cranky child. On those days Bill didn't stick around any longer than he had to; he took his board to the beach and surfed until he was blue with cold.

His old man didn't ever say he was sorry. Not even after that time he hit him because he couldn't find the screwdriver. The damn thing was right there in front of his face, hanging on the fucking tool rack, the one Bill made for him in shop class. He worked on that sucker for weeks, mitering the corners just right, laminating the woods so carefully, the cherry and walnut and mahogany. The Phillips was hanging there, and his father was staring right at it and couldn't see it.

He wondered what Don *was* seeing, when the damn screwdriver was right there in front of his nose. Maybe right at that moment the cancer was zapping a cell in his brain, short-circuiting a synapse, offing a few zillion neurons. It must have been something like that for his father to hit him. The blow had been so unexpected that Bill didn't have time to be afraid. It hurt, but not that bad; he'd taken worse from Todd Lewis.

No, what really knocked him over was the shock of

it. By then, he'd forgotten how scared of the old man he was when he first arrived. He'd given up expecting his father to manhandle him. Don didn't have to—his size and his quietness were scary enough. He had a look that could pulverize you, a way of hinting at the consequences of crossing him that made you think twice about trying it.

There was this book Bill had to read for English class about a guy who tries all kinds of shit to escape his fate—*Appointment in Samarra*, it was called. The time Don hit him was kind of the same thing; the blow had the force of destiny behind it, and it shocked him because he'd forgotten all about it after he'd figured out that Don wasn't ever going to throw him across a room or beat him up the side of the head or whip his ass, or do any of those things he talked about so casually. If you have strength, you hardly ever have to use it, Don said, unless you run into some idiot that wants to prove how tough he is.

After his father hit him that one time, Bill felt sort of relieved. If that was what it was like, he could take it. And he went into his room feeling pretty good about it, considering. Then later, when his old man didn't remember anything about what had happened, he began to get a little worried. Was it the tumor? Probably not, he thought. Don had said the doctors got it all, and there didn't seem to be any new lumps on his neck—Bill checked sort of surreptitiously every day. No, he figured, Don was just pissed off about something—problems at the marina, maybe, or a fight with Peggy, or just not feeling better than he did.

His old man didn't like being sick, that was for sure. On days when he seemed to feel okay, Bill could relax. Don was just like he'd been before the operation, and Bill was sure that the doctors had fucked up royally, like maybe they told the wrong guy he had cancer, got the lab reports mixed up or something. On those days, his father came home from the marina whistling. Let's go to a ball game tonight, kid, he'd say, or think you can beat your old man at chess? And they'd get out the board and go to it, and he never could—his father was just too good.

It wasn't so bad when Don was having the radiation treatments. Every day for a couple of weeks Peggy drove him to the hospital, and when she brought him home she stayed and made dinner for all of them. It was pretty neat, in fact, sitting around the table, just him and his dad and Peggy and Travis . . . sort of like those dopey old TV shows like *Father Knows Best* or *Ozzie and Harriet.* His dad would be kind of quiet, and Trav would be chattering away and Peggy would be pushing second helpings of everything on all of them, especially Don. Sometimes she stayed overnight, and Travis bunked in with Bill. Those nights, Bill never had any trouble falling asleep. But other times, when there was nobody there except him and the old man, he hardly slept at all. He'd lie there in bed, listening for the sound of Don shuffling around in the kitchen or the bathroom, and then he'd kind of doze off, until a while later, when he'd wake up and not hear anything at all. Then he'd get up and go across the hall and look in Don's room, get close enough to the bed so he could hear his father's light snore.

One time Don wasn't there, and Bill was pretty shook up until he found his father sitting out on the porch, watching the sky intently. He couldn't convince him to come inside, come back to bed, so he sat out there with him while the night waned and the sky lightened. When the sun rose in the eastern sky, his old man looked peaceful and satisfied: Well, there it is, he said, there's another day starting, and then he let Bill lead him back to his bed.

When his mother told him what the doctors had said, he wasn't really surprised. He knew it could be in your brain, or anywhere else in your body, and you'd never know it was there until it was too late. A tumor could be growing under your skin for a long time before you noticed anything was wrong. Maybe it was already there, lurking in some hidden place inside his father, when Bill came to live with him. Maybe it had been there for years; maybe it was already in Don's brain when he left Bill and his mother. Maybe that's why he left them, because the tumor was making him weird, the way it was doing now.

His mother and father together—now that was really weird. When she'd come to see them, the two of them were so lovey-dovey with each other that Bill wondered why they'd gotten divorced in the first place.

Bill couldn't actually remember anything that happened before the divorce, except for a hazy memory of a night when he woke up with really bad diarrhea. He must have been real little because he was wearing those kid pajamas with the seat flap and he couldn't get it undone by himself. He went into their room to tell them, but they didn't see him; his father's back was turned, and his mother was pounding on it with her fists. She was yelling so loud she didn't hear Bill's plea, and he couldn't help it, he had diarrhea, so he went in his pants.

That was a stupid memory to have about the only time you were ever a real family, but Bill couldn't help it, he was stuck with it. He was a little nervous when he heard his mother was coming to visit them— he half-expected her to start yelling at his old man like she had that time he messed his pants. But she didn't do anything like that, even when Don was being difficult, or expounding on something his mother felt totally the opposite about, like gun control or nuclear disarmament. His mother was definitely for both—she was always signing some petition or marching in some demonstration. And his father was just as definitely against them. Bill wasn't sure gun control was such a great thing, but he knew damn well he didn't want to get blown up by a bomb or fried by radiation.

It was a funny thing about radiation. It could kill you or it could help you. He thought it might be working on his father. Since a week or two after the treatments, Don was a lot better. Oh, he couldn't go ten rounds with Ali, but Don and Bill had gone sailing that day and his dad worked the ropes and handled the tiller. It wasn't a big boat like *Pandora*, in fact it was Bill's little sailing dinghy, but there was a stiff breeze and it wasn't exactly a cinch to handle. They went out pretty far from the marina, and it looked like a big storm was headed their way, but Bill wasn't worried. He could handle it if he had to, and even if he couldn't, he'd have still felt completely safe on the water with his father—in any water, or any weather. Even sick, the old man handled a boat like it was part of him.

His mom had told him his father was going to die, but maybe he wasn't, not for a while yet. Bill didn't like to think about it; when he did, he wished he was a little kid again, too young to understand. Or else old, so old he'd seen plenty of people die and he was used to it. He couldn't be a baby again, but maybe he'd be a grown-up when it did happen. At least grown-up enough so he didn't have to live with his mom again. Not that it would be that terrible, probably. They got along a lot better now than they used to. She was still asking him dumb questions, like how do you feel, Billy, how do you *really* feel, but now sometimes he didn't mind telling her.

Still, he'd just as soon stay where he was: home, with his father. He knew it couldn't last forever. He knew his dad was going to die. But maybe it wouldn't happen for a long time.

27 The first stage of construction was finished, but Don hadn't had any luck raising the second-stage financing. Sales were down some because his inventory was low; he didn't get around as much as he had, up and down the coast, locating the kind of boats people who knew something about sailing wanted. In a few weeks the kid would have his license, he'd let him drive. They'd go around to a few yards and take a look.

Driving was difficult; his eyesight wasn't as good as it had been, and he was supposed to get glasses, but he kept putting it off. His own driver's license had expired and he forgot to send it in for renewal, which meant he had to take another test and another eye examination. He wasn't sure he'd pass, so he kept driving on the expired license and hoped he didn't get stopped.

His service department had plenty of work, but it wasn't getting done. Ricco's guys had been fighting among themselves, now that the construction crew was gone, and Ricco was boozing it up lately, too, coming in still drunk from the night before or so hungover that he was worse than useless. The yardbirds ignored their chief and slacked off, shot craps while

Ricco slept it off in the supply locker or waved their
long knives at each other, shouting curses and insults
in Spanish and Portuguese. Ordinarily Don went
among them and broke up the fights, but now he
didn't. Like he told the kid, don't make promises you
can't keep or threats you can't carry out. And he
wasn't sure, if it came right down to it, that he could
keep those damn spics from turning their knives on
him.

He didn't seem to be getting worse, but he wasn't
getting better, either. His headaches weren't as fierce,
but he ached all over and had little appetite for food.
Strange, since he seemed to have acquired a gut, loose
flesh around his midsection that he'd never had before. Of course, he wasn't getting as much exercise as
usual, that might account for it. He'd been an active
man, walking the two miles between the marina and
his house twice a day, scrambling all over the boats,
swimming a mile in the ocean every morning. But
now it was even hard to walk a few yards; his bum leg
dragged behind him and threw his stride off, and the
effort needed to keep it moving along was exhaust-
ing. Goddamn, he thought, I used to be able to work
all day, booze and screw and party all night—now I'm
lucky if I can get it up at all.

A side effect of the radiation, the docs said. It'll
come back when you're stronger. Don't force it, don't
get yourself all worked up about it; the impotence as-
sociated with radiation therapy is temporary.

Maybe. Or maybe the part of his brain that controlled his cock got knocked out by all the rads. That's
what they called the invisible cancer-killing rays—
rads. It sounded like some kind of a screw or nut,
something you'd find in a drawer in a hardware
store—Hey, mac, give me a few molly bolts, and while
you're at it, toss in a couple of rads.

It happened the first time with Anne. He hadn't meant it to happen, any of it. He hadn't been fooled by her story about a business trip to L.A., but what the hell. She knew there was trouble and she was worried about the kid.

About him, too, he guessed. She might have stopped hurting, but she hadn't gotten over him. She was good with the wisecracks, and could joke about stuff that went on between them back then, but she still loved him. He'd seen the pain in her eyes the first time she saw him. He'd seen her wince a couple of times when he said something mean. He hadn't meant to, but it was right after the treatments ended, and he was burned out and peevish.

The first night she was there, he and the kid had an argument about something, and the kid went off to his room to sulk. She got up from the couch and started to follow him.

"Leave the kid alone," he said. "He'll come around."

She stayed in there with him for a while, and when she came out he heard the kid's door lock behind her. "What's the matter?" he asked. "Bill still got a wild hair up his ass?"

"He said he wants to be alone," she replied, and began to make up the couch.

"Let him do that himself," Don said. "If he's going to lie in his bed, let him at least make it."

"He wants to sleep in his own room tonight, so I'll take the couch."

She changed into a gown and robe, and they sat up and talked for a while, and then he said good night and went into his bedroom. He couldn't sleep; he got up and shuffled around, and the noise woke her up.

"Do you need anything?" she asked, coming into his room.

"A little company, maybe, if you're not tired."

"I'm not," she said. "Go back to bed, and I'll make you some warm milk."

"Add a little brandy to it as long as you're up," he said, and she came back a few moments later with a tray. She sat on his bed and watched him drink, and when he was finished she took the cup from him and stroked his face. Her hand felt soft and cool, and he took it to hold in his own, and then he kissed her.

It was a sweet, sad kiss, full of nostalgia and love—on both sides, he had to admit—and it went on for a time. She leaned forward and he could see the curve of her breasts beneath her robe. She still had wonderful breasts, round and firm; she saw how he looked at them, and she guided his hand there. One thing led to another; he had a fierce erection, stronger than it had been since the operation.

"It's been a long time," he said, and she saw the desire in his eyes. She stood up and began to remove her nightclothes. As she did, he saw all the familiar curves of her body; she watched him watching her, and wanting her, and she took a long time undressing. She came to bed then, and he touched her bare skin. He wanted to be inside her. He wanted to close his eyes when he came, and when he opened them again he wanted it to be twenty years ago, when he was young and healthy and life had so many possibilities, all of them shining and golden. But his erection went away before he even entered her.

"It's okay," she whispered. "It's nice being here like this, close, just the two of us." Soon she was asleep, her hand tucked under her cheek in the old way. Like a child, he thought, like Billy sleeps, her arms and legs pulled in close against her so no one could hurt her while she slept. He wanted to wake her, to lay his head on her breast and tell her how scared he was, not of dying but of getting sicker first, of being helpless.

He wasn't ready to die yet. There was too much to do. Boats to sail and a good woman to love, a business to build and a son to finish raising.

Don't let it hurt—that was what Billy said when he had to have a splinter removed from his finger or a cut washed out with green soap that stung. Promise me you won't let it hurt, Mommy, and Anne always had, even when she knew it was going to.

He wanted her to promise him that dying wouldn't hurt, that Billy wouldn't forget him, that she had forgiven him for the bad times. He wanted comfort; perhaps he wanted absolution. But he knew that if he woke her she would cry, and he would have to comfort her, and so he let her sleep.

He never tried to say those things to Peggy. She was stronger than Anne was, and she wasn't the crying type, but she had plenty on her mind already. She must be wondering what was going to happen to the marina if they couldn't raise the money they needed to complete the expansion. He'd raised the subject with her once lately, and she told him not to worry about her, a tax loss for this year was actually what she needed, since she'd made a lot of extra money during income-tax season. She was one strong lady, and she would probably even understand why he'd tried to make love to Anne that night.

Still, he didn't think he'd tell her—no reason to push his luck, what was left of it. Peggy wasn't the jealous type, but it didn't do any good to stir a woman up unless you had to. She'd probably know, anyway. She knew a lot of things he never had the words to say. She could tell by the set of his shoulders whether he'd had a good night, if he'd been able to sleep. She knew when he was cold, or tired, or hungry. She knew when he was frightened, too. Sometimes when they sat on *Pandora*'s bridge and watched the sun go down she reached over and took his hand and talked about the cruise they were going to take someday with the boys, down to the Marquesas and to Tahiti and back through the Hawaiian Islands.

She knew when he didn't feel like talking, when he wanted to be by himself. She'd kiss him good-bye, pat the boy on the head, and go back to *Pandora*. He wondered what she thought about, the nights she spent on her boat, with her boy safe and asleep in his bunk, the water lapping at the dock and the bumpers sliding back and forth between the hull and the pilings. Did she dream about Nat McCarthy the way Anne, Don was pretty sure, still dreamed about him? Or did Peggy dream of strong, healthy men she had not met, who would dance all night with her and then love her fiercely until morning?

He wondered if Peggy would be there when he died, and the thought made him uneasy. He wasn't sure he wanted her there. He knew he would not return to the hospital again, no matter how bad it got. He wouldn't have more radiation, he wouldn't take the pills that gave him the dry heaves or the other ones that made his vision cloudy. He wouldn't let them stick him full of tubes and pipes and needles, or hook him up to the machines that whooshed up and down in time with his breathing. He would not be connected to a screen that told his life in graphs and numbers, flashing with every stumbling heartbeat, every grasping breath.

He did not know what he would do when it got that bad, but he knew he would not see the doctor again—the young, arrogant doctor who had told him it's your life, buddy. A true diagnosis—it was his life, his own, and if it came to that, he'd end it, before it tortured him more than any man could stand. He was no hero like his old man.

The kid, though—he wasn't sure what the kid would think if *his* old man didn't tough it out to the end. If, say, he took a dip in the ocean some morning, right after he saw the sun come up.

When Don was a little boy, his mother told him that dying was like going to sleep. He hadn't seen his own father die, but he was pretty sure the old bastard sat straight up before it happened and spat death right in the eye. He'd have called Don a gutless piece of shit for even thinking about sneaking out the easy way, and probably the kid would too. Hell of a thing to leave a kid like that, thinking his old man was a coward.

"Hey, Bluebeard, you look like you're ready to make the minions jump the plank!" Peggy had re-christened him when he'd grown a beard after the radiation treatments. Shaving wasn't easy with his bum hand, and the hair on his face somehow compensated for its lack on his head. Today he was wearing a patch to ease the strain on his bad eye; with his beard trimmed to a rakish point by the barber, he looked, she told him, exactly like the legendary pirate.

"Minions don't jump the plank, they polish it." He put his good arm around her waist and squeezed the soft fleshy part between her shorts and her halter— God, she felt good. Her skin bounced back from his touch with a satisfying elasticity—every part of her glowed with health and aliveness.

"You having a good day, hmm?" She inspected

him critically, as if searching for signs that he had deteriorated since she'd last seen him.

"Pretty good,"

"Feel like taking a drive, then?"

"Where to?"

"The wooden boat show at Newport Beach."

"What about the kids?"

"Bill said he'd feed Trav dinner and put him to bed after they shot some baskets. It was thoughtful of him to rig that hoop up behind the boat shed and rake it up so they could play on it."

"Did you happen to notice who got roped into helping him build the forms for the concrete, though?"

"Yes, but he mixed it and rolled it all himself. Travis loves it. He said it's the best birthday present he got this year."

"When were you planning on leaving for Newport?"

"As soon as I could talk you into it. It's almost closing time. Ricco's around, he can keep an eye on things."

"About time he did," he grumbled, but he allowed Peggy to get him a sweater in case he got the chills again, and lead him to the car.

"No arguments about who drives, Don," she said. "Let me."

"Certainly. Would I deprive you of the chance to run some poor sonuvabitch off the road? Not on your life, lady."

At the boat show they ran into Karl and his girl-friend, and after it was over they all went out for a drink together. Don hadn't seen much of Karl lately, and Karl wasn't sending much survey work his way, either. He knew for a fact that Karl was using another marina, closer to San Diego, near the commercial docks. When Don brought it up, Karl was embarrassed. Just until you get to feeling better, he said, but that was a couple of months ago and he hadn't sent him any customers since. Tonight, Karl couldn't seem to look him straight in the eye, and when Don made any reference to business, Karl changed the subject.

There was a band playing some disco crap, and Karl danced with Peggy while Don sat at the table and made idle conversation with the girlfriend. He drank more liquor than he should have, and snapped at Peggy more than he meant to. She drove them to the marina and he honked to signal Bill to come out.

"Damn kid, where is he?" Don fumed.

"He probably fell asleep. Let him stay on the boat, he can go to school from here in the morning."

"No. He belongs at home."

She sighed. "Have it your way. You usually do."

That stung. He put his hand over hers and said, "Hey, Peg, I'm sorry. I know I'm a real pain in the ass sometimes."

"Yes, you are." She smiled. "You know, that's the first time you've ever apologized to me?"

"Not true . . . I said I was sorry I called you a lardass once."

"I don't remember that."

"I do."

"I love you."

"I love you too. Go get the kid will you?"

"You sure you feel like driving home? I could take you, then pick you up in the morning."

"Nah, the kid'll drive, he wouldn't pass up the chance. Getting his license soon, wants the practice. Shake him out and tell him to get moving. I'll see you tomorrow."

That night he had a bad dream, and woke up disoriented, not sure where he was. He thought he was a kid again, back at Culver; he heard reveille being blown, and knew he'd get busted for sure if he didn't get his uniform on. But he couldn't find it in the closet. He crashed around his room, pulling clothes off hangers, tossing them in a pile on the floor. When Bill came in to see what was happening, he didn't know him at first; he thought he was Jack McRae, his old Culver platoon commander.

Bill led him back to the living room and sat him down on the couch. He brought him a sleeping pill and some orange juice. Then he changed the sopping bedsheets and hung up all the clothes Don had thrown around the room. He helped him into the bathroom and waited until he peed and rinsed his hands and face. Then he walked him back to the bedroom, and turned the covers back so he could get in.

"Sometimes Mom does this for me when I get sick," Bill said. "She says you always feel better with clean sheets."

"Miss your mother much, sport?"

"Once in a while. But I'd rather be here."

"Good. I like having you here."

"You do?"

"Beats a poke in the eye with a sharp stick. Get along to bed now, you got school tomorrow."

"Okay. You want me to leave the light on in the bathroom?"

"Sure, if you want to. When you were a kid we always left the light on for you. Yeah, go ahead, leave it on."

"Goodnight, Dad."

"G'night, son."

28 Several things happened in November that convinced Bill his father was getting better.

The first sign was the return of Don's appetite. Bill figured it was the cannabis they'd given his old man that made him hungry all the time.

"Man, that's the weirdest case of the munchies I ever saw," he said one night while his father was fixing himself a snack. "My father, the world's first peanut butter and banana pothead."

"You got a better idea?"

"Yeah, maybe." The next day Bill checked a cookbook out of the library. He sort of liked messing around the kitchen—"Only in self defense, you understand," he told Don—and some of the meals he prepared weren't too bad. He experimented, trying to find things his father would eat and that were nutritious, too. Some of them tasted terrible, but a few weren't bad, and Don started to gain back the weight he'd lost in the hospital.

Another thing was that the old man's hair had grown back—not only what the radiation had destroyed, but even in places where he'd been going bald for years. Personally Bill didn't think getting bald was so terrible, but his father was ultrasensitive about it so he went easy on the wisecracks.

Don was sleeping better at night, too, and there hadn't been any Looney Tune times, the strange interludes when his father was confused and disoriented, for a couple of weeks. At Thanksgiving they took the *Pandora* to Coronado for a couple of days; the pallor disappeared from Don's face, and his radiation burns faded.

The old man was taking hold again, a fact that became eminently clear when Bill got a midterm warning in chemistry. He thought about not giving it to his father, but only briefly—the warning was bad enough, but if he lied about it and got caught, the shit would really hit the fan.

"Looks to me like you've been slacking off, kid," Don said when Bill showed him the note from school. "You planning to make this a habit?"

"No, sir."

"Think you might need to spend a little extra time bringing your grade up?"

"Yes, sir."

"Glad to hear it. You won't mind missing the Chargers game Sunday, then."

Shit. His dad had gotten a pair of fifty-yard-line seats, and he'd been looking forward to the game. The old man went with Ricco instead, without so much as a "Too bad, sport."

Shit. He guessed he deserved it, but still, shit. Those chemistry labs were a bitch and he'd been goofing off in class. When the teacher called him, his mind was a total blank . . . he was off somewhere, cruising the Pacific, completely spaced. Studying at home was no picnic, either. Don didn't go out often at night, and when he was home the TV was on most of the time; it was easier on his eyes than reading, he said, which was understandable, but that didn't explain why the volume control was always at maximum. It could be his father was getting deaf, Bill thought; he didn't know if it was a symptom of the cancer or a side effect of the treatment. Or maybe he was trying to drown out something else. It was hard to tell with Old Stoneface, he never gave you a clue to what he was really thinking.

Still, Don seemed to be getting stronger every day. Peggy pushed him about seeing the doctor again, but he refused. "Anybody can tell I'm getting better," he told Bill. "The radiation shrunk the tumors, like it was supposed to—I don't need the medics to tell me that."

Christmas was coming up and Bill didn't know what to do about it. He didn't like the idea of leaving his father alone in the house, even though the old man was looking pretty good. "Listen, when I need a wet nurse I'll tell you," Don said when Bill brought up the subject of staying in California over the holidays.

"But Peggy won't be here either." Bill said.

"They're only going to be away for a couple of days. I'll be fine. What do you think, your old man needs a baby-sitter?"

Peggy's father was having an eightieth-birthday party in San Francisco and, as she explained to Bill, she really had to go. "Don't worry so much," she said. "I won't be gone long. We'll have Christmas together and I'll be here New Year's Eve, too—we're going to a party. Travis is going to stay up north for a few days with Nat, and I'll be here to look after Don. Go to Seattle and have a good time. You've been a real help to your dad—to me, too—and you deserve a vacation."

"You're going, just like you planned," said his father. "And no arguments. What's the matter, you think I can't manage by myself? Seems to me I made out pretty good by myself for more years than you got on you, sport. You go up there and keep your mother company. But don't give her any trouble, or I'll bust your ass."

Billy didn't plan on giving his mother, or anyone else, any trouble. He was looking forward to taking some long, swooping runs, feeling the snow sting his face and the moguls disappear under the tips of his skis. To sitting around and bullshitting with Chris. To making Christmas cookies with his mother. To getting away for a little while.

"I'll be around when you get back, you know," Don said. "I'm not going anywhere."

The night before Bill left they exchanged their presents. Don gave him new ski boots and a copy of Bowditch's *Small Boat Handling and Navigation.* Bill gave his father a hand-laminated wooden case for cuff links, change, and all the odds and ends he emptied out of his pockets every night. He had chosen the woods carefully, planing and sanding and polishing them until they gleamed.

At the airport, his father hugged Bill with his good arm and rumpled his hair. "Have a great vacation, kid," he said. "Don't break any bones on the slopes, hear? We've got some cruising to do when you get back here."

"Yeah. Listen, take care of yourself, will you?"

"Sure thing. Take care of your own self."

He'd only been home for a couple of hours when he felt a strong urge to talk to the old man, just see how he was. "Hey, Ma, can I call Dad to tell him I got here okay?" he asked.

"I forgot to tell you, he called while you were at Chris's. But sure, call if you want to."

Bill could tell by the way Don teased him that his father was glad to hear from him. "Well, well. I was just sitting here enjoying a nice cold beer and thinking how quiet and peaceful it is without you around. No rock and roll music, no lousy singing in the shower. And plenty of beer left in the fridge. I guess there's nobody around to sneak it out when they think I'm not looking."

"Hey, Dad, I never . . . well, yeah, I did. Last night. I thought you wanted one so I opened it, but you were asleep and it was stupid just to throw it out."

"Yeah, sure. Everything okay up there? How's your mother?"

"She's okay, we're all fine. I just thought I'd call and make sure you hadn't busted up the Canterbury tonight, taken on some big palooka while you were putting a few drinks away."

"They don't make many palookas bigger 'n me, son."

"Yeah, I forgot, you're the original Paul Bunyan, right?"

"Big enough to keep you in line, anyway."

"Sure, Pops. Well, listen, I'll see you around."

"'Less I see you first. Thanks for calling."

"Nada. Night, Dad. I'll call you on Christmas."

"Okay. Give my best to your mom."

He called again on Christmas afternoon, but there was no answer. He felt afraid, suddenly, and tried the *Pandora*. He knew Peggy's number as well as he did his own. When she answered she sounded kind of sleepy.

"Who? Oh, hi, Bill, how are you? Good . . . that's good . . . you did? How super . . . I'm glad you like it, Travis picked it out. Yes, your father's here. No, we weren't sleeping. Just a minute. I'll get him."

Don came on the line and Bill was glad to hear his voice. "Hello, kid . . . I'm glad to talk to you, too, even if you do have a lousy sense of timing . . . No, I wasn't sleeping, I was showing this mouthy broad here that there are better things to do in bed than talk—ow, Peggy, quit that! You okay, Bill? . . . That's good . . . fine, fine, never better. Will you quit worrying? Everything's fine . . . Yeah, I'm eating okay. Peggy cooked this damn goose, just for the two of us, somebody had to eat it. Did you get a lump of coal in your stocking? . . . You didn't, huh? Guess they screwed up and gave some other kid your coal. Poor bugger, he's probably been behaving like a perfect kid for weeks now, and he gets a lump of coal and you get skis and tapes and a new leather jacket. That kid's been waiting for Santa Claus forever, and you're sitting pretty—well, that's the way it goes, some guys luck out and some don't . . . Yeah, I'll be there at the plane to pick you up, 'less I got a hangover. Peg and I are going to tie on one on New Year's Eve, I haven't been pie-eyed in too damn long, that's just what the doctor ordered . . . Sure, I said I'd be there, didn't I? Yeah, me too . . . Merry Christmas, son."

The day before New Year's Bill went skiing at Crystal with Chris. It was a fantastic day; the sun was shining, and when he looked up to the summit of Rainier, he figured the Indians were right when they called it a sacred mountain—if there was a God, and He ever came to earth, He'd be dumb not to make Mount Rainier His throne.

On the lift he bumped into Clary Redman. She'd gotten cuter, he thought . . . hell, she'd gotten beautiful.

"Bill!" she cried with delight. "Oh, Bill, I'm so glad to see you! When did you come home? How long are you going to be here? Are you going to Ingraham next semester?"

She was just the same as ever, a living Chatty Cathy doll, but he enjoyed listening to her, and they skied together for the rest of the day. He felt a little guilty about deserting Chris, but he looked down as they rode the chair up the mountain and saw his friend at the end of the lift line putting the make on some girl he didn't know, and he figured it's every man for himself, pal.

"I heard your dad was sick. Is he going to be okay?" Clary asked.

"Yeah, he's a tough old goat, he'll be fine. Hey, Clary, you still going with Todd Lewis?"

"Oh, no . . . he turned out to be a total creep."

"Always knew he had it in him. Say, look, I promised my mom I'd get the car home by seven o'clock, and I'm leaving tomorrow . . . I don't suppose you want to go to a movie or something tonight, do you?"

"Sure I do."

"You do? With me?"

"Mmm hmm." She smiled at him. "Or we could just stay home and play with Mudge."

"Your folks going out?"

"Uh huh."

He rounded up Chris and they got in a last run before their lift tickets expired. In the car he was relaxed and pleasantly tired, but he kept a close watch on the road while Chris smoked some weed and changed the tapes in the deck. He didn't want any dope—he felt great, and besides, he'd promised his mother he wouldn't smoke or drink when he was driving. He'd gotten his license on his sixteenth birthday, and for the past few weeks he'd been chauffeuring his old man around. His father was a bitch of a backseat driver, but if Bill turned the car radio up loud, he couldn't hear him.

He knew right away something was wrong. He could tell as soon as he walked into the house. His mother was sitting in the wing chair by the fireplace, and there wasn't a single light on. She was playing music, that old stuff she hummed sometimes, the songs she said she'd fallen in love to, when she was young.

She didn't hear him come in. He saw her first, with the light from the fire casting deep shadows on her face. She was singing along with the record, and the tears were streaming down her cheeks, and he knew.

"It's Dad, isn't it?"

She nodded, but kept singing, in a high clear voice that broke just before she stopped. He waited until the song was over. "He's dead, isn't he?"

When she turned her face toward him, he noticed that she was old. Older than she had been that morning, older than he'd ever seen her. She held her arms out to him but he turned away. Her grief was hers, and his was his.

She got up and went into the kitchen to make cocoa, and when she came back with the cup he asked her, "How did it happen?"

She shook her head. "I don't know exactly. Peggy came to the house and let herself in. She'd called him this morning from San Francisco and told him she'd be back by lunch time. He wasn't at the marina so she went looking for him. He was in the bathroom, half dressed. He'd been shaving, or maybe trimming his beard. They said an aneurysm, or a blood clot . . . it was probably very fast, a few seconds and then he collapsed on the floor. Peggy said he looked surprised. She said he thought he was going to beat it. He'd started having the headaches again a few days ago and she wanted him to go back to the hospital for more radiation, but he wouldn't."

He said he'd be there when I came back, Bill thought. He said so. The sonuvabitching bastard promised.

"He did it his own way, Billy. You mustn't feel guilty, he wanted it like this. He didn't want you to see him suffering. This is the way he wanted it. He would have chosen it if he could. Quick and quiet."

"Alone."

"Not really, Billy. You were with him, in his heart."

"That's not the same." He made a fist of one hand and punched the palm of his other one. "I knew I should have stayed, but he wouldn't let me. It wouldn't have happened if I'd been there."

"Oh, Billy, darling, that's not true. Don't do this to yourself. Be glad for him that it happened this way."

I wish I never knew him. I wish I never went down there and never saw him and never lived with him. He did it to me again, the sonuvabitch, Bill thought.

"Oh, Billy, he loved you so damn much," his mother said.

He never knew anything could hurt this much. He wondered if dying was as bad as this, and he thought it probably wasn't. He thought it was Don's pain he was feeling . . . that when his father died it all slipped away and somehow ended up in him. That made it easier; he could take his father's pain. He could do that much for him, at least.

She wouldn't let him go back to California. "He didn't want a funeral, Bill. He wouldn't want you there while they put him in the ground. He's . . . there'll be a cremation in a day or so. Peggy said she'd send the ashes here. We'll do something. Scatter them over the Sound, maybe."

"I want to go. It's my home."

"Your home is here now, Bill. With me."

He knew she didn't say that to hurt him, but that didn't make it any easier. Talking to Peggy was almost as bad; it was like his mother brainwashed her or something. "It's for the best this way," she said. "The house, the marina . . . it's not the same without him. You wouldn't want to be here, believe me."

"You going to keep running the place?"

"In a few months, maybe. I'm not up to it right now. Ricco can handle things in the meantime, and Karl. He thinks he has a backer for us."

"I could run it," he said. "Not the business end, but the yard. Well, maybe not run it, but I could help Ricco out some."

"Not now," she said firmly. "But if I come back in the summer, maybe you can come down and stay with us on *Pandora*."

"You going somewhere?"

"I think I'll cast off for a while. Travis is staying with Nat for now. I think I'm going to head out to sea until I figure out how long it's going to be before I feel like getting up in the morning again."

"I know how you feel."

"Yes, I think you do. Bill, he loved you a great deal. You know that, don't you?"

He wiped his eyes. "I guess."

"Don't guess anymore, Bill Manning. Know. Be very, very sure. Your father loved you more than anything, anyone in the world. He was very proud of you, so you do him proud. Hear me?"

"Yeah, I hear you. Hey, Peggy . . . stay in touch, will you?"

"Of course I will." Her voice was husky with tears, and he could hear the sobs catch in her throat so he hung up the phone.

He walked down to the lake and turned south toward Seward Park. He walked for a long time, until the sky lightened and he realized it was almost morning. Across the lake to the east, the sun crept over the horizon. That's it, he thought. Another day.

Coming back, he looked up the hill; in the lucent dawn, he saw the weather vane on top of his house. Except it wasn't his, anymore. It wasn't where he belonged now. He belonged in California, sitting on the seawall with his father, waiting until the sun's last rays had disappeared over the horizon and his dad stood up and grunted his satisfaction: That's it, then, another day done.

He belonged out on the bow of his boat, hanging over the edge, staring down at the sea until his old man called him, his deep voice booming across the jetty: Get that thing made fast now and get your ass home for chow.

He belonged with his father, but his father was dead, and he wasn't.

He looked up again, to where the light gleamed through the trees and his mother waited. She had loved his old man, too, and he went up to see if she needed anything.

29 Some days it seemed that Bill had never been away. Anne thought he was quieter, more withdrawn than before; when they ate meals together or drove somewhere in the car, or worked at the projects Anne thought up to keep him busy, silence settled around them like dust on a windowsill. He rarely talked about California and never mentioned his father; she took her cues from him and steered the conversation away from those subjects, afraid to intrude on his grief or remind him of his loss.

When classes resumed after the holidays he enrolled in school; she held her breath and waited for the familiar summons from his teachers and advisers. When he brought home no academic warnings at midterm she called his school on a flimsy pretense to learn if he had destroyed or diverted them, and discovered that, in fact, he was doing respectably well in his classes and had caused no disciplinary problems. She asked him once if he wanted to "see" someone— Dr. Wilson, for instance—and although his "No" was delivered in a neutral and unemphatic tone, she saw for a brief second in his eyes a flash of something that could have been anger, or derision, or even fear.

Don't push the river if you have no life jacket, she told herself, and did not insist, or even bring the subject up again. As long as there was no reason to think that Bill had resumed his old habits, and as long as the points of dispute between them were resolved without rancor or abuse, she was satisfied, if occasionally uneasy. He was two years older now, she thought, and what he had been through in the previous months had further matured him. She experienced his silent grief for his father as a stab in her own heart, the way she had felt the pain of his childish illnesses and injuries.

She mourned Don in a different way. She had settled with him before he died, erased her anger for the times he had hurt her, emptied the last dregs in the vessel of her pain while he was still alive to receive them. Perhaps he had not acknowledged his failure to love her enough, or made apologies, but he had made amends, in his own way, by rescuing Billy. She had forgiven him. Sometimes she dreamed of him, and when, awake, she realized that he was dead—that she would never see or hear or touch him again—she remembered how much she had loved him. And since she could not now summon up the old anger, too, she knew that she, at last, was free.

"Aren't you taking the bus home?" Clary asked.

"I feel like walking." He adjusted the daypack on his shoulders and started toward home, walking swiftly, but Clary caught up with him at the corner. He would have crossed against the light but there was a traffic cop there, and he wasn't in the mood for a hassle.

"Mind if I walk with you?" Clary asked.

"It's a free country," he said.

They walked in silence for several blocks. Clary

sensed his mood and kept quiet—not without effort, he suspected. She talked the way other people breathed—effortlessly, constantly, without stopping. But today she didn't say a word, not the whole long three-mile distance to his house, which was only a few blocks from her own.

"Well, this is it," he said. "See you tomorrow."

"Sure. Hey, Bill?"

"Yeah?"

"I'm really sorry about your father."

"Yeah." He started up the stairs to his house and then he stopped and turned around. "Do you want to come in?"

She considered his offer gravely. "If you want me to," she said.

Inside, he dropped his books on the hall table. Clary followed him into the kitchen. He took bread and peanut butter and jelly from the refrigerator, set them on the counter, and made them each a sandwich.

"You don't happen to have a banana around here, do you?" asked Clary. "I have this thing for peanut butter and banana sandwiches."

"That's weird, I never knew anyone who liked . . ." The thing that lived inside him circled his solar plexus like an octopus enveloping its prey. He imagined it that way, cold and dark and many-tentacled, creeping out from his depths, slithering through his secret places, waiting until he was distracted to strike, to lash him and sting him and squeeze the life out of him.

"Uh, Clary . . . would you mind leaving? I mean, finish your sandwich first if you want, but—"

"No."

How could she do this to him? Didn't she know he didn't feel like having anyone around? Sure, he'd asked her in, but that was because she practically forced him, not saying anything all the way to his house, and then saying that, right out loud like that. Sorry. She was sorry about his father. If she was really sorry, she'd get the hell out.

He shrugged his shoulders as if to say it's up to you, do what you want, and went upstairs to his room.

"Bill? It's me, Clary. Let me come in, okay?"

He didn't answer and she pushed his door open anyway. Just like his mother. Was there any woman in the whole fucking world who knew enough just to leave him alone?

She came in and sat on the bed. "You really miss him, don't you?"

"Yeah."

"I know. When Daisy died I felt the same way."

"Daisy was a goddamned dog, Clary."

"I know, but all the same, I loved her. And she loved me, too. Remember how she used to follow me to school?"

"Yeah . . . hey, look, Clary . . . I know you're trying to be nice, and I know I'm supposed to say thank you, but I don't need this, you know? I really don't need this one fucking bit, if you want the truth." She cringed as if he had struck her and the hurt look in her eyes was like . . . like . . . like Daisy, he thought, after she'd been hit by the car. "I'm sorry," he said, more gently. "It's just that . . . oh, shit, I don't know. Sometimes I remember something about him, and it gets to me, and I get . . . weird."

"I guess it's not like losing a dog, no matter how much you loved it, is it?" said Clary.

"You can always get another dog."

"I guess so," she said. "Billy . . . do you still want me to leave?"

"I don't care," he said. "It's up to you. If you want to."

"Then I think I'll stay," she said.

In March Bill's grades began to slip and in April he started missing school. At first he complained of vague aches and pains, and Anne allowed him to stay home a couple of times. The third time it happened, she made him go to the doctor, who examined him thoroughly and could find nothing to explain the symptoms. Two days later, when Bill told her he thought he was coming down with the flu, she insisted that he go to school.

"There's nothing wrong with you," she said. "Dr. Abbott says you're perfectly healthy."

"What does he know, he's not me," Bill said sullenly.

"He knows as much as I know, which is that there's no reason for you to be feeling sick."

"So?"

"So get your books and hit the road, sport."

"Don't call me that!" he said angrily. "Just don't call me that."

"Okay," she said evenly. "Get your books, Bill, and go to school now."

He was moody and snappish for a few days, and then he seemed to calm down. Something like peace reigned until she received a call from the vice-principal of Ingraham High School. She left her office after lunch in order to be home at the time Bill usually returned from school. He expressed no surprise at finding her there; he tossed his pack on the hall table and went into the kitchen to fix his usual after-school snack. She followed him there, and poured herself a cup of coffee.

"I hear you've been suspended until after spring

vacation," she said. "You've been skipping for most of this month, signing my name to your excuses, and you've been asked to leave class twice before today for—what did he call it?"

"Substance abuse."

"What substance have you been abusing, Bill?"

"You know, so why are you asking me? You found the dope in my room."

"I haven't been in your room. Not when you're not in it, or when I haven't asked permission to come in."

"So? So what does that make you, some kind of paragon of virtue or something?"

"No, but my virtues—or vices—aren't what we're talking about here. Yours are."

"Well, we can start with the virtues, that'll only take a second, or should we get right to vices, huh?"

"Why don't we talk about what you're going to do for the next three weeks, until school starts again, instead?"

"Look, I already know what you're gonna say, Ma, so don't bother."

"Oh?"

"Yeah. You're grounded, you can't use the car, you don't get your allowance, and you do some work around the house, clean the basement or something. Oh, yeah, and you go talk to a shrink, and you do some extra credit work in chemistry and English because otherwise you're going to flunk them and then you'll have to repeat them next year or you'll never get into college or you'll grow warts on your palms or some shit like that. Spare me, will ya?" He got up from the kitchen table and pushed past her, and he was almost out of the kitchen when she said, "Am I as predictable as all that, Bill?"

He turned, and there was a look on his face that

was half scorn, half pity, a look so much like Don's that it sent a shiver down her spine. "Just about," he said.

The next evening at dinner she said, "You'd better set the alarm for tomorrow morning."

"What for? I'm not going to school, I'm suspended, remember? And I'm grounded, right, so I can't go anywhere. Why do I have to set the alarm?"

"Because you have to be at the cannery at eight a.m.," she said calmly. "They need somebody to work in the packing plant, a helper, to unload fish, clean up after the cutters, haul ice—your basic shit work, sounds like. And that somebody"—she smiled sweetly—"is you. Minimum wage, time and a half for overtime, and probably not much chance for advancement. Unless you work out, as Joe says, or want to keep working there instead of going back to school."

"Who the fuck is Joe?" he said. There was no question about it; she definitely had his attention.

"Joe Garcia is a man I know who owns the cannery. He's the one who's giving you the job. As a favor to me."

"Who says I'm gonna do it? You ever been in a cannery? That's real shit work."

"It's about the only thing a sixteen-year-old kid without a high school diploma is qualified to do at this very moment in history, given the fact that there is a lot of unemployment these days and there are very few other jobs available." She looked at him evenly. "It comes down to this, Bill—you take it or leave it. If you live here, you live by my rules. You go to school, you stay out of trouble, you do what's expected of you, and you get supported, with whatever advantages I can give you and whatever help you need to finish growing up and making a decent life for yourself."

"And if I don't? If I don't live by your rules?"

"Then you're on your own. And you can consider this little stint in the cannery as a going-away present. It's fairly representative of what you'll have to do to survive."

"There's other ways to survive," he said. "I could find some other job."

"Yes, but not by tomorrow, which is when, if you don't take this job, I want you out of the house."

"So what? I could stay plenty of places—Chris's, maybe. Or I could go live on the streets. Plenty of kids do."

"I've thought of that, Bill. I've thought of all the ways you might destroy your life if I throw you out." And all the ways you might if I don't, she said silently, prayerfully.

"And that doesn't worry you, huh?"

"It worries me quite a bit. But it's a risk I'm willing to take."

"How come?" he asked.

"Because I think you do want to survive. I'm just not sure you know it yet." She got up from the table. "I'm going to stay at David's tonight. Here's the cannery address, and you know David's number if you need me for anything."

He gave her a look of grudging respect, and then, unexpectedly, he chuckled.

"Care to share the joke?" she asked.

"It's no joke," he said. "I just thought I heard the old man clapping, that's all."

He stood by the Vega, jiggling the car keys, waiting for his mother to say a good-bye to the last wedding guests. Finally they stopped chewing her ear off and left, and she came toward him, tripping over her long skirt.

"I guess you're anxious to get going," she said.

"I want to get a decent campsite before it gets dark."

"Where are you going to stay tonight?"

"Cannon Beach, maybe, if traffic's not heavy."

"You have everything you need?"

"I think so. I didn't want to take much . . . there's a bunch of stuff down there I may want to bring back."

"I'll miss you," she said.

"Hey, lady, you'll be on your honeymoon. If David's any kind of man at all, you won't have time to miss me."

She grinned, and he grinned back at her. Then he held out his arms and she hugged him. "You'll drive carefully?" she asked.

"No, I'm going to go a hundred miles an hour except when I pass on a curve, and then I'll see if I can make a hundred and ten," he said. "Of course I'm going to drive carefully. And I've got the name of the island in Greece you'll be staying at that doesn't have any telephones and if I need you for an emergency I should call the American consulate there and they'll find you and—"

"Okay, okay, I get the message," she said. "Bill . . . I hope you find what you're looking for there."

"What do you think I'm looking for?"

"I don't know . . . some kind of peace, I guess. Some way to come to terms with your dad's death."

"I don't think it's that, Ma. I know he's gone. I don't like it, but I know it. It's just that, like, one day I had a place there, a home, a family kind of, you know, Peggy and Trav and Ricco and my friends, and the old man, of course. I had a life. And then the next day I didn't, and it was all wiped out, like some kind of tidal wave washed over it or something. I never got to say good-bye to any of it . . . and it was my life."

"I thought I was doing the right thing by not letting you go back."

"Yeah, well, maybe right then it wasn't such a hot idea. But I need to do it now."

"I suppose you do." She kissed him again. "Have a good trip," she said. "I'll see you in September."

He headed south out of the city. The summery drizzle had stopped and the air from the open window was cool and fresh against his face. The sky cleared, and suddenly there was the mountain, the throne of the gods, rising up from the foothills of the Cascades. One of these days I'm going to climb that big mother, he thought, just to see if you can see the ocean from the top.

27 million Americans can't read a bedtime story to a child.

It's because 27 million adults in this country simply can't read.

Functional illiteracy has reached one out of five Americans. It robs them of even the simplest of human pleasures, like reading a fairy tale to a child.

You can change all this by joining the fight against illiteracy.

Call the Coalition for Literacy at toll-free **1-800-228-8813** and volunteer.

Volunteer Against Illiteracy. The only degree you need is a degree of caring.